THE TURBULENT STORY OF A YOUNG
WOMAN WHO FOUND HER
"SAFE BRIDGE" IN THE STRENGTH
OF HER LOVE

In this romantic story, the celebrated author of
*Dinner at Antoine's*, *Senator Marlowe's Daughter*
and *The Great Tradition* re-creates the days of
great open fireplaces, tallow candles on rough-
hewn tables, unblazed trails, virgin forests and
sparse settlements—the adventure of life and
love in the unknown wilderness of Old Vermont.

"The story of Elizabeth Burr and James Anderson which I have told in *The Safe Bridge*,"
writes Frances Parkinson Keyes in her fasci-
nating Author's Note, "is true in every essential detail. Not only was each a real person,
but so is every other character I have tried
to portray."

"A GLOWING AND EXPERTLY
WRITTEN NOVEL."
*New York Herald Tribune*

# THE SAFE BRIDGE

## Frances Parkinson Keyes

AN AVON BOOK

TO
THE BEAUTIFUL MEMORY OF
Elizabeth Burr Anderson
AND TO
HER DESCENDANTS WHO HAVE HONORED
ME WITH THEIR FRIENDSHIP
IN WHOM
HER VIRTUE AND HER VALIANCE
IMPERISHABLY SURVIVE

AVON BOOKS
A division of
The Hearst Corporation
959 Eighth Avenue,
New York, N. Y. 10019

Avon Edition
First printing, July, 1962
Fourth printing, March, 1965
Printed in the U.S.A.

# THE SAFE BRIDGE

# PROLOGUE

## *The Distant Vision*

In THOUSANDS OF SCOTCH HOMES, through the latter part of the eighteenth century, the subject of immigration had become one of absorbing interest. A period of peace had brought prosperity to some classes and a desire for it to all; and whole regiments of soldiers, returning from colonial service, spread to eager listeners the tidings of new-world opportunities. Individuals and families sailed in large numbers, to accept the good fortune offered them; and associations were formed to purchase land for settlement, in order that entire communities might be established by persons already united by ties of acquaintanceship or relationship.

One such association, the Scotch-American Company, organized in 1772, sent out two commissioners, James Whitelaw of Whiteinch and David Allan of Sandy-Arms, "empowered to purchase in America a tract of land suitable for the construction of a Scotch city according to a model plan." After extensive travel and careful consideration they purchased a township called Ryegate on the Connecticut River, and returned to Scotland to make their report. This was so favorable that the following year over one hundred members of the Company set sail for the colonies: among them numerous skilled artisans sent out by a great cotton manufacturer of Glasgow, Archibald Burr, who foresaw in this enterprise an advantageous opening for himself.

But men and women battling to provide themselves with food and shelter are too hard pressed to evolve a "model city"; and though Ryegate long remained unique among New England towns in form of government, the

American Revolution, wrenching the colonies away from the Mother Country, interfered with its development as originally planned. Eventually, its dreams of glory forgotten, it sank into oblivion. The structure had lacked permanence; the plan had failed of fruition; the vision had been a mirage.

Yet years after Archibald Burr had made his luckless venture, his daughter, a blithe lass with a heart-shaped face and eyes the color of a deep loch, came riding into town. And with her coming, instead of with its founding, the real story of Ryegate began.

# PART ONE

## *The Dark River*

"I<small>T</small>—<small>IT'S COLD, ISN'T IT, J</small>EANNIE?"

"A wee bit chill."

"I—I don't think it's often as cold as this at home, do you, Jeannie?"

"Oh, aye."

"Then maybe I feel it more because I'm so tired."

"Maybe. 'Tis rougher going on horseback than in the coach. Come, let me take your reins a moment, dearie, while ye wrap your cloak around ye—so——"

The shriveled old serving-woman guided her horse nearer to the one her mistress was riding, and took the reins from the girl's small, unresisting hands. These were, indeed, almost numb with cold. Her fingers were so stiff that she could hardly tuck back the long lock of golden hair which had escaped from her red hood, and blinded her as it blew across her high-cheeked little face; much less could she draw more closely around her slim and shaking figure the full blue cloak which, swelled by the raw wind, billowed about her like the sails of a ship, as Jeannie helped her to fasten it.

"It seems strange, doesn't it, Jeannie," she said between chattering teeth as they went on again, "that beyond Hanover there should not be an open road over which at least a chaise may pass? Only this half-hidden trail through fields and woods! How do you know we are not lost already? Surely we have gone farther than

9

our good host told us our journey would take us before nightfall!"

"Nay, 'tis only that in a wilderness like this the way seems long. Andrew canna' ha' mistaken the path. Halt, mon, and tell us how far we have yet to go!"

The serving-woman raised her voice, which, resonant as it was, failed to reach the ears of a tall gaunt man riding ahead of the two women and momentarily lost to view. There was no answering call; and the encircling silence added a further element of dread to the young girl's unformulated fears.

"Andrew!" she cried, feeling that the trees were closing darkly in around her. "Why don't you answer? Where are you?"

"Here, Miss Bessie, not a stone's throw in front of ye. I had but gone around a wee bend. Must ye shake and shiver every moment that ye canna' stretch out yer hand and touch me?—As to the trail, it is so plainly blazed that even a wench as feckless as yourself could not stray off it. And we have now not above twenty miles to go, by my reckoning."

The sound of the familiar burr close to her ear brought reassurance to the girl, dourly as the words were spoken by the man who uttered them. She answered with a touch of archness which revealed how quickly she had succeeded in steadying herself.

"If you and Jeannie would only go clad in sapphire and scarlet as I do," she said lightly, "instead of in the dismal grays and russets which match this dread landscape so well that I cannot tell where it leaves off and you begin, it would not be so hard for me to see you!— Besides, you have been so surly ever since I beguiled the tedium of our stay in Hanover by a little harmless dalliance with the Indian lads at Dartmouth College, that I thought you might have chosen to desert me as a sign of your continued disapproval. Yet Dr. Wheelock himself was most benign. He showed me almost as many favors as he did to our Commissioners when they first passed through here years ago— It must have been hard for them to choose between lands offered them by two college presidents, even though they did finally decide in

10

favor of the property offered them by Dr. Witherspoon of Princeton!—If Dr. Wheelock had felt my conduct to be light, he would hardly have lavished so many courteous attentions upon me!"

"Your levity has led ye into trouble in the past, as ye well know, though it happens the Reverend Doctor does not. When I see ye surrounded by a score of young savages, all deep in your toils, must I be blamed for fearing lest it lead ye into more?"

"More likely it will be the only thing that will keep me from despair," the girl murmured under her breath. Then, with mocking, twinkling gravity, she turned again to her steward. "You must never lay more at the heart than you can kick off at the heel, Andrew," she went on, "so says our wise old proverb, and so say I, too.—As to the Indian lads, there were not a score of them—only seventeen! And they are not savage any more—in truth there are some arts in which they are well grounded! As to my levity, I went as regularly and devoutly as you to all the sacred services of Dr. Wheelock's conducting, and thought his earnestness must be an inspiration to all who heard him—especially his prayers in behalf of those who had contributed or might contribute to the building and maintenance of their college. I was moved to empty my purse of all it contained before I passed out of the meetinghouse every time I went there."

" 'Tis to be hoped that Colonel Johnson may profit by your prodigality," Andrew remarked dryly. "Yon is a gallant gentleman who furnished a goodly share of lumber for the college, and who has long and patiently been jogging President Wheelock's memory for the payment thereof. I have heard they had a lengthy correspondence, adorned with much compliment, but that at last the Colonel wrote the President a letter containing but one sentence: 'I thank you for your courtesy, but I would prefer the cash.'—Colonel Johnson was one of the first settlers of this upper valley, and a founder of the town of Newbury. Our Commissioners respected him greatly, and one of their reasons for selecting Ryegate as the site for our 'model city' was because of its nearness to this

11

settlement, whose citizens are godly men and women, strict in their observance of the Sabbath."

"When they pray God to forgive them their debts as they forgive their debtors!" sighed Beth whimsically. "Ah, well!—Can they not sweeten their severity with the excellent syrup which flows so strangely from their trees and makes such a fine sugar? I fill my own pockets with it now whenever I go to meeting.—Come back, Andrew! Must you view every jest that passes my lips as an evidence of sin?"

"Andrew has grave reason to be tried with ye," chimed in Jeannie. Her sense of sympathy was submerged now that she saw her charge riding forward again more buoyantly; and the network of fine wrinkles covering her chapped and frosty little face seemed to stiffen in every seam, as she screwed her mouth into a hard knot. "Your trifling with the Indians was bad enough, but the last straw came when ye stood, already hooded and cloaked for this journey, while the horses waited without the door, scribbling symbols on a frosty windowpane with the diamond in your ring! And then pressing your lips against the icy glass which ye had scratched! Those marks are there forever; and should the goodly tavern-keeper guess whose *kindly* hand wrought this damage to his property, his charges against ye will be heavy in both cash and kind."

"Which is the camel whose back is broken by this last straw?" asked Beth mockingly. "Thine, Jeannie dear, or Andrew's? And which is worse with which to ride up this bleak valley—a broken back or a broken heart? At least the hearts I etched upon the frosty glass are whole and intertwined, and stamped with the initials of true lovers. So let them stand! And may my thoughts of them help to heal the heart which, as you well know, needs much of mending and which is lonely as well as bruised!"

She brought out the last words with something of a sob, and bent her head to escape the biting flurry of snow which suddenly threatened to strike her in the face. The wind, which had died down for a time, was blowing a gale again now, whistling and moaning through the naked trees, to which only a few seared oak leaves still hung.

The narrow trail along which the travelers were winding, rough at best, was almost impassable where it had frozen into deep ruts; and on either side, the unfriendly hills rose menacingly, with patches of snow half covering their rocky cliffs and clumps of evergreen. Through the valley, clad in its dull November browns and grays, the Connecticut River wound and twisted, reflecting the dismal color of the sky in its swift cold current. Not a human habitation was to be seen, not a human being, except the gray spare figure of the narrow-faced man, riding silently ahead of the old woman and the girl herself.

The sound of the sob smote Jeannie's ears, and for an instant she pressed her narrow lips still more closely together, but involuntarily she felt her eyes blurring, and spoke forgivingly and with a forced cheerfulness.

"Come, come then, think no more of it! 'Tis no such great matter. And greet no more neither. It isna' like ye to grieve. When ye were a wee lassie, ye were always gay. Now you're a woman grown, can ye na' be gay still?"

"I'm wee yet," said the girl trying to smile, "that is, you always say so! I can put my head under your chin, Jeannie! And is a girl a woman grown when she's seventeen? If she is, perhaps that's what makes her grieve, to see how many troubles fall to woman's lot!" Then as the old servant did not answer, "Did Andrew say we had not above twenty miles more to travel, some hour ago?" she asked with desperation in her voice. "Surely we have come a hundred since then!"

"Nay, but a short ways. Deil take it, lassie, no journey hath ever before been long enough to suit ye! Yet for this one ye have neither spirit nor stomach!"

"Is this the same as bargaining for taffetas and velvets with Parisian shrews? Or playing the fine lady at the court of Naples? Or jaunting like a gypsy through the sunshine in Spain? How could I guess when Father spoke of sending me to our late rebellious colonies that all would be so different from those gay and pleasant countries where we had been before? He must have known—and yet he gave me no forewarning! Was that the act of a loving parent? Even in displeasure, he could have re-

13

membered that the good Lord tempers the wind to the shorn lamb, be that lamb ever so silly!"

Again Jeannie did not answer at once, and when she did it was with painful hesitation. "Children myst aye honor their parents," she said at last. " 'Tis not for ye to say, Miss Bessie, that your father be harsh or what he should or should no' tell ye!"

"Sure, it was prudent not to tell me that he was sending me into a wilderness! If he had, I should never have come! There is naught about this journey which hath not been terrible—the raging sea—the barren land—the heavens which have emptied their wrath upon us night and day! Even before we left port, desolate enough in all conscience, came that horrible reminder that in the midst of life we are in death! Did you not notice the great funeral passing slowly along just as we were sailing? I have not spoken of it to you before, but today—today I cannot get it out of my mind! I could see it plainly from the ship, for it was so big and grand and black that it seemed to stretch down the road for half a mile at least! All the horses that drew the coaches, as well as those that drew the hearse, were black-draped and had great waving plumes on their heads! I cannot believe it is a good omen to see a thing like that, leaving harbor on a long and perilous voyage!"

"Dinna' talk of omens!" exclaimed Jeannie sharply. "What can ye think yon funeral was to ye?"

"I—I do not know. But I felt—oh—I can scarcely say what I felt! Surely you must have marked it?"

"Yea, I marked it."

"And did you know of any great personage who had died?"

"Nay, but I had no time for idle gossip with the neighbors. Nor have I second sight. Cease chattering, Miss Bessie, and put such gloomy thoughts out of your mind."

"My thoughts are all gloomy."

"Then 'tis best ye keep them to yourself."

"I will, if you do not wish to share them and thereby make them lighter."

The girl's horse stumbled in a deep rut, and lurched forward. She leaned over, and patting it, spoke to it kind-

14

ly as she pulled it up again. Then for a long time she rode forward in silence, her reflections as desolate as the bleak and frozen country through which she was passing. At last, noticing that the trail had turned abruptly to the left and led down a hill jutting in the direction of the river, she lifted her head and called again to Andrew.

"I can hardly see—it was day but a little while ago and now it is almost night! Is there no gloaming in this wretched country? Where are we headed? Is that the Connecticut River? And are we going to cross over it now?"

"Aye, into Vermont. Our journey is well-nigh over."

Through the obscurity a covered bridge, its unpainted wooden frame blackened by inclement weather, loomed ahead of them. The girl turned to Jeannie.

"It looks like a coffin," she said, shuddering, "an immense coffin, stretched all the way across the River Styx."

"Nay, it is a bridge, and as ye have just said yourself, the river is the Connecticut."

For the first time that day the girl laughed. " 'A rose by any other name,' " she quoted softly. "Maybe," she added aloud, "but I feel as if I were going into a great grave. Yet what does it matter? Come, let us enter it all together!"

They plunged abreast into the hooded opening, their horses' hoofs thudding softly against the creaking boards. A darkness so complete as to be overwhelming suddenly engulfed them. The girl caught her breath, but conscious that, at last, her companions no less than herself had been seized with a sense of the supernatural and were shivering with fear, she stifled the scream that tore at her throat for release. She had hardly conquered the shattering impulse to cry aloud when the dreadful moment passed. A faint and distant glimmer of light began to filter through sable surroundings.

"A gleam from heaven," she whispered. "See, Jeannie, we are almost across the river! It was a good bridge, after all, despite its frightening form. It hath carried us safe over the river, and we must speak well of it.—Look, I can see the shapes of houses ahead! What is this celestial village, Andrew?"

"It maun be Newbury," Andrew replied in a voice deep with relief. "If I be right, we hanna' more than seven miles more to go now."

As he spoke, there was a slight stir in the dead grass near the road, and the travelers were aware that a creature of some sort was moving furtively along beside them. The density of the dusk made it impossible to guess whether this was a human being or an animal; and the soundlessness of its footsteps added to the spectral effect of its shadowy form. A creeping chill zigzagged through Beth's body as she realized that the apparition was stealthily drawing closer and closer to her; and the horror which she had mastered while crossing the river almost overwhelmed her again as she felt her horse quivering underneath her. Then it reared back, whiffing and whinnying with fright, and she was aware that an unseen hand had laid hold of her bridle.

"You go Newbury?" a guttural voice asked thickly. "You stranger, not know way? Joe take you. Joe ver' good guide."

"It be the deil himself!" shrieked Jeannie. "Dinna' harken to him, Miss Bessie! He will lead us straight to hell!"

The last remnants of her self-mastery had been shattered by the gruesome spectacle of the sepulchral bridge; and from then to the moment when she had become conscious of the mysterious movements on the roadside and the presence of a shadowy being, she had been a prey to a panic which had mounted rapidly towards frenzy. Now she shrieked again, still more loudly, "Say your prayers, lassie, and gallop for your life!"

"Be quiet!" commanded the girl sternly, steadying her own voice by a supreme effort of will, "and sit still! Your only danger is in chattering and flight!"

She peered into the darkness, then forced herself to laugh reassuringly. "This is no ghost—it is an Indian!" she exclaimed. "I can see his headdress—and his fringed leggings! You did not expect moccasins to make a noise in the grass, did you? He has probably been hunting.— Have you, Joe?"

The apparition responded instantly, and with a human

16

heartiness which revealed that pride had shaken his racial stolidity. "Yes, Missie, much big hunt. Heap bear, heap wolf, heap panther in woods. Joe hunt them all, catamount too. Catamount climb tree, Joe go under boughs, put gun on shoulder, run eye through sights. Joe say to catamount, 'You kill me? I kill you? Maybe both?' Joe shoot gun, jump high, jump wide, catamount pounce, Joe shoot again, catamount die! Look, Missie!"

Beth bent forward. The man's features were not discernible, but there was no mistaking the friendliness of his approach, and as her eyes became accustomed to the darkness she could see that he was short, thickset and swarthy, with broad shoulders and wide haunches; and gradually she also distinguished the outlines of a huge limp animal which the Indian had been carrying slung over his shoulders and which he now held up with pride for her to admire.

"Good shot!" she said enthusiastically. "And now the hunt is over and you are going to take the catamount home?"

He grunted out his satisfaction. "Yes, Missie. Joe take catamount Joe's cave show Molly Squaw, Molly dry meat, make coat."

"And is your cave on the road to Ryegate? Could you show us where to go without passing out of your way?"

The Indian grunted again, and tugged gently at her horse's reins. This time it did not resist, but responded with surprising docility to Joe's hand. He reached out and possessed himself without difficulty of the two other bridles. The nags which Jeannie and Andrew were riding fell quietly into step.

"Joe take you," the Indian said again reassuringly. "Joe ver' good guide." He looked back once, with a glance of contempt which fortunately they did not observe, towards the mute and cowering servants; but Beth, who noticed it, guessed that with the swift instinct of primitive people he had divined their fear of him and despised them for it.

"We are very grateful to you, Joe," she said gently. "We are all very tired, for we have come a long distance today—all the way from Hanover. Did you know that

17

some of your young braves are studying at Dr. Whee-lock's college there? They were very kind to me."

"Young Indian brave like young paleface maiden. No like old paleface woman much," Joe volunteered with brutal frankness. "My boy Toomalik maybe go Hanover some day Joe think." He lapsed into unembarrassed silence, padding quickly and noiselessly along through a small settlement from which only a few lights shone forth, and in which they encountered no passers-by. Only when they had gone beyond it did he jerk his head back towards Beth again.

"Newbury," he said laconically.—"Missie no talk much."

"I'm Scotch, Joe. The Scotch and the Indians are some-thing alike—neither likes chatter. We ought to be good friends."

"Friends now," stated Joe emphatically.

"Thank you, Joe. You won't forget now, will you?"

"Indians no forget, Missie. Scotch too?"

"Scotch too!" Beth assured him gravely. "But, Joe, you're not going out of your way, are you? You said your cave was in Newbury."

"Near. North. Near Oxbow, Colonel Thomas Johnson's place."

"And are you a friend of his also, Joe?"

"Heap friend. Heap friend General Bayley too. My folks, Colonel Johnson's folks, General Bayley's folks. Joe same friend George Washington!" He brought out the portentous announcement swollen with pride. Then, as if this vaunted glory warranted a lapse from reticence, he warmed to his subject.

"Joe and Molly visit George Washington his wigwam. George Washington shake hands with Joe. Bimebye bad paleface man come Newbury, want to shake hands with Joe. Joe put hand behind his back, Joe say, 'This hand shake with George Washington. No shake hand with bad man. Joe keep hand clean.'"

"'He that hath clean hands and a pure heart,'" mur-mured Beth softly; and then aloud, "That's right, Joe—that's what I'm going to do, too.—Oh, you are going to leave us here? Is your cave over there?"

The Indian nodded. He had released the bridles, and now, still ignoring the two servants, he reached for Beth's hand, took it in his, and made a sign with it in the air before placing it to rest against his heart. Then laying it down again, he pointed towards the river.

"North. North. West. West. Moon come heap quick. Can see road. Good-bye, now. Joe find pretty Missie again. Bring catamount skin present. Good-bye."

"Good-bye, Joe! Thank you again, and do come and see me soon.—Where shall Joe come to see me, Andrew?"

The steward did not answer. Peremptorily the girl repeated the question.

"Did you hear me speak, Andrew MacPherson? Answer me this minute!"

"Ye will be lodged at Master Cameron's," said Andrew sourly, "but never think——"

"Master Cameron good man, another heap friend Joe," the Indian said cheerfully. "Joe come quick, maybe bring two catamount. Good-bye!" Almost as silently and suddenly as he had appeared, he vanished. The darkness swallowed him completely, leaving no trace of the direction he had taken. Beth turned to her followers imperiously.

"Have you no courtesy—no gratitude?" she asked hotly. "The man was friendly and kind and helpful. And you had not even a civil word to give him. My father shall hear of this."

"Aye, that he shall," said Andrew heavily, "and know that his daughter still chooses strange company."

A quick retort rose to the girl's lips, but she checked it. "Let us talk of that another time," she said quietly. "But for now, tell me more of those friends we are to make who are of my father's choosing. Do you know aught of the family with whom we are to lodge at Ryegate?"

"'Tis a good family," said Andrew, as sourly as if his mouth had been filled with alum. "The Camerons. Master Cameron is a judge, and hath married the daughter of one of the rebel generals, John Stark of New Hampshire—a great man despite his misguided ways."

"I know of him, and of his wife, Molly, who is a very
19

brave woman," the girl answered thoughtfully. "So Judge Cameron has married his daughter?"

"Aye, his daughter Elizabeth. She should be well fitted to receive ye."

Darkness closed in upon them. The biting wind, dying down, left behind it a still, clear cold. The flurries of snow ceased, and the heavy clouds began to break and scatter across a velvet sky shot with silver. From behind one of the looming mountains a golden moon, huge and heavy, rolled slowly upwards, bathing the bare fields and the rough road with its liquid splendor. Some of its radiance penetrated to the hearts of the three weary travelers, comforting and sustaining them as they plodded ahead in its pathway. At last they saw the scattered lights of another settlement shining before them; and Andrew dismounted, slowly and stiffly, and walking towards the door of a little house with undrawn curtains, he lifted the knocker on the wide clapboarded door.

There was a sound of bolts being shot back, and of a heavy latch being lifted. The door, creaking in the cold on its iron hinges, opened slowly. From within, the wayfarers could see an enormous log fire which blazed and leapt on a huge hearth hung with cranes and kettles; and silhouetted against its vivid glow, the tall dark figure of a man.

Andrew approached him. "I am MacPherson, the agent of Archibald Burr, the cotton manufacturer of Glasgow," he said, "and I have with me Master Burr's daughter, Elizabeth, and her serving-woman, Jeannie, who is my wife. Can ye tell me how much farther it is to the house of Judge Cameron of Ryegate?"

The door opened more widely, and the tall dark man came forward. With the firelight behind him he stood revealed as a somber but somehow splendid figure, clothed with dignity and power.

"This is Judge Cameron's house," he said slowly. "He and Mistress Cameron are gone to Prayer Meeting, but they will return anon. They charged me, if the Scotch guests they were expecting came during their absence, to welcome them. I am James Anderson, their hired man."

20

## TWO

Miss Bessie, darlin', 'tis time ye were wakin'."

The girl stirred slightly under the patchwork quilt which covered her, drew it up more closely about her, and turned over, her eyes still shut. She had slept, she knew, for hours and hours. And yet, she was still so completely engulfed by the exhaustion of her long journey that she could not shake this off and rouse herself. The old woman bent down, and brushing back the yellow curls, laid her gnarled hand on the warm cheek almost hidden by the soft hair.

"My bonnie bairn! it grieves Jeannie to fret ye—but it's gettin' late."

Beth flung up her arms, and wound them around her nurse's neck, drawing her over the bed.

"Come back here, Jeannie dear," she murmured drowsily, "it's cold without you. What made you sneak off and leave me? I had a nightmare, and when I waked, crying aloud, and reached out my hand to touch you for comfort, you were gone. I dreamed I saw that funeral again, that I followed it to the churchyard, and that just as the coffin was being lowered into the grave, I sprang forward and tried to raise the lid. But it was nailed tight and fast, and though I screamed that I must know who had died before the earth swallowed it up forever, I was held back by powerful unseen arms while the earth was shoveled over it." She paused, shuddering again at the memory of her vision. Then, feeling a slight quivering of the form which she embraced, she opened her blue eyes wide, and pressed her lips against Jeannie's.

"What is the matter? Did you dream too?" she asked in a startled voice.

"Nay, but ye must rise. I've fetched water and laid out your clothes. Mistress Cameron thinks you're a wonderful sleepyhead—and the men have been gone to work so long, 'twill soon be time for them to return to dinner."

The girl laughed, and sat up, swinging her feet over the side of the bed. "Is that my bath?" she asked merrily, pointing to a small wooden tub standing on a braided rug before the unpainted dresser; "and if it is, how can I bathe in this cold room? You've built no fire for me, Jeannie."

"And how can I build a fire for ye, dearie, when there's neither stove nor fireplace in the chamber? I did fetch ye some hot milk—there's no tea in the house—but it has grown chill while ye chattered. Be quick, while I get some more."

Shivering, but still enjoying the novelty of her surroundings, Elizabeth stepped into the shallow tub, scarcely larger than a bucket, dashed the water over her soft face and slim white body, and rubbed herself to a rosy glow with a rough huckaback towel. Then she leapt back into bed again, cuddling down like a baby. Jeannie, coming back with the reheated milk, scolded her gently.

"Nay then—drink this and then put on yer clothes."

"Myself?"

"Aye—try it."

The girl laughed, and slipped the chemise which Jeannie handed her over her head. "That's simple enough," she rippled, "my arms must go through the two little holes, and my head through the big one, whether I put it on myself, or you do it for me! But stockings—they twist so! And I cannot lace my own stays—or dress my own hair—or fasten my frock. Is it a game you're playing with me—or a riddle?"

" 'Tis neither, dearie. I should have made ye do it before, on shipboard. But I couldna' bear. Come now, you're trembling."

"And you're *crying!* Why, Jeannie, what's the matter? Of course I'll try if you want me to."

The little hands, numb with cold, seemed to be all thumbs. But Jeannie stolidly withheld her help, turning her head away, her shoulders shaking. Elizabeth's amusement began to give way to mild rage.

"I cannot reach those buttons, Jeannie; and my curls are all tangles. What's come over you? It isn't fun any more!"

The old woman swung about suddenly, and clasped the girl to her with a violence that hurt. "I canna' bear it," she sobbed, "my bonnie little lambie, I canna'. Come, Jeannie'll show ye. Reach your hands back so, darling, and ye'll find the buttons—ye that Jeannie's dressed since ye were first laid in her arms, a new-born babe. Take the comb like this, dearie, and pass it through your hair, gentle-like, this way, up—and then down—and over again—see——"

Elizabeth snatched the comb from her, and tossed it down on the dresser. "Jeannie," she said quietly, "something dreadful has happened—something you're afraid to tell me. I felt it all day yesterday, coming, as we were riding up the valley. What is it?"

"I canna' say it."

"You must. If there is something I've got to know—something hard to bear—it will be easier if I hear it from you."

"Nay, darling, finish your dressing and go out to the warm fire. Andrew is waiting for you there. He'll tell you."

"You mean—you won't."

"I canna', Miss Bessie. 'Twas given to him to do. I would have failed."

The girl stood very still for an instant, then laid her hands on Jeannie's shoulders. "What do you mean, Jeannie?"

"Andrew will tell thee. Come, go to him. Thou'rt dressed now. I'll follow thee in a minute, when I have tidied up thy things."

"You won't even come with me?"

"Anon—anon."

"You're a coward, Jeannie." The girl opened the door, and paused, with her fingers on the rude, hand-wrought latch. "But I'm not. Whatever is going to happen to me, I'm not afraid." And she closed the door behind her, and entered the living-room.

It was a typical New England kitchen of the early days of the Republic, serving every purpose except as a bed-chamber. A huge fireplace flanked with a brick oven extended across one end, and in the iron kettle hanging

23

on the swinging crane a savory stew was simmering. From great hooks fastened in the ceiling drying meat and apples and sliced pumpkins were suspended, a spinning-wheel stood in one corner, and on the scrubbed deal table an Indian pudding, a pot of beans, some mince pies, and several loaves of bread had been set to cool. But in spite of these signs of comfort and good cheer, the kitchen looked more bare and crude in the harsh morning light than it had in the glow of the tallow candles and the friendly shadows which had mellowed it the night before. Mistress Cameron was nowhere to be seen, and neither was Andrew. But, as Beth entered, the tall, powerfully built man who had welcomed her upon her arrival, and who had sat so silent at the supper table afterwards, came in through another door with a bundle of enormous logs in his arms, and, after throwing one on the fire, began to pile up the others beside it, without speaking to her.

"Good morning," she said pleasantly, "it's a chill day, isn't it?"

The man looked up, and stared at her for a minute, still without speaking. "Yes," he said at length, and went on piling the wood.

"I am not sure I heard your name right last night. Will you tell it to me?"

Again the man raised his head and stared. As he looked her full in the face, she was aware again of something arrestingly noble about him, uncouth as he was. But apparently he was conscious of no conversational necessities, for he muttered, "It's Anderson," almost as if asking, "What's that to you?"—"James Anderson."

"Well, James Anderson, have you seen my man Andrew this morning?"

"No."

"Will you find him, and send him to me here? I need to speak to him."

"Can you not find him yourself?"

It was the girl's turn to stare, and then to flush a trifle angrily.

"I do not run errands," she said coolly.

"Nor I."

24

"Do you not work here?"

"Yes—but not for strangers—or women. I am hired out to Judge Cameron to cut his timber and put it where he tells me, but not to wait upon his guests."

The man was horribly uncouth and blunt, but he was not, Elizabeth realized almost instantly, intentionally rude. It was more likely that he thought her so.

"No one seems to wish to wait on me this morning," she said with a little laugh, "though everyone has, all my life, so far! Even Jeannie has joined the mutiny. She made me dress myself."

"She made you *dress yourself!*"

"Yes. I'd never done it before. She's been with me, you see, ever since I was born."

"You'd never *dressed* yourself before!"

"No—that's why my hair is done so badly, and my frock all awry."

The man shifted his eyes from the heavy silk gown to the tangle of bright curls above it.

"And in the midst of it—the mess I was making of dressing, I mean, in that cold room, with nothing but a bucket to wash in—she let me see that she was feeling very badly about something. She wouldn't tell me what it was, but she said Andrew would. So I came out here to find him. And you won't help me do that."

"Your man Andrew," said Anderson abruptly, "is out in the barn, saddling his horses. I have not seen him, as I told you, but he said to Judge Cameron that he meant to leave this noon—he and the old woman—that you were staying on."

The girl grew suddenly cold all over; but she forced herself to answer, almost indifferently, "There's some mistake.

"Perhaps."

"Jeannie never leaves me."

Once more Anderson's eyes traveled slowly over her face and figure. Then he moved towards the door, and went out. But, after he had closed it behind him, he opened it again, and came back to the place where she was standing.

"I'm sorry," he said awkwardly, "if something is troubling you. I will send your man Andrew hither."

25

Spring was sweeping up the Connecticut Valley, trailing pale green robes behind her over fields that had lain brown and wind-swept for weeks as they emerged from under melting patches of snow. Mayflowers had come and gone, shrinking between their clinging leaves, but dimly fragrant; wake-robins and adders' tongues had blossomed thickly, glossy and brilliant as they were scentless; more rarely, lady-slippers of purple-veined pink, and bronze-colored jack-in-the-pulpits had raised their shy heads in the woods where James Anderson chopped, and beside the brook where he sat to eat the dinner which he carried with him, in a covered pail, and to refill the rude canteen hung over his shoulder. He had worked in these woods for years, he knew them as few men in Ryegate knew them; and yet he had never noticed these flowers before. Did they grow about Newbury and Haverhill, he wondered, in the same profusion? Had they always been there? And the birds—had they sung like this every spring? Thrushes and whitethroats, preachers and tanagers seemed to puncture the silence with their sweet persistent notes.

Besides the singing of the birds there was another sound which Anderson sometimes heard. He had noticed it more and more frequently of late, and it had begun to haunt him. He heard it not only in the woods, but in his sleep. There was no joy in that note. It was out of tune with the rest of the spring melodies, yet it persisted. It sounded—what did it sound like? He did not know, and, involuntarily, he kept trying to think. Was it a child in pain? The idea was nonsense. The children of Ryegate went safely and happily, through the spring, to the rough little schoolhouse that was, perforce, closed through the long hard winter; and at night they slept, equally safely and happily, in their trundle-beds beside their parents' large one. Besides, it was not, after all, like a child's cry, any more than it was like the wailing note of a bird. It was a suppressed sobbing, the sobbing that betokens bitter, hidden anguish. The anguish of—a woman! Yet what woman did he know who could have a hidden grief? Not one!

He put the thought behind him; but the sound persisted. Sometimes he did not hear it for several days at a time, and he began to think he had imagined it altogether, and that it had ceased. Then it swept again, poignantly, across his consciousness. At last the time came when he could bear it no longer. He threw down his axe, and went to seek it.

He sought for a long time. When he thought he had almost found it, it eluded him. Then it stopped. For two afternoons he neglected his work, chopping very little, and walking about a great deal. On the third, his conscience pricking him, he decided to chop as long as it was light, instead of returning to the Camerons' for supper, in order to make up for lost time. And, going home in the fragrant dusk of the forest, staring straight ahead of him, he almost stumbled over what he had sought so long in vain. Lying on the ground at his feet, dressed in coarse homespun, was the tiny, slender figure of a girl. Her back was turned towards him, and it was growing dark; but even before he bent over her, and pushed away the blue sunbonnet covering her face, he knew that it was Elizabeth Burr.

She was asleep—asleep from sheer exhaustion. That was why she had not heard him, and fled at his approach. But it was she—there could be no doubt of that—whom he had heard crying, over and over again, as he chopped. He sat down beside her, very quietly, that he might run no risk of waking her, and tried, by piecing together the events of the last few months, to puzzle out the reason for the hidden grief of this mysterious girl, whose very elusiveness enhanced still further her irresistible fascination.

She had been merry enough, all that long winter, laughing at the blunders she made, trying hard to correct them as she laughed, entering into the life of the Cameron household as if she wished to live no other—soon as if she never had lived any other. Before spring, the girl who could not dress herself in the fall could spin and sew and cook and scrub almost as well as Mistress Cameron herself, better than most of her neighbors. She even learned to milk, to set the milk in brown earthen pans, removing the cream with a skimmer and storing it into an earthen crock until it was sufficiently refined, and then churning it with a dash churn into fine butter, with a peculiar nutty flavor, better, she declared, than she had ever tasted in Scotland. Early every Saturday morning she rose to heat the brick oven, kindling the great fire for which James Anderson brought in logs of wood four feet long and over, until it was heated. Then, together, they drew out the fire and ashes with a long-handled shovel, and baring her little white arm, she held it in the oven while James counted to a certain number, to test whether the proper degree of heat had been reached. After that was assured, in went beans, brown bread and Indian pudding; next pies, pumpkin, apple and mince, and finally the cake, made from the "one, two, three, four" recipe which Molly Stark had given her daughter when she married. By afternoon, all was cleared away, and the girl was at the loom or wheel, making cloth for trousers of Scotch gray, by mixing the wool of black and white sheep, blue and white frocks to take the place of coats, shawls and aprons, blankets and coverlets. The first time that Wells Goodwin, the lanky traveling shoemaker, with a shock of sandy hair above his friendly, freckled face, came through Ryegate after Elizabeth's arrival, she had put out a small silk-shod foot for him to measure; but the second time she had on stout woolen stockings of her own making, and laughed with him over the change.

"You'll never find me in those flimsy things again, Wells," she said merrily, "nor in a silk frock, either. I've made my first homespun."

"You're a wonderful quick lassie—lady, I mean," he amended. But she shook her head.

"I like lassie better—'tis such a friendly word. And why do you and all the others call me Mistress Burr? I was christened Elizabeth." And she began to hum

"Bonnie Sweet Bessie, the Maid of Dundee."—"I came from Glasgow instead of Dundee, to be sure," she finished, stamping her foot down into the new shoe, "but never mind. I'm bonnie and sweet and Bessie, am I not?"

"You are all of that," Goodwin declared slowly, and watched her as she tripped across to the hearth.

"Could I do a Highland fling in these shoes of yours that wear so well and are so heavy, Wells?" She wondered, "I might try!" And before his astonished eyes she began to dance, swiftly and lightly, her little light, flexible body fairly flashing to and fro. Anderson, coming in with the wood, had found the two together so. She dropped a curtsy.

"Will you dance with me, James?" she asked archly.

Never had the mysterious spell she cast over him been so strong. No other maiden in the settlement, however lovely, had seemed so bewitching as she did at that moment, yet he answered her soberly enough.

"Nay—I have never danced."

"Will you not join Master Goodwin then, and watch me do so?"

He refused even that. Dancing was frowned upon in the settlement. But since Wells had not told her that, neither would he. And afterwards he wished that he had stayed beside the shoemaker, and feasted his hungry eyes upon her.

She went to church and singing school, and sang the solemn hymns which she learned there, to the great improvement of the local choir; but she sang, too, the ballads of Scotland which many of the good folk in Ryegate had scarcely heard since they left the Old Country, and, because of this, some of the more strait-laced among them were inclined to doubt her orthodoxy. But "Father" David Sutherland, the earnest and eloquent "Priest of Bath," who sometimes came, on a great occasion, to preach them a sermon—speaking without notes and adding greatly to the effect of his addresses by retailing the facts and anecdotes with which his memory was stored—laughed their doubts to scorn from the first moment he laid eyes on her. And his word carried great authority, for he had won the title accorded to Protestant ministers in the settlements only when eminent ability and long and efficient service had given them an intellectual as well as a spiritual dictatorship.

" 'Tis a good child," he said conclusively, "your little Scotch lady of whom I have been hearing. How does it come that she stays so long with you?"

No one could tell him. The old serving-woman and the steward who had brought her up the valley to visit the Camerons had gone away again the morning after their arrival, without speaking to anyone. The Camerons themselves, if they had wondered at this abrupt departure, or at the fact that Andrew and Jeannie had not returned for their charge, had never said so; there were some among the settlers who thought the Camerons had been prepared for this, by letters from overseas; but it was difficult to ask questions when no information was volunteered.

"And the little Scotch lady herself—is she silent, too?"

"She is never silent. She is chattering and jesting and singing godless songs from morning until night, as we have said, and proverbs and Scriptural passages come so trippingly from her tongue that it cannot be she really marks their worth. We greatly fear she is light-minded as well as lighthearted. And yet—she tells nothing in her chatter and her maxims."

"So the child is wise as well as good," the old Priest muttered, under his breath. Aloud he said, "Has she wealth?"

"The steward who brought her left gold for her use, and since then a packet has come for her. She gave all the clothes away to ne'er-do-weels and beggars and some of the money—so much that the Camerons have prudently taken the rest from her, and hidden it—under the great boulder in their orchard, so 'tis thought. We are not sure. But certain it is that her thriftlessness cannot be denied."

"So—generous as well. And very fair—bonnie in the true sense of our good Scotch word. I know not when I have seen a sweeter or more blithesome face—I must talk with her."

It happened, during this conversation also, when the

30

Priest brought it about, that Anderson came in with wood. Elizabeth sat by the hearth, small feet crossed in front of her, small hands folded in her lap, small head bent a little. She was listening respectfully, intently even, to all that the clergyman was saying to her, but she was apparently saying very little in return. As the hired man advanced, she looked up and smiled.

"Do you know my good friend James Anderson, Priest Sutherland?" she asked. "Son of the James Anderson who was carpenter to the Company when it first came over. He sees to it that we are never cold, and is clearing great tracts of land, that more homes may be built from the lumber, and more corn raised as soon as fields take the place of forests. Will you not sit down, James? Our reverend guest has taught me much. Surely he has something to say to you as well."

The clergyman looked at her swiftly, his piercing glance sweeping over her from head to foot. He had not intended that another should be included in their talk as yet. Surely the girl had known this, or at least guessed it. But her head was bent again, and he could not see her eyes; her hands were as demurely crossed as ever.

And this time Anderson did not refuse to remain. He sat down beside her. Afterwards he wondered, in his troubled fashion, if he had done a stupid thing. For the Priest of Bath, though friendly enough, had, after all, little to say to him, and not much more to Elizabeth. When he had taken an early departure—much earlier, as a matter of fact, than he had originally intended—and Beth, curtsying almost to the floor, had opened the door for him and closed it behind him, she turned to Anderson with a little laugh, which had, he fancied, a slight catch in it.

" 'A friend in need is a friend indeed,' " she quoted gaily. "Thank you, James."

"Why should you thank me?" he asked, looking at her with the comprehensive stare with which he still occasionally enveloped her.

"For nothing, bless your dear stupid heart," she said, and laughed again. But she, as well as Anderson, would have been surprised if she had known that Sutherland, riding home towards Bath in the darkness, was laughing, too.

"And clever, also," he chuckled to himself. "Well, well, I must see more of the girl. They shall not, those good people over there, crush that fine spirit with overmuch zeal and piety."

After that, he came to Ryegate more frequently than he had made it his custom to do before, and once he took Elizabeth home with him, to spend a week with Mistress Anna Waters Sutherland, the wife whose talents, education and devoted piety so well fitted her to be his worthy helpmate. The little house where the Camerons lived seemed strangely empty to Anderson till Beth came back, crowded though it was; for their turn had come to "board the schoolmistress," and she was staying there also, sharing Elizabeth's bed with her.

The visit in Bath strengthened the friendship between the old clergyman and the little Scotch lady as nothing else would have done, for there he had her to himself; but still she told him no secrets; and though every visit that he paid to Ryegate after that brought him a warmer reception from her, it was to Peabody Ladd, the traveling vendor of musical instruments, even more than to the shoemaker or the preacher, to whom she gave the most joyous welcome. Even the appearance of Indian Joe, who never let a week go by without coming to see her, laden with gifts, and sitting motionless on his haunches for hours at Master Cameron's fireside, made her less happy than the mocking volatile musician, though she always spoke of Joe as her "first friend" and watched for his coming. Ladd came less often than the others, and never to stay long, for the settlers had little use for his wares, and scarcely more, it must be confessed, for him; so he paused only for a meal or a night's lodging on his way to some larger and more friendly spot, where his gypsy ways and wagging tongue gave less offense. But he brought with him news of distant cities, where he bought fiddles and flutes and rude harmonicas, and of the men and women who played upon them in the places where such accomplishments and such amusements were not frowned upon. And, for the first time, he found in the little hamlet

32

among the Vermont hills an eager listener to his tales. Once, in the middle of one he paused.

"The students at Master Wheelock's Indian Academy at Hanover—Dartmouth College, I believe we must call it now—were making merry the night that I was last there," he said, "and one of them, going to a frosty window, saw something upon it which Jack Frost had not etched, and called to his fellows and to me to help him decipher it. The work had been done with a diamond, and I made it out to be two hearts interlocked, with lovers' knots around them, and the letters B.K.—E.B. beneath them.—Hast jewels, little Scotch lady?"

"Aye, gems of thought," she retorted quickly—very quickly, James considered afterwards, "which I will not show to thee. They might dazzle thee."

"My eyes are dazzled already by the brightness of thine."

"Then shut them, and open thy prattling mouth, and I will give thee sugarplums to stop it."

She was beginning to use the provincial "thee" and "thou" more freely and frequently, Anderson noticed, though she did not do so consistently. But they came now quite naturally from her lips, as she stood twisting molasses candy into long honey-colored ropes. She broke off a bit and dangled it in front of Peabody's face.

" 'Twill stick thy mischievous jaws together," she said, smiling, "which will be well. Thou'rt a chatterer. James, here, is more discreet."

"And hence," mumbled Ladd with difficulty, "thou dost feed him no sweets. The moral is plain."

But for all his volubility, he never spoke again of the writing on the window, or hinted at questions which she might not wish to answer. Instead, he played, between his stories, upon the instruments he carried with him, sometimes far into the night, when all the household except Elizabeth had gone to bed—unless it were James, who brought in wood a log at a time, instead of one great armful, and listened, off and on, to the tales and the music. The little schoolmistress would half waken, long after she had first gone to sleep, to feel her bedfellow

33

quietly slipping in beside her under the patchwork quilt and homespun blankets.

"Why do you fancy the fiddler so?" she murmured once, drowsily.

"He fiddles away my fancies so," the little Scotch lady answered. "I am sorry I woke you. Next time I will be more careful." And she put her arms around the schoolmistress, snuggled close to her. "Sweet dreams, dear Joan."

Joan told Anderson of this afterwards. "She says that he fiddles away her fancies!" she exclaimed. "What are they then, her fancies?"

"I do not know."

"Ask her."

"I cannot—no more could you!"

"What are they then, her fancies?" Anderson was asking himself the same question, as he sat beside her now in the forest twilight, permeated with the scent of the pine needles, waiting for her to wake, turning over all these events in his mind. Why were they driving her out into the woods, over and over again, to cry out her heart alone, when, to everyone, she had presented so gay and brave a front? Who had harmed or hurt her? What was this mystery that enshrouded her? The deepening dusk brought him no answer, the sleeping girl beside him did not stir. At last he leaned over, and shook her gently.

"Little Scotch lady!" he said in a low voice, that he might not startle her. "Little Scotch lady, 'tis getting very late! You must wake and come home, Mistress Burr."

She trembled, caught her breath with a slight sob, and opened her eyes slowly.

"What has grieved you?" he asked abruptly.

The sob shifted to a laugh. She sat up, almost with a start, rubbing her blue eyes, smoothing down her tumbled frock over her supple figure, and straightening the tangled curls that clustered under the heavy bonnet which bound but could not confine them, and straightening her bonnet.

"Nothing has grieved me," she said quickly. "Where did you come from, and how did you find me, James?—I

34

have been dreaming, I fear—I often come to the forest
—not to chop wood, usefully, like you, but to dream,
like the idle creature I am. I greatly fear, from your question, that you have been dreaming too, else you would
not have asked so senseless a one."

"And do you always cry when you dream?"

"Do you always dream when you chop?" she countered
lightly. "I shall begin to think so! You're fancying,
James."

"Then it would take more than a fiddler to drive this
fancy away from me," he said, a trifle grimly. "Over and
over again I've heard—a strange sobbing. I thought at
first it was a bird—then a child—then I guessed it was a
woman, though I could not guess who. I've been searching—" It was seldom he made so long a speech. He
stopped, awkwardly.

"Joan is a tattletale with her talk of fiddlers and
fancies!" said Elizabeth, springing to her feet. "I shall
kick her in her sleep tonight! Come—catch me—if you
can!"

She sprang up, and darted off among the trees, flitting
through them as lightly and swiftly as a shadow. There
would not have been a chance for the man to overtake
her, in spite of his long, powerful strides, if a thorny,
blossoming blackberry bush had not suddenly entangled
her. She tried to snatch her coarse, full skirt free of it,
but the more she pulled and turned the more hopelessly
she found herself fettered by the sweet-smelling brambles.
The next instant, she was fettered in another way also.
Anderson's arms closed suddenly around her and, holding her like a vise, drew her to his breast.

She struggled vainly for a moment, then lay stiffly still.
"Let me go," she panted.

He had heard her laugh, over and over again; but this
was the first time she had heard him do so.

"No," he said, and laughed again, drawing her, if possible, still closer to him, "not until you tell me why you
come into the forest and cry."

"Hasn't even an abandoned girl a right—to a refuge?"
She regretted the words the instant they were spoken.

But they served their purpose. He dropped his arms instantly.

"An abandoned girl!" he repeated in dull amazement. *"You?"*

She saw that he had misunderstood her use of the word, and seized the opportunity it gave her.

"Yes—and in another minute you would have kissed me. Aren't you glad you escaped the contamination?"

It was her first false move. He swept her into his arms again, the primitive violence of his longing for her, pent up for months, breaking suddenly in a torrent of passion. "I love you—love you—love you—" the words were jerked out between the hot, rough kisses with which he covered her neck, her forehead, her cheeks, and, over and over again, her mouth, as he pressed her face against his with one powerful hand while he held her close in the hollow of his other arm. But for all the response he got, he might as well have embraced a woman who was rigid in death. And when at last he let her go, he found, that instead of tingling with exultation, he was stammering with shame, almost with fear.

"Forgive me—I didn't know that was going to happen—didn't mean to hurt you. I'm some kind of a dreadful brute to do that to you. Please, little Scotch lady——"

It had grown dark, but the moonlight, filtering in through the pine branches, showed him a face that was as white as chalk under the soft boughs of the tree against which the girl was leaning, as if to gather strength. She put her hand against her smarting cheek, and closed her eyes wearily, and Anderson felt as if his heart was being torn from his body, and that his own anguish was as nothing even then, compared with hers. But, when she opened her eyes again, there was neither anger nor terror in them, nothing but gentleness, and, to his stunned surprise, she slipped one cold hand into his.

"Don't feel so," she said kindly. "I know you didn't mean to do that. We'll forget—both of us—all about it—and be good friends again. I had no right to taunt you, so you must forgive me, too. Any man—who was human—would have acted as you did. But you misunderstood—what I told you before that. When I said that I was an

36

abandoned girl I meant a girl who was deserted, deserted by those she loved and trusted most—except one person, who couldn't help her, who didn't know she was in trouble. But perhaps you would think I *was* a wicked girl—my father did."

Anderson waited silently.

"I didn't realize it when I left home. He offered to send me to the New Country—on a pleasure trip. He had often sent me on such trips before, to Italy and France, and Spain, when Andrew, his agent, went for him on business. He has connections all over the Continent—and he is very rich and powerful. Jeannie, my nurse, went always, too—to take care of me." The girl caught her breath again. "I was always very happy, traveling like that, and I learned a great deal. I thought America would be more wonderful still. I have always loved adventure, and I had never seen a land that was wild and free."

Still Anderson waited, dumbly.

"The morning after we got here, when you called Andrew to come to me from the stable, he told me that I was—banished."

*"Banished!"*

"Yes, forever. He and Jeannie had known that I was to be, all along. They were to bring me here—and abandon me. I saw a funeral wending its way into the country as we left port. I thought—I feared afterwards that—it was the funeral of—someone I care for very much. But it was my own."

"Your own!" repeated Anderson stupidly.

"Yes. A mock funeral." The girl was forcing herself to speak mechanically, as if she were repeating a lesson—a hard lesson—which she had learned by rote. "My father had given it out that I was dead. I am—to him. And to my—my mother. I am never to go home any more. I am never to hear from him—or—or—my mother—except indirectly, again. Four times a year they will send me clothes and money. I shall never wear the clothes. I shall never touch the money except to give it away. Andrew told me about these—arrangements that morning, before he left. The Camerons knew it before that, Jeannie was afraid to tell me. She didn't even have that

37

much mercy—to warn me, the least little bit, beforehand how far my father's power could reach——"

"Oh, you poor little child!"

"So you see I was abandoned. And everyone in Scotland thinks I am dead. All—all my friends. No one will ever know that I'm not. It gives me an awful feeling—to think of that long, black procession—and that empty coffin lowered into a grave and—and everyone believing that I lie in it. I see it all the time—empty—and wish—it were not empty. I dream about it when I go to bed at night—almost every night, almost all night——"

"Good God!"

"I haven't meant not to be brave about everything. But sometimes I have come into the woods. I do not see the funeral so vividly here. And it is good to be alone. I never am, you see, at the Camerons'. And when I am alone—I can't seem to keep the tears back. But I didn't mean anyone to know I cried. Indeed, indeed, I didn't."

Again, though very differently, the man put his arms about her. Waves of tenderness and compassion seemed to be surging over him, almost drowning him. And this time she did not stiffen, or try to fight herself free. Instead, she dropped her head on his shoulder, and resting there, began to weep again. Clumsily, brokenly, too deeply moved to find coherent speech, always difficult for him, he strove to comfort her; and, after a long time, the bitterness of the outburst passed, and was supplanted by less and less frequent and violent sobbing. At last she raised her head.

"You haven't asked me," she said, "why I was banished."

"It doesn't matter," said Andrew slowly.

"Then you don't think I'm wicked?"

"Oh, my God, no!"

"You did—for a minute."

"I made myself—because I wanted an excuse to—to get hold of you. I've loved you so long, you see—ever since that first morning. But I knew, even when I took you and kissed you, that it wasn't you who were wicked. It was I—trying to pretend that you were so that I could feel you in my arms."

38

"I was banished," said Elizabeth clearly, "because I went and spent the night in the barracks of the man I love—an English officer who was stationed in Glasgow, and whose regiment had been ordered to leave for the Indies in the morning. It was our last chance to be together."

The man to whom she spoke was probably slow of wit, certainly slow of speech. But in this, the greatest moment which had illumined his dull life, he spoke swiftly, almost before the words had left the girl's lips, thinking more swiftly still.

"Do you feel me so far beneath you," he asked gently, "that it makes you tell me half-truths like that, which are really lies? I *am* far beneath you, I know, farther than ever after having failed you as I did tonight, too far to reach up and touch the hem of your dress—but still not so far that I deserve that. I have not, perhaps, as fine a sense of honor as the Englishman who loved you so much that you could trust yourself to him completely. It is natural that you should think that I have not—when I have insulted and hurt you. But I love you too, as I have said—and honor you more than any woman in this wide world. Won't you tell me the rest of the story—to show that you've forgiven me—and that you trust me, too?"

The moon had slipped under a cloud. In the tense silence that followed his speech, he could not so much as see the girl's face. But she took the hand she was holding and laid it against her lips. It touched, as she did so, her soft, wet cheek.

"You—believe me!" she whispered. "You believe that —that I'm telling you the truth when I say I wasn't bad. Oh, God bless and keep you always! I shall never feel abandoned again!"

## FOUR

IF SHE HAD HAD HER WAY, she would have told him all
there was to tell before they had stirred from the silent
shelter of the forest. But he was firm in his determination that she must have rest and food, and one night's
sleep at least—preferably more than that—before she
tried to say what was in her soul.

"Why, Jim? You asked me yourself to tell you."

"Aye. But there is no hurry. I am asking you first to
come back with me to the warm hearth, and let me heat
you some milk; and then that you will wrap yourself
snug in your patchwork quilt, and dream of life instead
of death; and tomorrow to see how much more real sunshine is than moonlight, and work than anguish. Then
some day soon you will bring me my dinner, and dinner
for yourself as well; and we will eat it by the brook
that runs through the woods where I am chopping. And
after dinner I will lie at your feet and smoke, and you
will talk to me."

Once more, rebellious at submitting to his will instead
of following her own, she attempted to dissuade him.
But the quiet sanity of his plan prevailed. He would not
listen to her, she saw, until her emotional despair had
quieted sufficiently for her to do justice to herself and to
her lover in relating what had passed between them; and
finally she suffered herself to be taken home. During the
next few days she steadied herself, finding immeasurable
comfort in the knowledge of Anderson's complete confidence in her, satisfied, now that she knew she could unburden her heavy heart, to postpone, after all, the moment of her confession until she had entirely regained
her shattered self-control. Meanwhile, without impatience
and without again suggesting that she should come to
him, Anderson waited for her, every day, beside the
brook. When the noon hour had come and gone and
she had not appeared, he went back to his woodcutting,

chopped until dark, and then walked quietly back to the Camerons' house, thankful that the forest silence was no longer pierced by those strange muffled sounds of sobbing, content to bide his time.

More than a week had passed before she finally came; and then he heard her singing—singing one of those gay little Scotch ballads that she loved so well—before he saw her, advancing through the dappled sunlight under the sturdy pines and spruces, towards the space which he had cleared. Two earthen jugs were hanging from a strap across her shoulders, and she carried an open basket, linen-covered, in either hand; her homespun was discarded for a rose-colored muslin frock which he knew was one of those she had brought from Scotland. His heart bounded with thanksgiving. He would not have known how to express it; but it was this that, inarticulately, he had hoped for—a feast, not a fast; triumph, not tears. He sprang forward to help her, returning her smile with a shout of welcome.

"I had a feeling you might come today. Here—let me take those."

"You—you did not think it strange that I did not come before?"

"No."

"Nor think that perhaps I would not come at all?"

"I was sure you would come. And now that you have, what have you brought me?"

"Oh—'sugar and spice and all things nice'——"

She spread the linen cloth, laid the food out temptingly on it; hesitated, and then, divining his wish, knelt beside it, asking grace, with him kneeling beside her. Afterwards they ate, hungrily and heartily, speaking little; and together laid what was left neatly back in the basket. At last he lighted his pipe, and flung himself, full length, at her feet. Inadvertently, he laid his head on the full folds of her skirt, spreading wide about her. He had not dreamed that any stuff could be so soft, that there could be such fragrance and freshness in any garment. And she did not draw it away.

"Did you know the woods in Scotland?" he finally asked, at random, as she did not speak, and he guessed

41

that even now, though longing to confide in him, she was uncertain how to begin. His question gave her the opening wedge for which she had been seeking.

"Not virgin forest like this. There were woods, of course, on my father's estate in the country, and on the estate of his neighbor, Oliver Latte."

"And Oliver Latte was thy lover?"

"Nay. He was but my suitor."

Anderson smiled faintly.

"There is, then, a difference?"

"A difference!" exclaimed Beth vehemently. "A difference between a man who is eyed with favor by a girl's parents because his land adjoins theirs, and the two together would make a pretty property! A man whose mills are bigger than her father's and therefore serve to shame and threaten them! A wizened stingy snob, without the wit to woo or the strength to seize a lass unless she were fair thrown into his arms—as my father and mother threw me to their own purpose! A difference between that and——"

"You will tell me of the difference?"

"I am going to tell you everything," she said impetuously, "even that I might have married the Auld Clootie—for surely he was loathsome to me as the deil himself! But it was very hard ever to hear, that if I did not wed according to their wish, I would dishonor my parents by my willfulness, and might bring ruin on my father's head. I felt hamshackled as any leckless beastie!"

He knew that the Scotch vernacular was seldom used by one of her rank. Therefore, her lapse into it betrayed to Anderson, far more significantly than her now easy and frequent use of provincial colloquialism would have done, how deeply she was moved. He forced himself to speak quietly.

"But you escaped?"

"As far as the length of a tether! This dowy suitor of mine could not dance for ague and rheumatism, but he took me one night, because I would give him no peace till he promised, to a grand ball to which I had been bidden—as had my dear companion, Maisie, late married, and very happy so, to a young mercer, Duncan Baird. She was a very sonsy lass, and had acquaintance with half the English officers quartered in Glasgow. Duncan never saw aught amiss in that she should make merry still, though she was wed. A good soul he was, and would have been a husband after my own liking, had Maisie not found him first, and had my heart not so soon been given away to one of those same soldier lads, a young lieutenant, whose name was Basil Keith."

"You met him at this ball?"

"Aye,—he was known to Maisie already, though he was but newcome to Glasgow. As it chanced he had brought with him letters of introduction to my father from men of standing in the English town which was his home and where there were great industries. So my father had no choice but to receive him civilly, and he talked with much witting about the manufacture of cotton, and professed no little interest in it. But his own property was small, and though his station was honorable it was not grand; and all this, which my father speedily discovered, was little to his liking. Besides, when Basil visited us the second time, he spoke less of cotton— and more of other things. And the third time he came, he forgot to speak of cotton at all."

"And after that your father's looks grew black when Basil Keith came courting, and you thought it easier to meet him elsewhere? At your friend Maisie's house, perhaps?"

"Yes, that was it. How could you guess so well? I went there every evening when Basil was not on duty, and he met me there. Maisie and Duncan were wont to leave us in their drawing-room alone. They were all and all to each other too, and they saw how it was with us."

"And how was it with you?" asked Anderson in a low voice.

"We loved from the first moment we saw each other," Beth whispered vibrantly, "and after that more and more each time we met, each time our fingers so much as touched. Oh, if you could have seen Basil, you would never have wondered how I felt!—He was very braw, almost as fair as I am, with blue eyes and golden hair,

43

and skin as rosy and tender as a lassie's! He was slim and straight and tall, and wore his scarlet uniform as if it had been part of his own graceful body. And he was a gilpy lad—always merry and gracious. When he spoke to me, I loved to listen to his voice, and when he laughed, I loved better still to listen to that, and when he was silent and smiled into my eyes, with a bright and tender light in his, I loved that best of all! When I danced with him it was like floating away to fairyland; but when he kissed me, he lifted me up to heaven!"

The dark uncultured man, stretched out beside her, winced. But she rushed on with her story, unobservant of his pain.

"We were never grave together, and we never spoke of the future—we were so happy, and the present was so sweet and fair. There were whole weeks—like that. How could we remember, in our joy, that after word comes weird! I think my father must have guessed that we were meeting and that we were far ben with each other. But if he did, he never made sign nor spoke sentence. He bided his time, having learned that the regiment was soon to leave. But he bided it too long!"

"You mean——"

"One night I had but left my own doorstane when Basil stepped out of the street-shadows, and spoke to me, frightening me beyond measure, for I had never thought to see him there. As Maisie's house was so near, I had always gone to it alone, or with Jeannie—there was no danger—and Duncan fetched me home again late in the evening. It was safer, we knew, that Basil should ne'er be seen abroad with me. But now he was waiting for me with such desperate tidings on his lips that he had been driven to telling them to me all of a sudden and all in a breath: His regiment had been ordered away. He was leaving for the Indies in the morning. He might be gone for years. We had only that night."

They had only that night! It was easy, appallingly easy, for Anderson to visualize what happened then, even before the next frenzied words came tumbling from the girl's lips: That Basil, pulling himself together, half-led, half-carried Beth, frantic as she was with grief and fear,

44

to Maisie's house. That Maisie and Duncan were told the "desperate tidings" too, and, stricken with sympathy, left the two helpless young creatures once more together in the dim little parlor which had sheltered them so often. And that at last, when, very, very late, Basil tried to tear himself from his sweetheart's clinging arms, she would not let him go.

"I begged that he would take me with him to the barracks. I knew it would not be so hard to say good-bye there, as in that room where we had so long been happy together. He asked me if I could not feel, even if I did not know, why I should not go with him, and his voice was stern and shaken, as I had never heard it before. I—I knew what he meant. But I told him, and I told him truly, it did not matter, that it would comfort me, after he had gone, to think that I had stayed with him as long as I could—till—till morning. At last he said, if Maisie and Duncan would go with us, I might walk back with him, but that I could not stay."

So the slim, fair boy, with his smiling eyes and his scarlet coat, had, in truth, possessed a fine sense of honor, as Anderson himself had said, hoping, rather than believing, that it was so. The strange choking feeling in his throat lessened, as if sinister fingers which had been grasping it were relaxing their hold.

"It had been a lowering evening, with cold, biting showers, that came and went, without threat of fury. But we had hardly reached the barracks, when a great wind arose —no such tempest had smitten Glasgow in years—never since I was born. It uprooted trees, it struck down buildings, it shattered pavements. The men and beasts who ventured out in it were maimed and killed. It was a gowk storm, sent from heaven as a portent. Even here you may have heard of it."

"Aye," said Anderson heavily, "tidings of the Great Storm of Glasgow reached the settlements by the same boat on which you came. I remember them well. Master Whitelaw himself, and my father had letters— I know that it was as you say."

"So you do not wonder that Basil could not bear, after

all, to send me from him? Out into that raging gale? The barracks were at least a shelter!"

"No—I do not wonder."

"The sentries looked another way when we went in. They worshiped Basil, and they understood. And after that, when it was found that I must stay, Maisie and Duncan kept watch. Belike there were officers who knew that I was there, but none came to disturb us. We were left to ourselves—to our sorrow and to our joy. And in the darkness of those last hours that we had together, we made a pledge."

"A pledge! And of what sort?"

"We plighted our troth to each other! 'I promise,' Basil said, 'that I am yours—forever and ever. That I will be faithful to you, and love you always, and find the way to claim you for my own. So help me God. Amen.'—And I said, 'I am yours forever and ever. I will be faithful to you and love you always, and wait for you until you come to claim me for your own. So help me God. Amen.' —And when the storm was over, and I could leave, we said good-bye. But then it was morning!"

She was, for the moment, powerless to go on. Anderson forced himself to speak.

"And your father?"

"He was waiting for me at our doorstane. He asked me harshly where I had been. I answered that I had been safe with Maisie, that the storm, as he well knew, had raged so the night before that I could not venture abroad. He told me he had just been to Maisie's house, that there was no one within. And then, without warning, he called me a dreadful name. I could not help crying out. I was so very tired—stunned and hurt. But I didn't shrink away. I told him again that I had been with Maisie, and as I said it I looked him in the face."

"I am glad you did that. It was like you. And then——"

"He sneered and said it was a likely story. 'How shall I believe you,' he asked, 'having myself found her house empty?'—'Her house was empty *because* she was with me,' I said, 'I did not tell you I was at her house.'—'And where were you?'—'At the English barracks.' "

46

There was a long pause, in which the girl's breath came and went quickly, but during which she did not speak.

"And then?" said Anderson at last.

"He repeated—that dreadful name. 'And Maisie was with you, I suppose,' he said, 'all the time you were there?'—'Yes.'—'If your purpose was to be with Maisie, why did you go to the barracks'?"

"And you told him——?"

"I told him that I had gone to the barracks to be with Basil Keith, as he had doubtless guessed already. But I said, too, that I had not been with Basil—in the way my father thought."

"And did you tell him of your pledge?"

"Yes. Word for word. And still he could not see I spoke the truth. 'What did this interloper need with lovers' lines,' he cried, 'when he could have you at your own cheap price? Go back and ask him now if he will marry you today—and if he answers yes, then will I believe he has not taken his way with you already!"

"And you had to tell your father that he could not!"

"Yes—that the ship had sailed, that I had watched it out of sight before I had come home. And then he seized me violently, and struck me. 'And so the thieving boy has fled!' he shouted. 'And you are leavings for my honored neighbor! And when your brat is born, belike you think——' "

"Elizabeth! For God's sake, stop!"

Anderson had leapt to his feet, his face livid. He was almost beside himself with horror and compassion. In his effort for self-mastery he turned away, that the girl beside him might not see how completely he was unmanned. She misinterpreted his gesture.

"I told you long ago that I was banished—and buried," she said bitterly. "The charge you also knew—or part of it before. Now you know it all. My father dragged me to my room, and locked me in it. When I was released it was to be taken on board the ship which brought me to this country. So you see I have come to the end of my story. But I have told it to you because it seemed to me your due, and not to make complaint or crave your sympathy. Full well I know that I must dree my weir alone."

She had risen too, and stood with her hands clasped behind her. As Anderson swung suddenly around, he saw that she was facing him with the same steadfastness with which she must have faced her father. He laid his great fingers on her shoulder, and drew her towards him with quiet strength, looking down from his immense height straight into her eyes.

"Nay," he said tenderly. "You are wrong. We shall dree it together, you and I."

# PART TWO

*The Building of the Bridge*

## FIVE

NOT ONCE, IN THE MONTHS that followed the day when Anderson had listened to Elizabeth's story, did he refer to it, or to their strange meeting. Not once did he try to touch her, or even to create an opportunity to see her alone. But he stayed on in the Cameron household, through the blossoming spring, long after Joan, the little schoolmistress, closing the door of the rough little schoolhouse on the hills behind her with a joyful bang, had left for the short midsummer vacation; and he was still there when she returned in the early fall. The chopping and clearing were done, for the time at least. The following winter, logs would be drawn out of the woods again, and it seemed possible that he might still be there then; for plowing and planning, haying and reaping, threshing and harvesting time came and went, and he worked steadily on, with no question of departure; and when there was no other work for him to do, he took his turn behind the counter of Judge Cameron's thriving little store, serving the customers, no matter how querulous or quarrelsome they might be, with patience and judgment. Indian Joe and Peabody Ladd, Wells Goodwin and David Sutherland came and went, but he was always there. The elders of the church, and the old cronies of the village, gossiped and speculated about the little Scotch lady; but his stubborn silence was never broken. His patient devotion, his inarticulate tenderness, enveloped her like a soft robe of healing. The sparkle of her gaiety towards others did not grow dim; but with him, she let herself gradually drift into the quiet communion of understanding that needs no badinage of wit to stimulate it, the unexpressed trustfulness of complete companionship.

Long since, they had become "Lisa" and "Jim" to each other. "I cannot call a lad of your inches 'Jeamie,'" she had once said laughing, "and 'James' smacks so of kings and Bibles!—But 'Jim' suits you—and it suits me, too!" He also had groped for a nickname that pleased him, and once he had ventured on "Beth." Then seeing a swift look of pain cross her face had questioned her gently.

"You don't want me to call you that?"

"I—had rather not."

"Is that what your parents called you?"

"Nay, I was always Bessie to them and to Jeannie; and to all my friends—save one. It was Basil who called me Beth."

"I understand. Then I shall never name you so again. Do you like Lisa?"

The deep comfort of being able to speak to him freely! After that, she went to him, instinctively, with every task beyond her own strength which she had undertaken—unless he had forestalled her by coming to her first with proffered assistance. And she was not slow at undertaking tasks. The hard winter had, necessarily, confined her almost entirely to the house and barn; but, in addition to the domestic talents she had already revealed, she now disclosed a "way with bairns" which enlarged her field of usefulness to an extent that would have spelled drudgery to anyone who loved children less dearly, and immeasurably enhanced her usefulness to her hosts. There were already three toddlers in the Cameron family when Beth became a member of it; and when another wee lassie put in a premature appearance, it was Beth who cosseted the fragile little creature throughout the first perilous weeks of its precarious existence, and tended the elder brothers and sisters while Mistress Cameron lay abed. The Judge had vowed that he would name his next child Thomas Jefferson in honor of the prophet of democracy who was his idol; and though a man of less rigid opinions might have been swerved from his purpose by the infant's sex, the mite was inflexibly christened in the way he had determined. But Beth thought of softening the inappropriate appellation by calling the poor little mite "Jeffie"; and it was to Beth rather than to her own mother that the baby long instinctively turned.

By the time there was a hint of spring in the frosty air, "Jeffie" was a sturdy little suckling; and when she had been tucked peacefully to sleep in her cradle by the hearth, Beth bundled up the older children and took them with her out of doors. She had become enthralled with the manufacture of maple sugar, and was seldom far from the wooden trough, the sap-yoke, and the huge iron pot hung from a pole, which were used in its making. When the milder weather came she did not stay within four walls at all if she could help it. Jim met her often, a sturdy and rosy-cheeked little figure, scouring the hills during the spring rains, for the tender calves and lambs who strayed from their mothers, wrapping them, when she found them, in her huge woolen apron for shelter until she could gather them in safe by the hearth. Sometimes she stood all day in the open shed, dipping candles, often as many as two hundred at a time, while Jim helped her handle the heavy kettle and feed the blazing fire. Again, on fairer days, he would discover her on the bit of grassy clearing which they called the "bleaching ground" that ran back of Cameron Lane near a little brook, laying out linen cloth to whiten, and wetting it afresh each morning. In early May came the sowing of flax, broadcast like grass seed, and in mid-July, the pulling of it, clear from the roots, the drying and turning and curing of it, in the sun; and the girl tied with swift fingers the rustling bundles of stalks, ready for the "flax-break" which Jim was to wield. When harvest time came, she proved to be a quicker reaper than he was, and he laughed with her about it, telling her that she did not leave the sweet-scented fields from the time that the red of the sunrise stained the morning star to the time that the evening star shone through the stain of the sunset. Still she did not tire under the long hours and hard work,

51

but grew brown and strong and hearty, and when they shared their bread and beans and buttermilk at noon she was as hungry as he and ate very nearly as much.

Their playtime was spent together almost as continuously as their worktime, sometimes alone, sometimes with the girls and young men who were numbered among their neighbors: Jim's cousins, the Symmes', General Whitelaw's sons and daughters, the Brocks, the Neilsons, the McKeiths. They all went to singing school and spelling matches; they took long walks to the mill which Jim's father had on the little stream running from Ticklenaked Pond, and to the granite quarries of Blue Mountain; they made up fishing expeditions to Wells River, where bass and salmon were plentiful, and excursions to Clay Island, in the Connecticut, where the remarkable deposits of clay stones were a never-failing attraction. Often they stopped to watch the boats, made of pine and oak, with masts which could be lowered as they passed under the low, hooded bridges, and white sails curving in the wind, being laden with lumber and other produce for their trips down the river, or unloaded on their return with iron and salt, sugar and molasses and rum. Sometimes as many as fifty teams, pulled by four and six horses, were drawn up along the wharf at one time, and the boatbuilders' yards were full of ships, not yet ready to leave the ways. Elizabeth's eyes grew wistful as she watched the heavy little craft vanishing from sight on their journey to the cities at the river's end; but she never spoke of her wistfulness to Jim, though she did not try to hide it from him.

Sometimes, to be sure, she rode off by herself, on Dobbin, the old gray horse whose stumbling slowness unfitted him for heavy labor, but which had served Judge Cameron so long and faithfully that he suffered it still to stay, though for the most part idle, in his barn. From the first, Elizabeth had fancied the heavy plodding creature, now half-forgotten and half-neglected by everybody else; and since the animal could not be put to other use, there was no grumbling from her host when she saddled and bridled it herself and jogged slowly out of sight, for she was always back again within a matter of hours, rosy and refreshed and ready for whatever task first claimed her strength and sight. Only Jim knew that when she slipped away like this, it was often to visit Joe, the guide, and Molly Squaw in their Oxbow cave, which no paleface but herself had ever been privileged to enter, and which she never described; yet she always showed him the presents of game and fish which the Indians gave her and regaled him with accounts of her visits. Even when on an occasion she found that both had partaken too freely of "fire water," and were rocking back and forth in their cups, heaping abuses on each other, she told Jim of the incident, confident that he would share her amusement without harsh and uncomprehending censure.

"It was too funny, Jim," she told him merrily, "Joe was saying to Molly, 'My folks General Bayley's folks, your folks nobody!' and Molly was saying to Joe, 'No! No! *My* folks General Bayley's folks, *your* folks nobody!' That is apparently the height of ignominy, Jim! It is terrible to have nobody for folks!—Am I your folks, Jim?"

"Thou knowest," he said quietly.

Her friendship with the Indians caused him no uneasiness. But once, when she came riding home on Dobbin, she was not alone, and then something seemed to catch at his throat and strangle him. Peabody Ladd was riding beside her, on a fine prancing black horse, and around his neck was strung some strange musical instrument the like of which James had never seen and on which Peabody was strumming lightly, and singing a lilting melody as he strummed. There was about him a carefree gaiety that was very charming; and the expression in his eyes and mouth as he looked at Lisa was unmistakable. Yet, as the girl caught sight of Jim, standing wretchedly beside the road in front of them, she urged on her aged mount and came towards him as rapidly as she could ride.

"I met with Peabody on my way," she said lightly, "and it was well met, too, for he is a good companion and a joyous one. He has been singing to me of Arcady, and hinting that we might ride on further together—and find it. But I have told him that home-keeping hearts are happiest after all, despite the pleasant fables of the poets, and I have brought him back to the fireside with me instead of going away from it with him. Do you think it is well, Jim?"

"I think it is very well," Anderson said gravely, "for all of us, but most of all for Peabody Ladd himself."

A tiny spark seemed to hiss for a moment between the two men. But in a moment it had flickered out, and it never flared again. Arcady was, clearly enough, a symbolic name for some place of enchantment; but it was not with Peabody Lisa would go, Jim knew, if she ever sought for it.—After that he watched the musician come and leave without anxiety.

And so the summer passed, tranquilly and busily, and melted into fall, that loveliest of all times in the Connecticut Valley, when one still, sunny, mellow day warm at noon, crisply cool at morning and evening, succeeds another; when the roads are bordered and the hillsides covered with maples aflame with scarlet and gold, crimson sumac, pale lemon-colored elms and bronzing oaks; when pines and hemlock, spruce and fir, shine among them with a dark, glossy green; when the twice-cut meadows are smooth as velvet, and great pumpkins lie placidly between rustling stacks of corn; when the harvest moon, a gigantic ball of translucent, golden light, rolls slowly across a dark blue sky——

Saturday morning was always the busiest time of the week; but Saturday afternoon brought respite, the sense of peace that comes from useful work well done, foreshadowing the Sabbath's calm. And, leaving a spotless chamber and a fragrant kitchen behind her, Elizabeth, fresh from a bath of hot water and soft soap in the old wooden tub, and dressed in homely, clean linen and wool of her own making, had taken her knitting, one day in early October, to the great boulder in the orchard, to sit for an hour watching the shifting lights of late afternoon playing over the green meadows where the Connecticut wound along in the distance like a broad blue ribbon, over the flaming hills and hazy mountains. There were few of the settlers who noticed this beauty of the land—it was fertile, that was enough for them. Fewer still who, after a hard day's work, cared to weary themselves still further by crossing fields and climbing hills. She was practically sure of solitude, and solitude, in spite of her increased contentment, was still very precious to her—solitude in this silent, complacent loveliness most precious of all. Jim might find her, to be sure—but Jim, then and always, would be welcome. Her knitting, forgotten, lay soft and warm under her small, clasped hands, and the laughter in her eyes died down, leaving only the unclouded depths full of deep contentment as she thought of him. Then she felt a pair of hands quietly folded over them, though she had heard no step behind her, she did not stir or speak for a minute; then she raised her own, and laid them against the face which she knew was bending to hers, though she could not see it.

"Jim?"

"Aye, Lisa—how did you guess so easily?"

"It was not hard. No one else would have sought me out.—Did you ever, in all your life, see so much beauty as lies beyond?"

"It is beautiful. But there is beauty, too, not so far off."

"Will you sit beside me," she asked demurely, "and take your hands down, that I may look at what delights me—and leave you less constrained in looking at what pleases you?"

He laughed, and brushing back her full skirt, seated himself beside her on the boulder.

"You are right, it is very fair," he said; "there is something in the sight and smell of a fruitful orchard, gay in the fall sunshine, that's wholesome and sweet, like a certain kind of a woman. I have never seen the ocean. But I have often thought that its blue waves, with the white foam cresting them, dashing clean and strong against the sand, must be like one, too."

"Why, Jim! Art a poet instead of a woodchopper? And where didst thou learn so much of women?"

"The trees are heavy-laden," he remarked glancing around the orchard, without noticing—or appearing to notice—the slight satire of her speech or her mocking shift to the vernacular, which he quietly followed, "there will be plenty of cider this fall, and apples to dry for pies —not to speak of parties to prepare them for the drying, by the hearthstone, besides quilting parties in the attic,

55

and husking parties in the barn. Wilt go with me to them, Lisa?"

"What wilt thou do when thou uncoverest a red ear?"

"Only what thou wouldst expect."

She laughed. "I am in more or less disgrace," she said, "I do not know that I shall be allowed to partake in much merrymaking. I forgot to cover the coals with ashes last night, I was so sleepy when we reached home after singing school, and this morning the hearth was cold, and I had to go to the neighbors' for ashes. Then yesterday I gave away all the flour and meal we had in the house, to a beggar woman with a child in her arms and another by her side, who came to the door and said she was hungry. I put out empty sacks over Dobbin's back in front of me, and rode down to Newbury to David Johnson's storehouse and returned before the lack was felt. But my good hostess thought I had been improvident for all that."

"Didst slip anything hard and yellow in with the meal?"

"Yes—but I did not tell her that. Those hard and yellow circles lie so heavy on her heart."

Anderson laughed again. "Why dost thou love to give so?" he asked.

"I know not. Unless, perhaps, it is because—there has been so little given me. I believe that women who lack of the joy of receiving always long to give that joy to others, when it lies within their power. From me, everything hath been taken."

It was her first voluntary reference to her condition. That it was an unmistakable sign of her affection for him, Anderson instantly sensed. He reached down and laid one of his great hands over the two little ones lying on the soft, neglected wool.

"Am I the only one to whom thou wilt give nothing," he asked, "when my want is greater than all the others?"

"And what is thy want, Jim?"

"Thou knowest," he said quickly. It was a phrase he often used, and to which she always found it hard to respond. Now, although she suffered her hand to lie under his, she said nothing, and after a moment he asked more lightly, "What other crimes hast thou committed?"

"I was sent this forenoon to watch the beans baking

56

in the great oven over yonder, and I wandered off to look at the view. When I returned a small brown bear was devouring them. He had come down from the woods, I suppose, and smelled them, and most cleverly had pulled them out. Thou'rt likely to go hungry at supper time, Jim."

"I am hungry all the time for what thou wilt not give me."

"At least, I let no one else steal it," she retorted. "Mistress Cameron was sorely put out. I did not blame her. Jeannie would have called me a 'bluntie' if she had been here, and I should not have blamed her either.—Jim," she went on after a slight pause, "hast thou noticed what fine houses there are in Newbury? Colonel Johnson's and those which he hath built for his sons, and General Jacob Bayley's, and others. I marked them again when I went for the meal yesterday. And now that it hath become the first capital of Vermont, and the legislature meets there, much entertaining will be done. I have thought that perhaps I might get a situation there as a serving-maid."

*"A serving-maid!"*

"Why not? Art thou not a hired man? What is the difference?"

"Thou knowest well the difference. Thy station and mine are not the same."

"That is very true. Thou art known and respected and trusted throughout the valley, whilst I——"

He closed his fingers suddenly and so violently over hers that she winced with pain.

"Lisa," he said thickly, "thou knowest that was not what I meant. It is well enough to talk in this country about all men being free and equal, but there are ways in which—they are not. Thou art a lady, while I——"

"Thou art a man," she said softly, "there are not many such.—Jim, thou art hurting me."

He unloosed her fingers quickly. "I am sorry. Forgive me."

"I did not mean my hand."

"Did I not hurt that?"

"Yes—but I scarcely marked it, because thou didst hurt my heart worse."

57

"I have tried to heal thy heart," he said under his breath.

"I know. And thou hast done so, as far as any mortal could—more than any mortal could, except thyself. But now thou dost hurt it again, by spoiling our friendship, which hath indeed been one of healing to me, with talk of being hungry for what I will not give thee. Thou hast not done so before."

"Is that not in itself some credit to me then, since I have longed to all the time?"

The girl's eyes filled with tears. She was not unaware how close to the surface, in that new country, men's primitive emotions ran, how few, save for fear of hell fire, made efforts to hide or suppress them. Therefore she could scarcely underestimate the struggle that this one had gone through.

"It is indeed. I only hoped—that thou didst not long to do so. That thou hadst put that behind thee, and were satisfied—with what I had given you."

"No man is ever satisfied with friendship only from a woman like thee, Lisa."

Again she gave him no direct answer. She was troubled, he saw, not only about him, but about other things as well. And when at last she spoke, it was to revert to the other things. "A guest who stays too long outwears her welcome," she said, "especially in a house which is always full to overflowing, and in Mistress Cameron's anger these last two days I have seen what I should have seen long ago. She feels, and has the right to feel, that I have dwelt with her long enough and wonders if she must put up with the exiled girl and her strange ways forever. Besides, I think there is a shortage of bawbeen in the family. Not so many folks come to the store as used, and it is my guess that the Judge hath had other reverses also."

"And so thou thinkest to become a serving-maid?"

"Yes—what else?"

He got his reply with staggering bluntness, her words unsoftened by sweet familiarity of form.

"Do you want for your wife a woman who loves another man?"

58

"I want you."

He leaned over her. "Lisa—Lisa—have I not been patient? I have loved you almost a year, and in all that time I have only once—and that time I begged your forgiveness. Have I hurried you or been ungentle with you? Have I made your hard life any harder for you?"

"You know that you have not. You have made what would have been unendurable into a fate that—I could bear. A lot that has been sometimes—almost happy. You have borne with me and shielded me. You have been the safe bridge carrying me over a river—a dark river of wretchedness and despair."

"And so, according to your loyal Scotch proverb, you speak well of the bridge which carries you safe over?"

"Yes—I speak well of it, especially in my heart, which no one sees, since I wear it not upon my sleeve; and in my prayers, which no one hears, since I say them secretly before God, and not openly before men."

"But, because the bridge is crude, and rough, and ugly, you cannot trust yourself to it for all time in spite of its safety?"

"Nay—I think not of its being crude and rough and ugly. I remember only that it is safe."

"Then—that is not the reason—the feeling that I am beneath you does not make you shrink away from me?"

She hid her hand in his again. "I do not feel that you are beneath me," she said tenderly, "and I do not shrink from you—as a friend. I go to you very gladly, as you know. But you are not satisfied, it seems, with that."

"And since I am not, you would rather be Thomas Johnson's serving-maid than my wife?"

She winced a little. "Colonel Johnson would look down on me, perhaps, if I were his servant," she said slowly, "I do not know. I hear he is a great man, and that is not the way of real greatness. However, if he did, it might be hard to bear. But if I married you, I should look down on myself, and that would be much harder still."

"It would degrade you to marry me?"

"Not in the way you mean. I have told you that already. But in another way—yes. What do we call the woman who gives herself for profit and not for love? Is it not a very ugly word? Do you want to make me call myself that, Jim?"

It was his turn to wince. But he answered her steadily. "And what do you call the woman who brings light and joy into a man's life? Who raises him from a poor uncouth creature to some semblance of decency and knowledge? Is that nothing for a woman to do?"

"It is much. But it is not enough."

"Have you any hope at all," he asked suddenly, "of—deliverance?"

"You mean—of belonging to Basil?"

"Aye."

"How could I have? When he returns to Scotland, if he does not die of fever or in battle in the Indies, he will be told that I am dead. He may have returned already, have been told that already. And that would end every-thing."

"Have you tried to write him?"

"Over and over again. But it is difficult to find trusty messengers, as you know. Indeed, I am beginning to think that it is impossible." A dry sob rose in her throat, and she locked her hands together. "I have done what I could. I should not like to tell even you to what length I have gone in the hope of reaching him."

"And you have had no answer?"

"None."

"I do not wish to hurt you. But is it not possible that he hath forgotten you?"

"Do you think it likely?"

There was no vanity in the question, only a honest surprise.

"Nay," muttered Anderson, "it is as impossible that a man should forget you as that he should be content to be friends with you. But, as you say yourself, he may be dead."

"It is possible, of course," said the girl slowly.

"And so you will never marry, for the sake of a hopeless memory? Never have a home—a man's arms about you —your own children at your breast?"

Again she winced a little. But she shook her head.

"Never is a long word, Lisa. Your exile is hard enough,

God knows! Will you, of your own doing, make it harder? — This is a fair country—a country of great promise— you grant that yourself. You love these hills and valleys already. You find some joy in them. But would you not find much more if you were mistress of your own home, wife of a man who loves you, the mother of children who will love you as much?"

"For God's sake," she said hoarsely, "stop talking about children."

There was a long silence. The shadows, deepening on the hills, turned the bright colors about them to violet and gray. With the sinking of the sun, the crisp autumn coolness began to creep over the mellow orchard.

"So that is it," said Anderson at last slowly. "I should have known—seeing you with Jeffie—you've been thinking of—of what childlessness is going to mean to you."

As he spoke, Beth sobbed again, this time aloud. Then suddenly she unlocked her hands and leapt to her feet. There was such anguish in her face that Jim was startled. But when he sprang up also, and tried to put his arms around her shaking shoulders, she flung herself free of him.

"Of course, I have been thinking of it!" she cried. "But it is Basil's children I am hungering and thirsting for! The children of the man I love!" Then, with the swift con- sciousness of the blow she had dealt him by her outcry, she stretched out her hands to him in quick contrition. "Jim, dear," she whispered, "I am sorry. It was worse for me to say that than it was for you to kiss me that night in the woods. But you goaded me to it—just as I did you. Please forgive me."

"Marry me," was all he answered.

"I can't—you know I can't," she returned. "I'm sorry I said what I did. But it was true, all the same."

Six O'CLOCK WAS THE BREAKFAST HOUR in the Cameron household. At that time, the milking already done, the men came in from the barn and gathered round the big table, set, near the hearth, with porridge, smoking hot from the iron kettle which hung on the crane, cornbread, and bacon. On Mondays and Tuesdays it was generally Elizabeth who cooked the meal, in order that Mistress Cameron might begin the washing and ironing earlier, going back and forth from the well outside, with the sweep and buckets on its curb, to draw the water for her task. But on the Monday following the afternoon which she had spent with Anderson in the orchard, the girl did not appear, and after the busy housewife had gone into her chamber to search for her, she returned, bustling and frowning, with a slip of paper from which she read to her husband.

"This was pinned upon her pillow," she said indignantly, "the scatterbrained lassie hath left me in the lurch, with all the work that there is early each week to do without her help! And Jeffie wailing so that I know not how to silence her!"

"Mistress Burr is thy ward and not thy serving-maid, is she not?" asked Anderson, taking the small sheet up from the table where Mistress Cameron had flung it down, "and pays good gold for all that she receives, besides giving away much besides." The couple had not noticed the look of dark anxiety which had passed over the man's face when he heard that Lisa was missing. Now they did not notice the look of relief which supplanted it as he read the brief note. "It is a long time since she hath had an outing. And now she hath but taken Dobbin and gone to see the Priest of Bath, starting early that she may be gone but one day. She was not only disappointed but worried when he did not come to preach yesterday. She feared he

62

or Mistress Sutherland might be ill. Besides, she wished to talk with him. She did well to go."

"That fellow grows presumptuous," said Mistress Cameron sharply as the door closed behind Anderson; "the girl hath him bewitched—as she hath half the men in this village. But 'twill do him no good. She is as proud as Lucifer, and would rather die an old maid than marry one whom she fancies beneath her."

"Anderson is the best worker that we have ever had," replied her husband briefly. "I shall be sorry when he leaves—as I suppose he will before long. He is under no obligation to stay here, save the one which he hath created himself. For he loves our ward, without doubt. But, as thou sayest, so do others." And to avoid further discussion, Master Cameron discreetly followed his hired man to the barn.

Elizabeth was already well on her way by the time the altercation provoked by her departure began. The sun had not yet risen when she set out from Rÿegate, and following the River Wells down the valley to the village that bore its name, had crossed the Connecticut into New Hampshire. By the time the day had fairly begun she was riding up beside the Ammonoosuc towards Bath. She was almost distraught with perplexity. Anderson had scarcely spoken to her on Sunday, and her carefully laid plans to avoid him had proved needless. But she was very well aware that his silence would be of short duration, that he had bided his time as long as he would, and that he now felt that the hour to press his suit had come. If nothing that she had said to him beside the boulder had altered his determination to marry her, there was nothing she could say that would. If she had lied to him, and given as the reason for her refusal the fact that she felt him to be beneath her, he never would have importuned her again. She knew that well enough. But he had deserved better than falsehood at her hands. The safe bridge! he had been that indeed, and not for one minute was she unmindful of the help he had given her, or ungrateful for it. But gratitude would not longer suffice him; and for no shadowy memory of a man, who, if still living himself, believed her dead, would he forego his claim upon her. He

63

was contented to accept her without her love—in fact, he would accept her in any way in which he could get her. And he intended to get her.—

She was tired of fighting, and this meant a new struggle —was it best, perhaps, to give up the struggle, and decide the question that was racking her in the way which would mean supreme joy for him, and a sure harbor of refuge for herself? For with him, she knew, lay peace. By Sunday evening, she had almost decided that she could. But that night she dreamed, as she often did still, that she was in Basil's arms again, that he was kissing her as he had done when they plighted their troth, and wakened with outstretched arms, still believing the dream a reality, a fire of ecstasy running through her. Then she remembered—and huddled down in the bed again, to lie, staring ahead of her for hours, in a dry-eyed agony. At last, while it was still dark, she rose and dressed, and saddling old Dobbin herself in the cold dawn, started for Bath.

"The Priest will tell me what to do," she said, over and over again to herself, as she watched the shallow, sunny little river, slipping merrily along over its stony bed. "I will tell him the whole story. I was a fool not to do it when he first came, as he meant I should. He would have helped me all this time, and I need not have suffered so much. He will know what I must say to make Jim give me up. Or if it is right that Jim should not give me up, he will tell me that and I will follow his counsel. But oh, God, let him not tell me that!"

Almost unconsciously, she slid from the saddle, and, her bridle over her arm, knelt by the dusty road, her head pressed against Dobbin's smooth gray side. "I belong to Basil," she whispered, "even if he's dead, I'm his. Even if he's forgotten me I'm his. I shall be—all my life and after I die. I can give my body to Jim, but Basil would still have my spirit. And then I'd be—a harlot!" She brought the harsh word out aloud, not shrinking from it as when her father had called her by it. "Dear God, let me not be that!"

The old gray horse stood patient while the girl wept and prayed beside him, turning his head inquiringly once or twice to see what ailed his mistress, and then pulling at the spears of tough late grass that still grew by the rough road, and swishing at imaginary flies with his long, unkempt tail. His sober gait, when at last she suffered him to start on again, having led him to a stump where she could mount unaided, bespoke his relief that, whatever had caused her to behave in so strange a fashion, it had apparently passed. And it was characteristic of Elizabeth that once her outburst was over her spirits rapidly rose, and that by the time she had mounted the hill which led to the parsonage, she had dried her tears and was singing, "Bonnie Prince Charlie"—a tune which always set even poor staid Dobbin off at a gallop!

She fastened him to the hitching post and walked over to the square-built, substantial house which stood upon a crest, overlooking a broken series of undulating woods and pastures, beyond which rose the mound of Sugar Loaf, the cone of Black Mountain, and the majestic slopes of Moosehillock. Never, it seemed to her, as she gazed out at them, had she seen the deep blue lights and shadows on the distant mountains mantle their grandeur in such sapphire splendor; never had she seen the trees flaunt their fall foliage so recklessly. Only the tall pointed firs rose dark and austere in a landscape riotous with colors ranging from the deep magenta to pale rose, from tawny russet to golden amber. All the leaves of yellow and vermilion seemed to have caught each other's fire; the hilltops, the roadsides, the ravines through which the clear brown brooks trickled, were all aflame. Lisa caught her breath at the glory of the scene before her as she paused on the wide stone doorstep of the dwelling-place which faced it; and as she raised the knocker she whispered, under her breath, " 'I will lift up mine eyes to the hills, from whence cometh my help.' "

There was no answer to her summons; and after rapping a second time, she lifted the latch and went in. The tall maple secretary at which the Priest usually worked, and which stood just inside the front door, was closed, instead of being open and covered with papers; and with a sense that something unusual must have happened that he should leave it so shut and secret, she looked first through the chilly empty parlor and then through the

65

warm empty kitchen, calling as she went, without finding anyone. It was not until she passed through the rear of the house to the orchard that she found Mistress Sutherland in the back yard, her baby in a basket at her feet, and two toddlers at her side. She was hanging out her washing, which shone white as snow in the morning sunlight, and she hailed her guest with delight.

"The little Scotch lady! Bless thee, my dear, how glad I am to see thee! I have been wondering how I should get a message to thee."

"Is the Priest ill?" faltered Elizabeth, stopping short, "or—or——"

"Would I be here, instead of at his bedside, if he were, thinkest thou? Nay—but he hath been called away."

"Called away! Hath—hath he again been honored by a great church in New York or Philadelphia which seeks him as its guest preacher?"

"Nay. He hath been called to the Old Country. It was very sudden—so sudden that he had no time to send word to the good folk of Ryegate that he could not preach there yesterday. He told me also that he wanted to talk with thee before he left."

"He hath gone to the Old Country," repeated Elizabeth stupidly, "why?"

"A mission of great import to the church hath been entrusted to him. It is a tribute we were far from expecting. It grieved him sore to leave the Sunday School for bairns which he hath started— Hast heard of this new venture? He is the first to undertake it in the settlements, and it promiseth much. Also he fears that in his absence there may be back-sliding amongst those wine bibbers hereabouts whom he is exhorting so earnestly to reform. But, for a' that, he couldna' refuse to go."

"And—how long will he be gone?"

"A matter of all winter at least. Wilt come and cheer my loneliness sometimes? David hath promised to keep a diary on shipboard which should make good reading for us to peruse together in the long winter evenings."

The girl sank suddenly down on the grass, pressing her hands over her heart.

"What ails thee, child," asked Mistress Sutherland

briskly, "art sick? Didst breakfast before thou didst start on thy trip?"

"No," Elizabeth answered faintly, "I—I think perhaps that is the trouble. I feel a little queer."

"Of course, thou wouldst feel queer!" exclaimed the good woman indignantly, "to take a ride of such length on an empty stomach, a chill morning like this! Sit still, while I fetch thee a drop of hot brandy and water to revive thee first—and then a solid meal before thou speakest another word to me. Thou'rt white as a sheet!"

But even the hot drink and the good food did not bring the color back into the girl's cheeks as the clergyman's wife expected. Her concern was shot through with a sudden suspicion.

"Why didst thou come to seek David?" she asked shrewdly, when they were settled in the comfortable kitchen.

"I wanted to talk with him."

"So much that thou couldst not wait until he could go to thee?"

Her visitor was silent.

"Was it perchance about James Anderson that thou didst wish to speak?"

The girl gave a little start. "Why dost thou think that?" she asked wearily.

Mistress Sutherland laughed, her fears set entirely at rest. "Because it was of that same braw lad that the Priest meant to speak to thee! What ails thee, Elizabeth, that thou art so offish?"

Again the girl did not answer.

"Dost fancy he is not thy equal? Remember that God is no respector of persons."

"Oh, no! It is not that!" She hesitated a moment and then said slowly, "I have never said aught of my own family. But my mother was Jane Lockhart Scott—hers was no mean family——"

" 'No mean family!' " echoed Mistress Sutherland, visibly impressed. "Well do I ken that it is not—Thou art then kin to that noble poet who——"

"Aye," said Elizabeth carelessly. "But what I mean to say was—my own mother, in marrying, stooped somewhat beneath her, for my father is in trade—though far richer than she ever was before she wed. So why should I not do the same, were there question of it?"

"There is no reason why ye should not," said Mistress Sutherland approvingly. "And James Anderson comes of good stock. His mother, who as a maid was Agnes Symmes, was a very handy lass, and I have read in the Company's book that she was paid no less a sum than thirteen pounds, seventeen shillings and threepence for services rendered it, for reaping, washing, ironing, mending and making——"

"And yet Jim did not wish me to be a serving-maid," whispered Elizabeth under her breath.

"And for the exercise of other accomplishments which she possesses," continued the clergyman's wife with growing enthusiasm. "She and Elizabeth Stewart were the first two brides of Ryegate, and Agnes bought from Newbury many things against her wedding, which were charged to her in the Company's book, and for which she paid in further services—ribbons, pins, gauze, and such fripperies; plates, mugs, candle-snuffers, a spinning-wheel, and other sundries which she required for housekeeping. The Reverend Peter Powers performed the marriage ceremony, and all the colonists attended the young couple to their home with great joyousness. James —the father of thy suitor—had done well as carpenter for the Company and built the meetinghouse where thou goest to hear my husband preach, and also as Captain of the Ryegate Militia during the War with England. And he hath prospered since, so I hear. He owns not only his farm but his mill, and has proved himself a politician of parts. To be sure, he is often paid for his services as carpenter in grain or in goods brought from seaport towns, but he hath put by some money as well for he is very frugal, and he hath served as one of the Commissioners of the Company since General Whitelaw hath resigned that office. There are only six children, and all will have a goodly inheritance at his death. Meanwhile James the son, who loveth thee, hath been industrious and hath saved his wages these last years. He could give thee a comfortable home. Moreover, he is a professed Christian; that is worth much in these unrighteous times, when the young needlessly abandon the sober ways of their elders and indulge in idleness, heresy, and frivolity."

"I know all that," said Elizabeth slowly.

"What more, then, dost thou want?"

"I want to love him, if I am to wed him," she sobbed, and laying her arms down on the scrubbed deal table, bowed her head upon them.

For the first time since she had known the little exile, Mistress Sutherland regarded her with an expression of scorn instead of kindness and sympathy. She knew next to nothing of the girl's upbringing; but there had been unmistakable signs of both wealth and culture about her upon her arrival, and it took more than the shedding of silk garments and the adoption of colloquial speech to obliterate these. And wealth and culture, in the simple vocabulary of Mistress Sutherland, spelt ungodliness.

"What dost thou mean by love?" she asked harshly. "The sinful lusts of the flesh?"

Elizabeth shivered, the vision of the night before appearing to her again like a living presence. She could have sworn that she felt Basil's lips on hers, that she heard his voice calling her—"Beth—Beth—Beth—my darling, my own little love—" and the answering flame of her own longing for him leapt again within her. Was this longing a "sinful lust of the flesh"? She sat, her face still hidden, motionless and rigid.

"Hast read the marriage service of the English Church? Though we have turned from it as smacking overmuch of Rome, there are parts of that which thou mightest do well to consider. 'The holy estate of matrimony was ordained first for the procreation of children, to be brought up in the fear and admonition of the Lord,' it saith; 'secondly, as a remedy against sin, that such persons'—and that means all men, my child—'as have not the gift of continency might marry and keep themselves undefiled members of Christ's body.' There is no word about love there! And thou mayest jeopardize the salvation of James Anderson, if, failing to have thee for his lawful wife, he should be led into temptation by another woman. Homes must be built and tended, land cleared and made fair and fertile, and children reared, if this valley is to prosper. With self-denial and self-chastisement must this be undertaken—and thou talkest of love!"

"James loves me—is that then wrong?"

"Nay—he is a man—and as I have pointed out to thee, his love for thee, which is righteous, will save him from unrighteous love, unless thou deny him. And thou wilt love him, too, in as far as it is seemly and proper that thou shouldst do, once thou art married to him. 'Twould be immodest and forward if thou didst so before."

Mistress Sutherland's face assumed an expression of contented reminiscence, as if the memory of her own courtship filled her with a self-satisfied complacence. And, as the bewildered girl before her made no immediate reply to her pronouncement on the proprieties of amatory progress, she decided to indulge in a brief personal narrative which would point a moral and adorn a tale.

"It was while Father Sutherland was temporarily ministering to the Church of Thurso in Caithness, which was my home," she said primly, "that he formed an attachment to me because of my sincere piety and what he was pleased to call my amiability. Had the thought ever entered my mind that he had been drawn towards me because of any partiality I had betrayed for his society, or worse still, by the practice of conscious allurement on my part, I should have been too sunk in shame to listen to his addresses. When he made them, however, my conscience was clear, and he proceeded in so respectful a manner that I was completely reassured on the score of my own conduct; and I told him I would deliberate on his proposal, whereat he at once withdrew. After lengthy and prayerful reflection, I gave him a promise of eventual marriage; but as the friends with whom I had taken counsel were of the opinion that we should not immediately join hands, we parted for the time being with mutual regret. Soon after this Father Sutherland left for Ireland, where he had been offered a church in Newry—a town where the Protestants were very destitute of religion and the situation most uncomfortable. But he remained there in all patience for some months, when he received a letter from his worthy friend Mrs. Lockart of Glasgow, informing him that some acquaintances of hers who had gone to America had commissioned her father to send them a preacher, as they were not favored by the means of grace. She entreated Father Sutherland to go to them, and as was natural, he viewed this offer as a call from Providence to enter an extensive sphere of usefulness. So he communicated with me, and I at once expressed my willingness to accompany him wherever he went, and partake of all the troubles he would have to encounter. Our next meeting was truly gratifying; and as our attachment now met with the approbation of all those with whom I was in any way connected, we were shortly afterwards united in the holy bonds of matrimony. We had entered it soberly and advisedly, and have indeed found it an honorable estate. I have tried ever to be a dutiful wife, submitting myself to my husband according to the precepts of Paul the Apostle; and I have had my reward in hearing him say, more than once, that he marveled at my fortitude in leaving friends and native country, and engaging with him in so bold and enterprising an undertaking as that on which he was bent. Moreover, he has often stated that his most valued moments have been spent in my esteemed company, and I believe spoke the truth."

"I am sure he did. I have heard him say you were the glory of his house, the joy of his life, the desire of his eyes and the precious partner of his bosom," remarked Lisa demurely. "He must, indeed, have found pleasure in his hours with you."

Mistress Sutherland shot a suspicious glance at her. "His language was but Biblical on those occasions," she said a little shortly, and with a slight blush, "after the manner of the Song of Solomon, which, as thou well knowest, celebrates the joy that Christ hath in his church."

"I have heard that said. But it was written, after all, centuries before our Savior lived, by a joyous youthful king who put no curb upon himself. So I have sometimes wondered if there might not be another meaning to it—if

71

it might not indeed have been a love song, voicing the ecstasy which a man had in the possession of his beloved and hers in being so possessed."

Mistress Sutherland gave a horrified exclamation. "Breathe not such words aloud!" she said in consternation. "Canst thou for one moment suppose that in the Holy Scriptures, which are of divine revelation, there could be included a book setting forth the delights of a carnal life! 'Tis well thou didst say this only to me, thou misguided and reckless child! Should the Council hear of such heresy, it would go hard with thee!"

The girl's tired head swam. This was not quite the same doctrine that her father had preached when he sought to make her marry his wealthy and elderly neighbor; but the burden of the same song rang through it. Love as she understood it was not an essential for marriage in the eyes of Archibald Burr and Anna Sutherland. Her own passion for Basil, which she felt was the most beautiful experience she had known, was described in ugly words— "a sinful lust of the flesh." Must a woman turn towards her children with deep emotion, but shrink from her mate? Every instinct within her told her that this bond should be the deepest and strongest of all! Yet her instincts were unguided, they might be playing her false——

"Do you think the Priest would speak as you do—if he were here?" she faltered at last faintly.

It was the last thing that he would have done. But Mistress Sutherland did not realize this.

"Of course he would," she said with decision. "He would tell thee first to cleanse thy heart of all voluptuous thought, thy mind of every heresy. And as regards the rest, I have often heard him declare that he believes the married state to be preferable to the single, and that when circumstances will, with any propriety, allow young persons with proper partners in view to marry, they ought to do so. And that he thinks thou hast a proper partner in view I well know, for it was of James Anderson that he wished to speak with thee, recognizing the mind and worth of the lad. I told thee this at the outset. I am giving the only counsel that he would give himself."

"Even if—even if he knew I loved someone else?" were the words which rose to the girl's lips. To the Priest she would have uttered them, and he would have guided her wisely. But to his wife, who, she instinctively knew, would have scant patience and less sympathy with her story, she could not speak. She guessed, quite rightly, that Mistress Sutherland would use this only as a further argument for her marriage with Anderson—a means of grace against a pitfall of possible indulgence. Still trembling a little, she got to her feet.

"I must go home," she said; "it is Monday, and Mistress Cameron will have need of me. I thank thee for all thy kindness and good advice. I will consider it well."

## SEVEN

Frame houses were rapidly supplanting the log cabins of earlier days all through the valley; but here and there occasional rude huts remained, on lonely stretches of road or back up on the hills; and between the settlements of Bath and Wells River there were several of these primitive shelters. From one of these, far distant from all the others, Elizabeth had fancied, as she had ridden towards Bath in the early morning, that she had heard sounds of distress—a faint moan, a fainter call. She had reined in Dobbin and listened. Everything had been still again. She had shouted, but no answer had come. So she had decided that she had been mistaken, and gone on her way. There were countless tales of strange sounds heard in these woods, which were never explained; many of them, no doubt, were made by the wild creatures which still ranged through them; but there were others too, of far more mystic characters. One story which Lisa remembered with especial vividness, was of a child sent on an errand by her mother. The little girl informed her neighbors, when she reached their house, that she had heard, in a certain place which she described with great minuteness, strange and beautiful music, which seemed to come from every direction, filling the entire air, about and above her, with its harmony and volume. She had stayed listening to it, she said, until it died away. The neighbors paid scant attention to her narrative, feeling that it was a fantasy of her own imagination; and when her errand was done she started on her return journey. But she never completed it; and when her parents, distressed at her prolonged absence, went, after nightfall, to seek for her, they found her lying dead, without any sign of injury about her, upon the spot she had so ecstatically described.

"If that could only befall me—that or something like it!" Lisa whispered desperately to herself as she rode along. "Why should not God send singing angels out to greet me? If I could die like that all my sorrows would be over! Why should the only sound I hear be one of wailing—though mayhap in those wails I may yet find my weir!"

The thought obsessed her; and when she drew near the log cabin on her way back from Bath, she was conscious that her heart was beating very fast, that it was filled half with dread and half with hope. She stopped and listened again. At first there was only silence around her, silence everywhere. But presently she was conscious of soft padding footsteps. There were no signs of life, no glimmer of light from the little hut; but someone was coming with a stealthy, unearthly tread around the bend in the road. The next instant, a leather-clad moccasined figure turned the corner, and with immeasurable relief she recognized her old friend Joe, the Indian scout.

"Evening, Missie," he said, grinning comfortably as he trotted towards her. "Why you out so late alone? Why you so 'fraid to look? You no frightened Joe, good Indian?"

"Of course I am not frightened of you!" she exclaimed. "But how could I know it was you, making that queer sound in the dead leaves?"

"All same sound I make first time I see you," he grunted teasingly.

"I know—and that time you certainly *did* frighten me! But just now I was—I was thinking of other things. And I have not seen you in so long, I thought you had gone away. The cave was empty the last time I went there. And I am sure someone told me that you were gone hunting moose.— Weren't you?"

"Indian Joe did hunt moose," the scout explained. "One day, two days, three days, lick chops, think all time of feast, then bad moose leave Vermont, go Canada. Joe wave hand say, 'Good-bye Mr. Moose, good-bye.' came home again. Moose Canadian moose, but Joe no English Indian, no French Indian—American Indian!"

Lisa laughed. She knew that Joe had served in Captain John Vincent's company of St. Francis Indians during the Revolution, and that his incomparable knowledge of the North Country, combined with his deep-rooted antipathy towards the British, had made him invaluable to such rebel leaders as General Bayley, General Hazen, and even General Washington. Now that the war had been over nearly a score of years, he still nourished the hatred to his former foe to such an extent that he could never set foot on British territory, though his erstwhile companions in arms had visited him more than once in an effort to persuade him to do so. His relinquishment of his prospective prey, merely because it had wandered over the Canadian boundary line, was an almost comic example of the lengths to which he was prepared to go to prove his patriotism.

"But where is Molly?" Lisa asked when her merriment had subsided a little. "She was not in the cave either."

Joe gave another contemptuous grunt. "Molly go Derby Line with Joe," he said. "One day Molly stay wigwam, Joe hunt. Braves come to wigwam, take Molly away Canada, think Joe go too afterwards get her. Ha, ha, ha! Joe fool 'em all, come home alone. Bimeby Molly come too."

"But, Joe, do you not grieve to be without her? Do you not miss her sorely?"

The Indian shrugged his shoulders. Lisa knew that there was, in point of fact, a deep abiding devotion between him and his mate, but evidently he was nursing a grudge of some sort about which he did not wish to speak. So she changed the subject, reverting to the one that had been absorbing her when his sudden appearance had so startled her that she had momentarily forgotten it.

"Joe," she said, trying to make her voice sound casual, "does anyone live in that cabin?"

He cast a disdainful glance towards it and grunted again. "No," he said so emphatically that the girl's suspicions were aroused. "People moved away, Wells River. Missie run along home."

"But I heard sounds from there, when I was on my way to Bath this morning. Sounds as if someone were in distress. I think I will just go and make sure."

"Missie not go near the cabin. Evil spirit there, maybe. Nothing else."

As the Indian spoke, an agonizing cry suddenly rent the air, followed by another, and another. He laid a restraining hand on the girl's arm, but she was already off her horse, tossing the bridle to him.

"Someone *is* in trouble. Fasten Dobbin for me, to that tree, Joe. Keep away from the evil spirits if you are afraid—but they can't hurt me."

As she ran up the slight incline towards the hut, a scream still more ghastly than any that had come before it rang out, echoed, and died away. But by the time she was pushing against the heavy door, flinging her whole weight against it to force it open, a silence that was ghastlier still had succeeded the terrible shrieks; her teeth were chattering as the door gave way, and she stepped into the room within.

It was cold, filthy, and apparently empty; Elizabeth glanced quickly about it, taking in the signs of squalor and misery that pervaded it like an unclean odor, as she tried to discover whence the cries had come. There was no one in sight. At last she stood stock-still and forced herself to speak.

"Is anyone here?" she asked as quietly as she could. "Anyone in trouble?"

The answer was a cry of anguish which seemed to come from a corner of the cabin, where an unpainted bed of rough-hewn pine stood with its high footboard turned facing the room; and, after the cry, came a groan, and then a sharp, shrill cry.

Elizabeth ran towards the bed. On it, lying in a nest of dirty rags, was a woman, her face already stark with approaching death. Beside her was a new-born baby, blue and shivering, but giving, from time to time, a tiny, whimpering gasp——

It was no uncommon thing, in the early days of the colonies, for one married woman to minister to another at the time of her confinement, without the assistance of a trained midwife, much less of a physician; and one of the valley settlers, George Corliss, had delivered his wife Joanna himself, since no other help was by, and then had been forced to leave her, weak and helpless as she yet was, to go foraging for food when her child was only a day or two old. The dread of Indian invasion was then still an omnipresent and well-founded fear; and about candlelighting time, on the evening after the young father's departure, several half-naked redskins stole stealthily into the Corliss cabin, stirred the flickering fire on the hearthstone into fresh flame, and squatting stolidly about it, held a long and solemn powwow. Joanna, clutching her baby to her sore and swollen breast, had lain motionless and breathless with terror, watching them throughout the endless night; but they left her unmolested, and towards dawn she fell into a light sleep from sheer exhaustion. When she wakened, with frenzied panic, it was to find that the Indians had gone away; but that beside her on her bed they had laid a gleaming knife, in sinister testimony of what they might have done and what they might yet do——

Elizabeth had listened to this story more than once, and her startled mind reverted, flashingly, to it now. But it was unheard of that any human mother should be left alone and unaided at the actual hour of travail: This was a far more terrible ordeal than that which Joanna had been forced to face; and with Lisa's sense of horror was mingled the sense of her own dreadful inadequacy. She lacked the most rudimentary knowledge of the exigencies of childbirth; that the succor of a young girl should be sought in such a situation would have been deemed a violation of all maidenly modesty. Though Jeffie had been hers to cosset and care for from the day of her birth, Lisa had been sent with the Cameron children to stay with the Whitelaws on the night the weanie had been born; and all had been put to rights in the chamber where Mistress Cameron had been brought to bed, before Lisa had entered it afterwards.

But even if she had not been trapped by pitiful ignorance, it was too late now, she soon realized instinctively, for her to save the quivering creature on the bed—if she had only stopped, earlier, that morning—there might have been time then to ride for help.—She said this, in her anguish, half aloud, as she sat beside the bed holding the woman's hand an hour later, when, under the latter's broken and agonized directions, she had done what she could to make the double death which was soon to come less gruesome. The mother heard her, and opened heavy eyes.

"No one would have come," she said, and closed them again, "I tried—for the baby's sake."

"Surely anyone would have come to thee in thy trouble! Any good woman!"

"Any *good* woman!" echoed the dying mother. "No good woman would come near me! *Good* women are not like that. Except thee. I think thou must be the little Scotch lady of whom I have heard so much, whose heart goes out to everyone." Her glazing glance fell on the girl in hopeless appeal. "Is there room in it for me—since I can do no more evil?"

"Hast thou done evil?" whispered the girl tremulously.

"Aye—there is no doubt of that. The everlasting torture that must come to me is well deserved. But that my baby must burn forever because it dies unbaptized—" She turned, writhing, on the bed, and clutched the poor little blue infant more tightly still. "Oh, God! is that just? The baby hath done no harm. Had I had care—and food— and fire—it might have lived! I have heard it preached, in the days when I still went to church, that hell is paved with the skulls of unbaptized babies.—Little Scotch lady, must my child perish for my sins?"

Elizabeth was not ignorant of the cruel theology of

the times. The doctrine of damnation, which Jonathan Edwards had preached, had already gone, like a scalding fire, over the colonies, so that she listened to it almost daily in her new home; and it but supplemented the tenets of the faith which she had learned in her old one. But her travels in foreign lands had taught her something of other faiths as well, and she remembered now what she had learned there.

"Thy baby shall not die unbaptized," she said gently, leaning over the bed, "in extremity, anyone may baptize an infant. I will do it myself. Let me take the child."

The woman looked at her in terror, as if fearing some new torment. "Is that true?" she muttered. "Art thou sure?"

"I am very sure. It is a recognized principle of the church. Come! Give me thy baby." She freed it from the clutching fingers that held it, and took it in her arms.

"There is still water in the pitcher," she said breathlessly. "Tell me quickly—what shall I name thy son?"

"I know not—name him what thou wilt."

"What is thy husband's name?"

"My husband! Thou sweet innocent! dost not know that I have not a husband? Would I be left to perish like this if I had?"

There is an instinct implanted in even the most sheltered of girls which tells them that there is a wickedness in the world, and, vaguely, of some of the forms which it takes; but they think of it, invariably, as something both rare and distant, which will never touch their own lives. The first encounter with it is invariably a shock, even when it is dressed in its most alluring colors; but when the acquaintance with it comes coupled with that of filth and suffering and death, it is more than that: it is a hideous and stunning blow. For a moment Elizabeth shrank, physically as well as spiritually, from the woman on the bed. Then a feeling of strange, mystic kinship with the fallen woman flashed, with lightning quickness, across her seared and stricken mind.

"Didst thou love him—thy baby's father?" she asked softly.

Two great tears—the first she had shed—rolled slowly down the sinner's soiled and ghastly cheeks.

"Aye," she said, "better than life itself. Better, as thou seest, than my honor. But I lost him. He found out—that he was not the first. God! Was that my fault? Nay—nay—nay—I was orphaned at thirteen—and men are men—when they sought me there was none to save me, none to show me salvation. And yet, he, who was as guilty as I—as guilty as all the others—turned against me——"

Elizabeth gave a little smothered cry. "If thou hast suffered *that*," she whispered, "thy child, since his father had neither name nor honor to give him, must have the name of one who was the soul of honor—whom I love better than any in the world." She dipped her free hand in the little pitcher, and sprinkled the cold drops over the baby's face. "I baptize thee," she said, *"Basil Keith* —In the name of the Father, and of the Son, and of the Holy Ghost. Amen." She laid the tiny form, already stiffening, back in its mother's arms, and knelt beside her. "That is the name," she said softly, "that my son would have had—if I could have belonged, as thou didst, to the man I loved. If it will comfort thee, I will tell thee my own story—but first let us pray."

It was a long time before she rose from her knees; when at last she did so the baby was dead; and when, hours later, she closed the door of the little cabin behind her, the tortured woman was dead, too. But on her cold face was the look of everlasting peace.——

The Indian scout, motionless as a graven image, was still standing by Dobbin's side. Without a word, he handed Elizabeth the reins and watched her mount. But before she rode away into the darkness he spoke to her.

"Evil spirit in cabin like I told Missie," he said stonily; "Missie better keep away."

Elizabeth turned, and answered him over her shoulder. "There was no evil spirit in the cabin, Joe," she said softly. "God sent the singing angels, after all."

## EIGHT

The WAGES OF SIN ARE DEATH. The wages of charity are often bitter condemnation. When it became known in the settlement of Ryegate that Elizabeth Burr had ministered to a scarlet woman, and that she had baptized the evildoer's child *in extremis* according to the rites of the Roman Church she was summoned to appear before the session, consisting of two clergymen from Philadelphia, the local minister, and three deacons, when it should meet in Ryegate at the time of the spring communion season, to be tried for heresy. The rumor that she had also been heard to affirm her belief that "The Song of Solomon" was a pæan of carnal love, and not an exposition of the mystic union between Christ and the church, rendered her predicament even more grave; though since this report was not confirmed, no formal charges were based upon it.

All through the second winter of her sojourn in the valley she waited for her trial, listening to the harsh comments made to her upon her conduct, and of its probable resulting disgrace—comments from which she had no escape, since the snow lay drifted deep over the meadows and in the woods, where, in the summer, she might have fled for solitude and refuge. Judge Cameron was worried about his failing fortunes, and sat brooding and silent, reading little, and telling none of the lively anecdotes with which his memory was stocked; Mistress Cameron was expecting another child, and was ailing and fretful. The atmosphere of the once cheerful house was gloomy as well as tense; but this was not the worst; the children who had always been Lisa's charge before, and who would have been of infinite comfort to her now, were kept apart from her as from one contaminated. She could not so much as bend over Jeffie to kiss her that Mistress Cameron did not snatch the wean away.

"Since thou hast seen fit to nurse a strumpet who hath

81

cast a leglen girt," [1] she cried, "take thy smirched hands away from my wee lambie."

Elizabeth thrust the child from her. "Aye, that I will!" she exclaimed vehemently. "Keep thy wallydraigle [2] to thyself and welcome! And when she next is ailing, cosset her thyself!"

The following day the bairn was hot with fever, and Mistress Cameron was beside herself. It was not past belief, she whispered distractedly to her husband, that the banished girl had bewitched the child in spite; but when night drew on, and Jeffie tossed in her cot and wailed for her lost friend, Mistress Cameron swallowed her pride and went abjectly to the small chamber where Lisa lay lonely and wakeful under her patchwork quilt, and begged her to take the child in bed with her.

"Till she is well again only?" Lisa asked scornfully, but with a palpitating heart.

"Aye. I will not trouble thee longer. But since she is so bounden to thy ways——"

The truce patched up between the two was a sorry one at best, and lasted only through the anxious weeks until Jeffie was well and rosy again. After that there was no mitigation of the girl's imprisonment; from the visitors whose comings and goings had once punctuated the long months so brightly for her, she could now look for little cheer. The Priest of Bath was still far off; and even if she could have forged her way through the snow to Bath and sought indirect tidings of him from Mistress Sutherland, she would not have done so; for the Priest's wife, she knew, sat in stern judgment upon her conduct, and was responsible for the untraced rumors concerning the "Song of Solomon." Wells Goodwin had been ailing with rheumatism ever since the autumn; he could not brave the elements, but must wait for warm weather to peddle his wares; and Wells, too, came of a family so strictly righteous that there was little doubt in Lisa's mind what his attitude would have been could he have expressed it. There remained Indian Joe and Peabody Ladd; and though

[1] Borne an illegitimate child.
[2] Weakling, the youngest of a brood.

each strove, in his own way, to divert her thoughts and lighten her burden, each failed to comfort her.

"Missie no be afraid of court," Joe told her gutturally, flinging a sheaf of fine furs down at her feet. "Joe's boy Toomalik kill man last year, court do nothing. Bah!"

"But, Joe, that was not the same kind of a court! And I have not killed anyone—I could not save a life, but I saved two souls. Thou seest, all is different."

"Bah!" said Joe again. "Church court mean, all same other court. My boy Toomalik love girl Lewa, Lewa marry Mitchell man. My boy Toomalik say, 'I shoot Mitchell, take Lewa all same my squaw.' Toomalik go one night, find Lewa and Mitchell on Oxbow beside camp fire. Toomalik make gun go bang, bang! Bad gun hit Lewa, not Mitchell, Lewa die. Court send for Toomalik, Toomalik say, 'Huh! no mean kill Lewa, mean kill Mitchell, Mitchell not killed, Toomalik no murderer!' Court think, court think hard, court think some more, Toomalik go free!"

"There is no moral in thy story," Lisa said listlessly, "and for that reason it pleaseth me. But it doth not help me."

The method of Peabody Ladd was different. He brought the strange instrument, the name of which the settlers could never remember, straight to the Camerons' fireside, and sat and strummed on it, looking across at Lisa with the bright roving glance in which was concentrated so much of his elusive charm.

"Thou knowest, bonnie Bessie, that Arcady is not really far distant," he said, softly and liltingly, his words hidden to all but her by the strumming. "We could reach it, thou and I, within a day or so. My horse goes swiftly even through the snow, and with a pillion added to the saddle——"

"Thou hast gone to Arcady before—with a pillon added to thy saddle?" she asked, her lips curling a little.

"Not to the same Arcady which thou and I might find together. If there have been wanderings before I knew thee, thou shouldest not hold that against me. Come, Bessie, we'll be gay together yet!"

"Gay, perhaps; but never at peace."

"Hast peace here? And what of heart's desire?"

"Until I find true love with it, I shall not harken to its call," she said, and rose as if to leave him.

"But thou canst hear the call?"

"Thou knowest," she said, borrowing Anderson's phrase.

"And hast thou no fire in thy veins?"

"Aye, that I have. But not quicksilver. I want a man with fire, too!"

There were stabbing points, half pain, half pleasure, pricking her all over as she walked away from him, but she did not once turn her head toward the place where he sat, still smiling and strumming, but not daring to detain her.

Anderson was not among those who came and went; he was always there. But though Anderson, his own heart heavy, would gladly have braved public opinion to comfort her, she turned on him in a biting rage which he had never seen her display before, at his first attempt do do so.

"Leave me alone!" she cried, her pale face flaming suddenly. "Thou'rt a godly church member like all the rest! In thy soul thou blamest me, too. It is only thy love for me that doth tempt thee to my side, against thy better judgment—a worthy love, forsooth, if it makes thee juggle with thine own conscience! That conscience which tells thee it would have been better to let a mother and baby —two human beings, created in God's image—die comfortless rather than get mud on my own skirts! Now that thou thinkest them muddy, keep away from them—they might brush thy clean leathern breeches as I pass thee by!"

"Thou knowest that I do not think thy skirts are muddy; only that thy judgment is rash and impetuous."

"Better that than it were cold and cruel! And I will tell thee something else—I would be willing to die, as that poor sinner died, without even the slight succor which she received, if I, like her, could have belonged, or could belong yet, to the man I love. Turn that over in thy mind, James Anderson, the next time thou tryest to stop me, for it is true!"

84

Anderson went white. But he answered her steadily.

"It is not true. It is a bitter grief to thee that thou couldst not wed him, and in the sharpness of thy grief thou believest sometimes—what thou hast just said. But it is not true. Basil Keith could not have tempted thee away from honor."

"He would never have tried! He was the soul of honor itself! But if he had not been——"

"If he had not been, thou wouldst have been strong enough for both. But I believe, as thou sayest, from what thou hast told me of him, that he was. Therefore do not make comparisons with a case where there was no honor on either side."

"There was love! Better unlawful union with love, than marriage without it! In the eyes of God, I believe, the sin is less!"

"The eyes of men, Lisa, reflect what is in the eyes of God—and in the eyes of men that woman was an evildoer, while if thou wouldst wed me, thou wouldst do good."

"Who made her an evildoer? It must have been the men of this valley, must it not? How do I know which ones?"

"And I know not either, as thou art well aware. Thou canst not hurt me by striking as wide of the mark as that. But I will leave thee alone until I find thee less sad, since thou wishest it."

He was as good as his word. Long before the winter was over, she would have called him back, to feel the relief of his sympathetic sanity about her. But she was too proud to make any sign, and he to come without one. It was not until the evening before the Church Fast of Thursday, in the communion season, which was kept as sacred as the Sabbath, that he sought her out again, finding her, as he had once before, sitting on the great boulder in the orchard, though the early spring air was still damp and cold, and there were melting patches of snow on the hillsides.

"I have brought a cloak to put around thee," he said, as casually as if they were in the habit of meeting every day. "It is too cold for thee to sit here, thus unprotected."

"Is it the cloak—or thou—that will protect me?" she asked, speaking sharply lest he should detect too much pleasure in her voice at seeing him again.

"Both."

"I thank thee. Nevertheless, I can wrap the cloak around myself, and accept thy protection the more gratefully the further from me thou dost sit while proffering it."

He handed her the rough woolen garment without a word, and turned to leave her. She called him back.

"Why dost thou go away?" she asked, stamping one small foot. "I am not so ungracious as all that! But I like neither to be—touched nor teased."

"Have I touched or teased you this winter once?"

"Nay—but thou art come to do both now!"

"Neither. Only to ask thee if thou wilt let me take thee when thou goest before the session on Saturday. First comes the baptism of those of mature years. Then the meeting of the session in the small room adjoining the main body of the church. After this meeting the elders will pass into the larger room and the preparatory sermon will be preached; and at the end of that sermon the tokens will be distributed to all those who are to be admitted to the communion on the Sabbath. If the decision of the session hath been unfavorable, thou wilt receive no token. But if thou hast withstood the test, we will go to the communion table together."

"And if it hath not?"

"I will go home with thee."

How much this meant to a man of Anderson's traditions and creed, the girl could not fail to know. Knowing it, she could hardly fail to be touched.

"Come thou here, James, and sit with me," she said gently, "and tell me why thou art willing to put up with so much bad temper and wickedness?"

He smiled, but shook his head. "I will not disturb thee now. No doubt thou hast need to meditate, and to collect thy thoughts. But I will be waiting for thee Saturday. Thou'll not disappoint me?"

"Thou'rt very good. And I will tell thee that I have missed thee sorely these last months. But I cannot accept this from thy hands."

"Why not?"

She hesitated a moment, then answered him frankly, without even turning away her eyes. "As well publish our banns!" she said, "if thou takest such a stand as this, publicly, when I am in disgrace, it will commit thee to me beyond any hope of withdrawal."

"Any hope of withdrawal! Thou knowest that my hope is not of withdrawal, but of the exact opposite!"

She laughed, at last, and motioned to him again to sit down beside her, the tension between them broken at last. "Thou wouldst wed me even if excommunicated?" she asked.

"Aye," he answered stubbornly, "if thou wouldst go, I should take thee straight from the table where thou hadst been rejected to some other minster who would make thee my wife before sundown."

"Then it behooves me to see that I am not excommunicated," she answered lightly, "for even if thou art committed, I cannot be. Let us not misunderstand each other there. I am making no promise."

"That is understood, of course. The obligation is all on my side."

"Then I do not see how I can deny thee."

"I did not intend that thou shouldst," he said, and left her. He had not expected to see her again before Saturday; but when the Thursday fast was over, she came to him in the barn as he was finishing his work, and suggested that they should walk over the hills together. And, as he looked at her in astonishment, she suddenly stood on tiptoe, and put her arms around his neck.

"I want to kiss thee," she said softly. "No—not to have thee kiss me—I dare not that, but to kiss thee, on the forehead, and say God bless thee for what thou art doing for me; and then to be out with thee, in this lovely country, together, as we used to be."

He bent his head, mutely, and she pressed her soft lips against his brow. Then, as he still stood quite motionless, "I am going to try to make thee proud of me—to justify thy faith in me," she whispered, slipping her hand in his. "Come, let us go."

A soft mist was rising from the valley with the twilight, and they could go neither fast nor far; but, without releasing her hold on him, the girl talked happily as they sauntered, her companion still silent beside her. "Thou knowest the tokens were first given," she said, "when the Covenanters were hiding from their persecutors in hills like these, and the ministers had to be sure that only friends and believers, and not enemies, came to the service. The little metal disc which was given them beforehand was their proof. There is one story that I have heard and that I have always loved, of a time when the fugitives had been almost overtaken, and one of them prayed, 'Oh, Father, hide us in Thy plaidie.' And just then a fog arose, and in the darkness they escaped. A fog something like this, I suppose."

"I did not know the tale. But I think our Father does 'hide us in his plaidie' when we ask it of him."

"And that he will so hide me?"

"I am sure of it."

Saturday dawned so clear and fair that it seemed almost as if summer had suddenly crept into the place but a day before left vacant by winter. And Lisa, looking out of her window at the warm beauty that had been spread over the earth, jerked open a long-closed drawer of her dresser, and pulled out of it garments which, folded between lavender sprigs and linen towels, had lain there unused for a year and a half. When Anderson knocked at the door, she flung it open and confronted him dressed in pale blue silk, a kerchief of fine lace and embroidered muslin about her neck, fastened at the breast with a jeweled brooch, rhinestone buckles on her high-heeled shoes, her golden curls piled high on top of her head. She looked inches taller; but what was more, she looked leagues lovelier than he had ever seen her. He flushed, and frowned a little.

"Put on thy homespun, Lisa," he said gravely, "and the shoes which Wells Goodwin made for thee, and take down thy hair. Thou wilt have no chance with the session dressed like that. They will harden their hearts against thee from the very first moment."

She laughed. "The rulers of the session are men, I suppose," she said, "even if they are Covenanters? At all events Indian Joe has reminded me that they are, and I am willing to take the risk that my gay apparel will be more seductive than shocking. Men's hearts expand before silk when they shrink before homespun—even while their lips are saying that they loathe the one and love the other! If I am to be cast out of the church, I shall go as Mistress Burr of Glasgow, and not as poor little nameless exile. For this one day I am going back two years. Come, let us start!"

There was no dissuading her; and all the way across the hills to the meetinghouse, sitting behind him on the pillion, her arm around his waist, she sang and chatted more gaily than he had ever seen her do. She sensed his bewilderment, although he said nothing.

" 'Tis well not to lay more at the heart than ye can kick off at the heel, Jim," she said. "So I am kicking now, with both feet, lest my heart should be too heavy.— But I have prayed, too," she added softly, laying her bright head for an instant against his shoulder.

"God grant that thy prayers may be answered, Lisa," he said earnestly.

The session had already assembled when they reached the church, and together entered the little side room where the meeting was being held. None of the sudden warmth of the day had penetrated into the cold building, and not one of the grim-visaged men, dressed in black coats, their high, black vests buttoned at the left and their high pointed collars partially hidden in the front by huge black cravats, rose or spoke, as the girl approached and stood quietly before them. She bowed gravely, then raised her head and faced them squarely.

"I am come," she said in a clear voice, "as you have ordered, to answer the charges of heresy brought against me by my neighbors. The nature of these charges is, I think, well understood by me. The first is that I have given succor to a harlot. The second, that by using the rites of the Roman Church, which is abhorrent to you, I have sought to save a bastard from everlasting damnation."

The words were crudely ugly coming from the soft red lips of a girl, even in a generation which never sought to soften its speech. Their ugliness, and the unexpected assurance with which they were spoken, smote every man present as surely as if the beautiful little creature, who looked so small and gentle and lovely, had suddenly struck him in the face with one of her tiny hands. They had been prepared for fright, for hesitation and evasion, from a cowering and ignorant girl. Not for this. The chief of the elders raised his hand to enforce silence; but the warning was little heeded. There was not one of the session who, at that moment, was not too thunderstruck to speak.

"This is correct, is it not? You understand, of course, that I admit the charges, that I do not seek in any way to deny them. If you do not, let me repeat this, that there be no mistake. The charges are true."

"Then thou art a self-confessed heretic," said one of the rulers harshly, finding his voice.

The girl turned to him swiftly. "Nay," she answered, "I did not say that. I ministered to the woman, and I baptized the child. But I am not an unbeliever."

"Dost thou not know the commandments?" asked another hard voice, "and that he—or she—who breaks them or connives with them who do break them shall be damned?"

"I do know the commandments," Elizabeth answered, "including the seventh. I know also the story of the woman taken in adultery, and the words that Christ spoke to the men who wished to kill her! 'He that is without sin among you, let him cast the first stone.' When Holy Scripture varies in its teaching from one book to another—which are we to follow—the law of Moses, who, our faith teaches us, was a man, or the law of Jesus, who, our faith teaches us, was the Son of God?" She paused a moment, and as no one broke the silence, she added softly, "I know also something of men, though I am very young. If this session had been in Jerusalem, that day, which one of you could have led the rest to do the stoning?"

The elder who had spoken first leapt to his feet, his

face brick-red. "Thou hussy," he thundered, "dost think thou canst insult thy judges and go unpunished?"

"I meant no insult. I but asked a question. That, as I understand, was not forbidden me. I do not desire to be heretical. Therefore, if the teachings of the church, and the practices of the elders are not clear to me, surely the session will not refuse to instruct me."

She paused, as if waiting for such instruction, and glanced with a look that was all docile receptiveness, from one elder to another. But no one spoke, and after a moment she went on, still more deferentially.

"There is still something else that I would ask. Our risen Lord showed himself first in the garden to another woman—a woman whose sins had been forgiven her, because she loved much. There was not more doubt of the fact that she had sinned than that she had loved—and that she had been forgiven. The suffering mother who died in the cabin had loved much—some man in this valley. He had deserted her. Did I do wrong, then, to seek to lead her at the end to Christ?"

"Thou hast said enough on this subject," interposed an elder who so far had not spoken. Anderson, listening to every syllable with a beating heart, could have sworn that his tone was edged with the conscious desire to probe it no further. " 'Tis no fit one for a maid."

"Your reverence will pardon me. I did not ask to be brought before this session, and the subject of the trial is not of my seeking. Let me speak of the child, then, instead of the mother—the dying baby, blue with cold, the little naked creature whose mother had not so much as a shawl in which to wrap it, who was not more than a skeleton because she had lacked for food. Never, so long as I live, shall I forget that awful sight. In my dreams I see it every night, and wake, shivering and weeping, because I think I hold it again in my arms. I told no lie to the dying mother when I said that in the church anyone could baptize a dying child, and that the baptism would be valid; that I had even seen it done. And this is true. She did not ask me which church—would not have understood me had there been time or need to tell her. There was only time and need, as I saw it, to bring the two

91

towards the light as best I could. 'Inasmuch as you have done it for one of these little ones, you have done it also for me—Suffer little children to come unto me, and forbid them not, for of such is the kingdom of heaven.' Which of you would have dared to disobey our Lord, and forbid that this dying child should be taken into the kingdom of heaven? If there is one, I will gladly be excommunicated by him as a heretic, for in his decision there would lie no shame for me!"

She took a step forward, and lifted her eyes. "When the mother and child were both dead," she said in a low voice, "and I was hastening to leave the cabin, that I might return and tell in Ryegate what had befallen me, I was arrested by the sound of angels' voices, singing all about me. They were the same, I believe, that sang when the little girl, whom you all loved, went peacefully to her death before she had been touched by sin or shame. They sang for the scarlet woman as gladly as for her. The scout, Indian Joe, who held my horse, and feared to enter the cabin because of the presence of evil spirts, which he believed dwelt there, heard them also. He waits without to witness to the truth of what I say, if you doubt it. There was joy in heaven because of one sinner who had repented. Is there none on earth?"

The elders of the session looked at one another. Anderson, leaning heavily against the wall, watched them with a thumping heart. The girl continued to stand motionless before them, her head still held high, waiting for some sign. At last, as no one moved or spoke, she bowed it.

"I thank Thee, Lord," she said, "that Thou hast softened the hearts of these Thy ministers toward Thy servant, a stranger in a strange land; and dedicate myself anew to Thy service, as Thou shalt reveal it to me. In the name of the Father, and of the Son, and of the Holy Ghost. Amen."

"Amen," said the elders of the session, in unison.

"Amen," said James Anderson last of all.

———

Side by side, with surging hearts, the boy and girl passed from the cold little room, and sat, with fingers

92

touching, near the place where Indian Joe had squatted motionless upon his haunches throughout the long preparatory sermon in the main body of the church; side by side, they advanced, after the service was over, to where the elders stood in front of the congregation, the applicants for communion passing before them in single file, receiving, upon identification, the small disc—the "token" which was to admit them to the sacrament on the following day; and side by side, at this latter devotion, they sat at the communion table which stood before the pulpit, a deacon at each end, surrendering to him the token again before they partook of the Body and Blood of Christ; and together, at last, they raised their voices and sang the Psalm of David, written in meter, with which the communion season was brought to an impressive close.

That man hath perfect blessedness who walketh not astray,
In council of ungodly men nor stands in sinners' way.
Nor sitteth in the scorner's chair, but placeth his delight,
Upon God's law and meditates on His law day and night.
He shall be like a tree that grows near-planted by a river,
Which in his season yields his fruit and his leaf fadeth never.

And all he doth shall prosper well, the wicked are not so,
But like they are unto the chaff which wind blows to and fro.
In judgment therefore shall not stand such as ungodly are,
Nor in the assembly of the just shall wicked men appear.
For why? the way of godly men unto the Lord is known,
Whereas the way of wicked men shall quite be overthrown.
Ye gates lift up your heads, ye doors, doors that do last for aye,
Be lifted up, that the King of Glory enter may.
But who is He that is the King of Glory? who is this?
The Lord of Hosts, and none but He, the King of Glory is.

## NINE

From the day when they took communion together after her trial, James Anderson and Elizabeth Burr were constantly together. She made no effort to avoid him, and he, in turn, did not attempt to make love to her. The settlement expected, as she had predicted, to hear the banns of marriage published in church. But Sunday succeeded Sunday without such an announcement, and another summer drifted on, and still it was not made. The man seemed to be content to continue to work indefinitely for Master Cameron; while the girl, on the other hand, did not again broach the subject of going out in service until Anderson spoke of it to her of his own accord.

"Hast thou given up thy idea of going to Newbury to work?" he asked her one evening as they were walking home from a quilting party together.

"I had given it no thought of late. Why?"

"Colonel Thomas Johnson's daughter, Betsey, has, as you know, recently been married to Isaac Bayley, the General's son—a match most pleasing to those two old friends, who first settled this valley together, I am sure! Her elder brother, Hanes, is opening the fine ballroom in his new house with an election ball on Thursday, next, and she and the happy bride-groom will be among the honored guests—indeed, he is to be one of the managers! I have heard it said that the Johnsons are short of help for such a grand occasion, and will be glad of any they may get. Shouldst thou choose, I can take thee down there that night, for I have received an invitation—doubtless because of the interest my father hath taken in politics, and his participation in these, Thou canst then see something of the leading families of Newbury, and judge for thyself whether it would please thee to go and live with either of them."

He handed her a stiff square of paper, elaborately printed. She read the superscription eagerly:

ELECTION BALL

The company of James Anderson
is requested at Johnson's Hall
on Thursday evening, the 8 inst, at six o'clock.

BEN PORTER,
ISAAC BAYLEY,

94

W. WALLACE JUN.,
W. B. BANISTER,
*Managers.*

Newbury,
    Oct. 1806 [1]

"A kind thought, Jim!" she said, giving the invitation back to him. "But thy great body is largely compacted of small, kind thoughts, neatly put together like a patchwork quilt!"

"Thou wilt come?"

"Aye, surely."

"Make thyself fine then, in that blue dress thou keepest laid away. There is much show of fashion in Newbury and Haverhill, I am told."

"But surely not among serving-maids!"

"I do not know that. But wear the gown."

"To please thee?"

"If thou dost choose to put it that way."

"I would do almost anything to please thee, Jim!"

He smiled a little ruefully. "There is ever that 'almost'!" he said.

But she was very fair to look upon when Wednesday evening came, and very sweet to him on the long ride down the valley beside the Connecticut, sitting, in the position which had come to seem so natural to them both, behind him on the pillion, her arm around his waist, her head on his shoulder; and he forgot the "almost" for the time being. His uncommon happiness made him talkative, and he told her, as they rode along, stories which he had heard of the early days of the valley, and of the men who had settled it, reaching back, from time to time, to make sure that her cloak was wrapped firmly about her, and stopping old Dobbin that she might shift her weight and not grow lame and stiff from sitting too long in one position.

"These are the meadows," he said, "where Jacob Bayley was plowing when Thomas Johnson warned him, by means of an ingenious device, that Colonel Pritchett and the Tories were after him. Pritchett's men were stationed on

---

[1] The first election ball held in Hanes Johnson's house actually took place in 1801.

the hills yonder, and could look down on the valley as easily as if it had been a map. He had summoned Johnson to come and see him, and Johnson, who had been released upon parole after his imprisonment in Canada, was bound to go, and also to hold no communication with his friend. He took a slip of paper, and wrote upon it 'The Philistines be upon thee, Samson.' This he gave to his brother-in-law, Dudley Carleton, and told him to go down upon his way without stopping. Bayley saw the paper, read it without lifting it from the ground, and calling to his sons, who were with him, 'Look out for yourselves, boys,' he went quietly down the field to the river, and so made his escape. When the British soldiers surrounded his house that night, it was only to find that their bird had flown."

"There is great friendship between these two great men, is there not?"

"Aye. There is a rumor that Mistress Bayley, who was Prudence Noyes before her marriage, was Johnson's half-sister, but that is likely only idle talk. I believe that there is friendship without blood-kin, which is the greatest of all."

As they approached the northern part of the settlement of Newbury, called the Oxbow, because of the winding bend of the river near which it lay, they could see horses hitched even in front of Thomas Johnson's house, and in front of the brick store of his eldest son, David Johnson, which stood across the street from it; while the yard surrounding Hanes Johnson's handsome new dwelling was thick with them, and the sounds of laughing voices and dancing feet, mingled with the scraping of fiddles, came through the open, candlelighted windows. James dismounted, and handed the girl the reins.

"Sit here and wait while I inquire whether we will be welcome," he said. "I will be gone but a minute."

It was, indeed, scarcely more than that; but, during his absence, two or three merrymakers and guests stopped and stared at her, as she sat quietly on Dobbin's back, and one of them, who had evidently begun to toast his favorite candidate even before he left his own house, raised a lantern to her face, and looked at her with insolent approval.

"What a pretty wench!" he said with a coarse laugh. "Get down, sonsy lass, and come and dance with me!" And, as she turned her head away without answering, he laid a heavy hand on her cloak, and gave it a vigorous tug. "Didst hear me speak to thee, sweetie?" he leered. "If not, I shall try other ways of opening thine ears."

"Thou'rt likely to get thine own boxed in the attempt," she retorted; and thrusting out one small foot viciously, kicked him full in his ample stomach. The man roared with a mixture of pain, surprise, and relish.

"Thou glaikit gilpy! I'll pay thee later for that! And would now, come not thine own cavalier."

Anderson noticed nothing. "I have seen Mistress Johnson," he said in a pleased voice, "a lovely woman still, though she must be well past middle-age, with all these grown sons and daughters. She was Abigail Carleton before her marriage, and I have heard it told that the blood of one of the Queens of England flows in her veins. Now that I have witnessed her graciousness for myself, I can well believe it.—She says that we are both to go up to the ballroom, and make ourselves known to her son Hanes and his wife, and to the bride and groom, and dance at least once or twice ourselves. Otherwise, since we are invited guests, she will hear naught of our helping. But I have told her that after we have had a glimpse of the merrymaking thou wilt go to the kitchen to help dish up pies and puddings and cakes, and I to the shed where stands a great barrel of rum to be ladled out."

"Wilt thou dance with me, Jim?"

"Thou knowest that I have never danced. But I will stand by and watch thee, and take pleasure in that, if thou wouldst enjoy it."

They tied Dobbin to the long hitching post, went up the cobblestone walk, and entered the wide hallway of the spacious dwelling house together. From either side of it, a great square room, white paneled and deeply carved, and crowded with company, opened out hospitably; and as they went up the broad and graceful stairway, they could not help but speak of how easy were the treads, how low and widely built. Turning, as they reached the top, they saw to their right an ample closet opened to disclose deep shelves stacked with wines and liquors, from which the guests were freely helping themselves; while directly before them was a noble double doorway, hung on huge hinges of iron in the shape of the letter "H." This doorway led into a great apartment with an arched ceiling vaulting over it and a high seat built all around it, which was, they knew, the ballroom, of which they had heard so much. It ran straight across the front of the second story, and was warmed, at either end, by a splendid fireplace. A yet greater crowd was gathered here, and beside one of the hearthstones stood a group of politicians, whispering and drinking together; around the other was clustered a gay little group of musicians. Peabody Ladd was among these, "calling out numbers" and flourishing his bow, and he paused to shout a greeting to Jim and Lisa as they stood hesitantly upon the threshold.

There was, as James had predicted, much "fashion" present, as the simpler Scots of Ryegate understood it. The early colonists who had founded Newbury and Haverhill were men of some wealth and culture, and the splendid service which they rendered during the American Revolution had brought them into touch again with the refinements of civilization which they had voluntarily abandoned a quarter of a century earlier. Yet a strong spirit of democracy dominated the gathering. Not only were the Johnsons and the Bayleys, the Chamberlains and Hazens, the Dows and Montgomerys present, but all the countryside, and Jim and Lisa were made as welcome in the ballroom as were any of the most distinguished guests. Indeed, the great General himself gallantly insisted upon leading up "the little Scotch lady"; and when their reel was over, a dozen swains were almost instantly around her. It was more than an hour before Anderson had the heart to remind her, gently, that they were needed downstairs.

"Oh—just a few more, Jim," she pleaded, laying her hand on his arm, her eyes sparkling, and her cheeks flushed more brightly than he had ever seen them, "I have not been in a ballroom since I left Scotland, and it seems more like heaven to me than all the meetinghouses put together in which I have sat Sabbath after Sabbath!"

Then, as he hesitated, she added mischievously, "Go to thy rum barrel! Since art not dancing, thou'll have more pleasure, and be of more use, there than here."

"I do not like to leave thee alone."

"Alone! Dost think I have lacked for company?"

"I mean, unprotected."

"But surely, in this great room, and with the General and our good friend Peabody present, no man will attempt liberties! And if, on the other hand, none shows me attention after thou art gone—for men are like sheep, and pursue a maid at a dance only when they are sure that one is leading—I will follow thee swiftly enough out of disappointment and spite, be very sure!"

Her argument seemed plausible; and feeling that they had no right to intrude on the gathering if one, at least, of them were not proving useful, he left her. His back was scarcely turned when Peabody called to her above the noise of his fiddle.

"Wilt not dance a Highland fling for us, Lisa? I did not dare ask thee before Jim, lest he should turn a black look upon me. But there are many here who can dish out puddings, and none who can tread as light as thou."

The bride, who had been dancing, stopped in the middle of her reel and clapped her hands with delight. She had overheard Peabody's plea and, swiftly, added her own to it. "Oh, Mistress Burr," she cried archly, "surely you will not refuse! 'Twill be a rare treat for us all! Come, let us clear the floor!"

It was a long time since Lisa had held the center of the stage alone and admired. She hesitated for a moment; but there was a teasing look in Peabody's eye which was like a challenge that she could not let lie. She flushed, bit her lip, and then nodded to him. She had not done curtsying to Mistress Bayley when he had struck up a Scottish tune which went to her head like wine; and instantly she had thrown herself with a zestful abandon which she had thought never to feel again, into the joyous "fling" of the Highlander.

She would, indeed, have been more than human had the enthusiasm that she aroused left her unmoved. It spurred her on to new harmonies of movement and of ecstasy. Over and over again, she danced, her full skirts blowing high above her tiny feet, as she kicked and pranced, her curls tossing, her arms lifted high, and when at last she sank down breathless, vowing that she could do no more, in spite of the cheers and clapping which rewarded her, Peabody would not let her rest.

"Thou must sing to us now! There is no dance here complete unless a concert goes with it."

"What then shall I sing? Some Psalm?" she asked wickedly.

There was a roar of laughter; Peabody called to her above it.

"Sing us 'The White Cockade'!"

She sprang up on a chair beside him, and rested her hand on his shoulder. "Play for me then—and everyone must join in the chorus!

"My love was born in Aberdeen—" she sang,
"The bonniest lad that e'er was seen,
But now he makes our hearts fu' sad—
He takes the field wi' his white cockade!"

Her gay lilting voice was drowned in a roar of applause. With mock gravity, she held up a small, admonitory finger.

"Now listen once, and then sing with me," she ordered. "Hark! it goes like this!

"O, he's a ranting roving lad,
He's a brisk an' bonny lad!
Betide what may, I will be wed,
An' follow the boy with the white cockade!"

"And follow the boy with the white cockade," caroled the General; and the next instant the room was rocking with the air.

"Now, then, give us the second verse!" Peabody shouted above the singing voices.

Again Lisa felt the challenge of his voice which she had no choice but to meet; and this time as her hand rested on his shoulder, it stole halfway around his neck.

"I'll sell my rock, my reel, my tow," she sang,
"My guid gray mare and hawkit cow,
To buy myself a tartan plaid,
To follow the boy with the white cockade!
O, he's a ranting, roving lad,
He is a brisk and bonny lad!
Betide what may, I will be wed,
And follow the lad with the white cockade!"

The girl leapt down from her perch to the sound of a crashing tumult. She turned, like a flash, to the bride.

"Will you go to the Highlands, Lizzie Lindsay,
Will you go to the Highlands wi' me?
Will you go to the Highlands, Lizzie Lindsay,
My bride and my darling to be?"

Peabody had caught the air instantly. He was fiddling with her before she had finished the first line.

"Thou little witch!" he muttered under his breath, when she had done. "Hast thou not something for the General, too?"

"Of course!" she retorted, and dropped a low curtsy before the famous man. "Come, Peabody, we must give him 'Bold and true——' "

"Aye, that we must!" flashed back the player. And again they were off in unison.

"O, bold and true,
In bonnet blue,
That fear of falsehood never knew;
Whose heart is loyal to his sword—
Seek Europe wide from sea to sea,
But bonny blue-cap still for me!"

"At your service forever!" General Bayley cried, immensely pleased, bending over and kissing her hand. "What hath this quick-witted little lady for us next?"

She hesitated for a moment. Among the young men and women who had known each other from childhood, a good deal of merry and open lovemaking was going on, and there was something in this unashamed demonstration of happy young blood, as natural and unrestrained

as it was harmless, which suddenly turned the girl sad.
But again she caught the ball which had been tossed to
her and after a whispered word with Peabody began another song.

> "When in my arms, wi' all thy charms,
>   I clasp my countless treasure, O,
> I seek nae mair of Heaven to share,
>   Than sic a moment's pleasure, O!
>
> "And by thy een so bonny blue,
>   I swear I'm thine forever, O,
> And on thy lips I seal my vow,
>   And break it I shall never, O!
>
> "And I'll kiss thee yet, yet,
>   And I'll kiss thee o'er again,
> And I'll kiss thee yet, yet,
>   My bonnie Peggy Allison."

"I'll join in a chorus of that too, gladly!" laughed a
tall, fair lad with a merry face, coming up beside her.

There was no offense in either manner or intention;
but there was, miraculously, a weird resemblance to a
face which she had seen before, close to her own, over
and over again. She grew suddenly faint, the dormant
memories of the nights when she had danced with Basil
suddenly and hotly awake within her.

"My next chorus must be in the kitchen," she countered, with a lightness she was still mistress enough of
herself to assume. "If I were Peggy Allison, I should take
up your gage—but I am Bessie Burr, worse luck. And the
lad with the white cockade is very far away."

"Sure, he is but in the shed, ladling rum. Call him up
again, if I do not please you."

"Jim Anderson doth not wear a white cockade," she
answered swiftly, "I spoke not of him. But that you will
let me go in peace, I will sing you one more song:

> "My heart is in the Highlands, my heart is not here,
> My heart's in the Highlands a-chasing the deer,
> A-chasing the wild deer and following the roe—
> My heart's in the Highlands, wherever I go!"

The girl was out of the room before the verse was completed, half-choked with sobs. The festive scene had brought up too many burning memories; and she had yielded so readily to the spell which Peabody Ladd never failed to cast over her, though usually she resisted it easily enough, that she was both dismayed and ashamed. She knew she would have done better to stay, soberly and safely, by Jim's side. And now it seemed to her she could not reach him soon enough. She was uncertain as to how to reach the kitchen, which she had not seen; but she groped her way somehow towards the narrow, dark, back stairs, with quick, hot tears scalding her flushed cheeks. She was feeling for the closed door at the bottom of the flight of steps, when she heard heavy footsteps behind her, and, in undefined terror, fumbled with shaking fingers for the latch. She could not find it. Turning quickly, she put her back to it, and threw her entire weight against the door. But it was of solid oak, and she did not turn the scales at a hundred pounds. She knew, as she heard a drunken laugh above her, that she was trapped. And the next instant a man's arms closed brutally around her.

"Wouldst box my ears and kick me?" he leered heavily. "Well, try it now, little Scotch lady, and see how much harm thou canst do me. I have watched for thee to leave the ballroom that I might cry quits with thee. Revenge is ever sweet, they tell me, but, by God, I doubt if any were ever sweeter than that which I am about to taste!"

Anderson had kissed her once by force, it was true; but his passion had been clean, and almost instantly conquered by his love. His kisses had left no stain. But the girl knew that if the lips of the brute who held her now had been wet with poison instead of brandy, there would have been no more danger for her in them than there was now. A red-hot iron, she felt, could not have branded her more openly. Her agonized struggle to free herself, hopeless though it seemed, delivered her. Her back was still towards the door, the man, holding her locked, leaning heavily against it. His great weight, thrown against hers, as he grappled with her, did what hers alone could not. The door gave way suddenly, crashing to the floor, hurling the man and girl with it. As it fell, the women in the kitchen, serving the feast, screamed aloud in terror. And Anderson, dropping his ladle, rushed in from the shed, and, brushing them from his path, reached Elizabeth's side, and snatched her to him.

For a moment he thought she was dead, and so did everyone else in the room. Her slight form fell limply away from him as he lifted her; her eyes were closed; her golden hair streamed vividly away from her blanched face. The stunned scoundrel who had fallen with her looked at her in terror, and then crawled, on his hands and knees, out of the house, before Anderson should remember him. The serving-women drew away, still screaming, too frightened to think or act clearly. Anderson laid her down, and loosened her dress, resting her unresisting head upon his shoulder, as he bent over and listened for her heartbeats. Then he looked at the panic-stricken women standing near him with immeasurable scorn.

"Give me some cold water," he said, "she has but fainted. Then go and tell thy mistress what has happened. She will not lack either charity or sense, as ye deem to do."

Under his hand, laid across them for the first time, he felt the girl's cold breasts grow warmer, throb, rise and fall again. Her delicate, blue-veined lids fluttered, and then opened slowly, over dull eyes that suddenly grew bright with terror.

"Lisa," he said gently, "Lisa, dost thou not know me? It's Jim. And Mistress Johnson is beside thee, too. No one can harm thee. When thou art better I shall carry thee to her house. Thou wilt be quieter there." And as she still looked at him with bewilderment and fear, he lifted her without another word, and carried her across the street and up the stairs into Mistress Johnson's own chamber, where he laid her down on the wide bed with the snowy counterpane, and high, carved posts that stood there. The Colonel's wife, who followed him, touched him on the shoulder as he gave up his precious burden.

"I will look after thy sweetheart," she said, her small high-bred features, slightly sharp and chill in repose, now soft with sympathy. "Come thou back and see her in the morning. She will be better then. Meanwhile, concern thyself with the man who abused my hospitality, and who frightened her. He cannot yet be far away. Thou'll find my husband's riding-whip in the entry as thou goest out."

## TEN

FOR A FEW DAYS THE GIRL LAY GRAVELY ILL. She had undergone a terrific shock, and the strong thread of her endurance, which had not broken under repeated strain, snapped suddenly, and raveled away. She was feverish, and in her fever she was delirious. That, at least, was what Dr. White and Mistress Johnson thought. But when they told Anderson of her wild ravings, his face, already white with anxiety, turned a shade whiter, and he demanded to be taken to her at once.

"She tells strange tales of happenings which I am sure have never befallen her, and which I understand not how she can invent. She babbles incessantly about the mails and the Indies, and asketh for a letter. Thomas hath told her that it is thought not one letter in three, going to and from the Old Country, reaches its destination, and then she wrings her hands and moans. She reproacheth herself for light conduct, because she did a Highland fling at Peabody Ladd's bidding, after thou hadst left the ballroom, and sang Scottish songs, which pleased the whole company mightily, as if she thought there were evil in so sweet and pleasant a thing. She calleth all night long the name of Basil, and weeps most bitterly. 'Tis a name we have never heard before."

"She will cease to call and weep when I am with her."

He was not mistaken. Elizabeth became instantly more quiet when he sat down beside her bed and took her hand. But the immediate explanation for this sudden change smote him through the heart.

"Basil," she whispered, "my own dear love—so thou art come to me at last."

He leaned over her, and forced himself to speak steadily.

"Basil is a dream," he said; "this is Jim—a reality. Come out of thy world of dreams, Lisa."

"Call me Beth."

"That I will not. Thou art Lisa, my sweetheart."

She looked puzzled, and passed her hand over her hot forehead. "I am Basil's Beth," she said in a troubled voice.

"Nay. Thou art Jim's Lisa."

At last she recognized him. But there was no joy with the recognition. She turned her head away, and would not look at him, and when he asked her the reason, she began to sob.

"I am ashamed," she whispered. "Oh, Jim, why didst thou leave me?"

"I have asked myself that a thousand times, and cursed myself for it. Nevertheless, there is nothing for which thou shouldst feel ashamed."

"I danced and sang."

"There was no harm in that."

"And listened to Peabody when he fiddled my thoughts away——"

"Thou hast long done that and, doubtless, ever will."

"And the man who tried to hurt me——"

She saw Jim's face darken and harden.

"I had mistreated him while I waited for thee in the yard."

"Only because he sought to insult thee. He will never do so again, or any other."

"I—I am not the sort of maid whom thou shouldst love."

"Thou art the sort of maid whom every man doth love—some righteously, and others evilly, each according to his nature. Therein lies the trouble. It is not well that thou shouldst be unprotected, as thou canst see for thyself. I trust that thou art cured now of thy talk of serving-maids."

She thought the harshness of his voice was for her, and shrank away again. The thought that he had ceased to care for her flashed through her mind, and she was dully surprised to find how much it would hurt her if he had. But the fear lasted only a minute. He called himself slow-witted, yet he always seemed to read her thoughts like lightning.

"I have told Mistress Johnson and the Colonel," he said, looking towards the lady who had entered the room and was standing by the doorway, and then towards the girl on the bed again, "that for nearly two years I have sought thy hand in marriage. Wilt thou confirm what I have said, Elizabeth?"

"Yes," she answered faintly.

"I have told them also that as yet thou hast not plighted thy troth with me. But that my heart has long been, and ever will be, wholly thine, they cannot doubt. Knowing this, they have given me leave to come and see thee as often as I wish until thou art well again. Just now thou art very tired, too tired to wish to talk much. I am going back to Ryegate, to tell the Camerons that my term of service and thy sojourn with them are both ended. General and Mistress Whitelaw have long wished, as thou knowest, to take thee into their household; I trust that when thou art recovered thou wilt go there. The Camerons have meant to be kind to thee, I know, though thou hast not always thought so. But sometimes they have not understood thee aright, and since their harshness after thy trouble in Bath thy spirit hath never been at rest there. As for me, now that I have publicly announced my hope to marry thee, whenever, and as soon, as thou wilt let me, it will be more seemly that I should return to my father's house—until, if ever, I may have one of my own. I must not leave Master Cameron without due notice, and without seeing that he is provided with other help. But when he is supplied, I will come back to see thee again, and thou wilt be stronger, and gladder to have me, I hope, than thou art now."

"I am always glad to see thee," said the girl, and

stretched out one hand across the counterpane. As she did so, the latch of the door clicked, and Mistress Johnson mysteriously vanished. Anderson walked closer to the bed, and taking the little hand, laid it against his cheek.

"God bless thee, my darling," he said huskily, "and keep thee safe always, and give thee to me in his own good time."

His departure left her alone with her thoughts much of the time, for the housewife of those days, no matter how prosperous her lot in life, was a busy one, and Mistress Johnson had little time to sit with her guest. The girl's reflections were sad ones. The Priest of Bath, who alone could give her helpful counsel, was still in the Old Country, and might not return for many months yet—perhaps not for over a year. The church, designed to give support and salvation to the sufferers who turned to it in their need, had sought to excommunicate her when she ministered to the fatherless in their affliction; only her own wit and her own beauty, not the inherent mercy of its ministers, had saved her; she knew this all too well, and would never seek refuge in that uncertain haven again. She stood so utterly alone that a fellow guest felt free to insult and terrify her, almost within earshot of the noblest men and women of the valley— had she been Betsey Johnson or Prudence Bayley, no man would have dared to raise his hand against her. And who, in Glasgow, would either of these women be in station, compared with Bessie Burr?

But she was, alas! no longer in Glasgow herself; she was, temporarily, through Mistress Johnson's kindness, a visitor in her house; and Lisa was almost ashamed to find how much it meant to her to have once more the luxury which, for two years, she had missed more than she admitted, even to herself. The finely wrought carving on the great four-posted bed; the mahogany highboy, with its brass handles, and the graceful lowboy with its knobs of opaque blue-white glass; the gilt-framed mirrors, hanging above them; the china toilet set, with its cheerful landscape scene wreathing the bowl and pitcher; the low, comfortable chairs with rush bottoms; the braided rugs on the brightly painted floors; the dainty meals brought to her bedside, served on sprigged china and heavy solid silver; the books and pamphlets given her to read; the sounds of a harpsichord, drifting up the stairs; even the ticking and striking of the great brass-faced clock which stood on the landing; the refinement and elegance of her silk-clad, soft-voiced hostess, an aristocrat from the crown of her well-set, proud little head to the soles of her small arched feet: she realized, with a little stabbing pain, how great a wrench it would be when she was forced to forego all these delights.

But she must, inevitably, leave them sooner or later, and return to Ryegate; of that there could be no possible doubt. And what welcome would await her there? What version of the abandoned dance in the ballroom, let alone of the episode on the kitchen stairs, what explanation or excuse for it, had reached the greedily critical ears of the Scotch settlement? Was she, as Anderson assured her, unable to do without protection? Her conscience was clear of the burden of actual wrongdoing; and yet, it seemed, she was ever running into danger, when she followed her own will. Where was there any hope of outer comfort or inner peace for her? Where, indeed—except in one place? What did it avail her to refuse, any longer, to go there?

Once a month at least, ever since her arrival in Ryegate, she had written to Basil Keith, at first finding letter-bearers where and when she could, more lately sending them direct from the Newbury Post Office, of which Colonel Johnson was himself in charge. And still, after two years, there was no answer to them. Every hope of seeing Basil again had left her. She turned her tired head, weary with endless, fruitless searching for some other solution for her problem than to marry Jim, to and fro on the cool, plump, linen-covered pillow beneath her, crumpling its snowy smoothness, her idle hands plucking at the counterpane, her breath, every now and then, coming in little sharp sobs. But the weariness, and the idleness, and the sobbing brought her no answer but one.

At last a letter came for her. Colonel Johnson brought

it to her himself, stamping into her room with great gusto, and waving it before her startled eyes.

"Here is what thou hast been waiting for so long," he shouted, and chuckled as she snatched it from him. He expected to be rewarded with a cry of joy; but when she had torn it open, and glanced at the signature inside, she fainted dead away. The Colonel, calling for his wife, tried to shake her back into consciousness while he waited, impatiently, for that lady's arrival.

"Dr. White hath bled this girl too much," he scolded, as his better-half, protesting against such vigorous measures, rescued her little guest. "She is more dead than alive."

"She would be, if left to thy treatment," retorted his wife. "What art thou doing now—reading her love-letter?"

" 'Tis no love-letter," answered the Colonel, reading busily. "She must have expected it would be, as did I. But there is no ill news in it either. 'Tis but a friendly scroll from the Priest of Bath, who tells her that he was only nine weeks on the ocean from Sandy Hook to Greenock Roads a fine quick passage—ten days of calm in which they made no progress, thirteen of wind when they were driven from their course, eight of fog, seven of violent tempest, the rest of favorable weather—what is there in all that to make a maid swoon?"

"Thou great numskull," said his wife good-naturedly, "ride thou up to Ryegate and bring James Anderson back with thee."

The lad came swiftly enough, and with little urging, to find that his sweetheart had gone from her fainting-fit into one of weeping, as violent as those which he had heard long before in the woods. But she stretched out both arms to him as he entered the room, and laid her head on his shoulder.

"I thought the letter was from Basil," she wept, "and it was only from Priest Sutherland, to send me his love and blessing, and to tell me that he had had a safe journey, and that his mission was prospering."

"And does it mean nothing to thee to know that thy good friend is well and thinks of thee?"

"It means much. But I thought———"

"Lisa," he said almost sternly, "dost not know by now that no letter will ever come to thee from Basil Keith? Wilt thou not admit it—both to thyself and to me?"

She would not answer him. He unclasped her arms from about his neck, laid his hands on her shoulders, and faced her squarely.

"Stop thy weeping and look at me," he commanded.

She quivered all over, her face averted, her sobs still shaking her whole body. He waited, without moving a muscle, without relaxing his steadying hold, without the slightest sign of either impatience or indecision. When at last she raised her eyes, she was as quiet as he. He smiled down at her, but there was something relentless in the smile.

"That is over," he said significantly, "for good. And so is my waiting." He paused for a moment, and then went on. "I have borne with thee a long time, and it has done no good, either to thee or to me. I am going away for an hour. Take up the letter for which thou hast shown such scant gratitude. 'Twill calm thy mind. When I come back thou wilt be able to tell me when thou wilt marry me."

"I cannot read———"

"Thou canst and shall———"

He opened the letter, spread it out before her, and watched her until he saw that she had forced herself to focus her mind upon it before he left her. At first she looked at the words almost unseeingly, and the sentences had no meaning for her; but gradually they began to take form before her dazed vision, and soon, to her astonishment, she found she was following the full and vivid narrative the Priest had sent her with attention and even with interest. It was written in diary-form, in beautiful clear script, and it made a chronicle amazingly complete and absorbing.

"Friday, October 24th. Weighed anchor early this morning. The wind rather contrary, but moderate. Of 70 passengers, none has yet had the smallest symptom of sea-

111

sickness. This is rather extraordinary. This evening promises fair. Little wind, but favorable."

"Sabbath, 26th. This day our public worship commenced. Upon application being made to the captain, he very readily and cheerfully gave his assent and offered the cabin if necessary. I endeavored to lecture, about 12 o'clock on deck, to the whole of the people, exceeding in all eighty people. We were interrupted repeatedly by the necessary attention to the ship. There was upon the whole as much attention given as I could expect. Towards the close of the discourse I got very sick and was obliged to go to bed immediately. In the course of the afternoon I recovered and having obtained permission, had public worship in the evening. Mr. Pringle performed, and agreed to perform alternative."

"Tuesday, 28th. This day nearly a perfect calm and the vessel sailed at the rate of a knot an hour during the whole day. Few of the passengers have been indisposed."

"Monday, November 4th. Since Thursday last was unable to write any. Friday was a very blowing day, nearly fair. Almost all the people were sick. I was confined in bed all day, really indisposed. Saturday was more calm, but the effects of the sickness remained. On Saturday night it began to blow very violently from the west, just ahead. It continued all the Sabbath, so that it was utterly impossible to have any worship. On Sabbath evening it was so tempestuous that it was necessary to lay the vessel to, after having shipped sea twice in large quantities. Being unacquainted with sea affairs, we conjectured from the dreadful rolling of the vessel, accompanied with a very high wind, that there was imminent danger, and under this anxious thought spent the night very uncomfortably. Whether it was because I wished it much or in answer to prayer, I cannot say, but these words prevented me from indulging the idea of instant destruction: 'The end is not yet.' Blessed be God, it was so. Morning came, and although the storm raged as violently as before, yet daylight was precious. The tempest continued till about 2 o'clock today, when we again got under way, after having been driven to leeward 31 miles. The wind now blows from the same point, but more moderately."

"Saturday, 9th. This evening the cook (a poor black who has paid more attention to worship than any sailor on board), when coming to worship was checked by the captain who upbraided him for being 'damned religious.' The poor man disregarded his taunts, but after worship was over he used such threats as I suppose will prevent him from attending again. Thus our temporary commander exhibits one lively trait of the character of the ancient Pharisees, he will neither enter into the kingdom of heaven himself and those who would he hinders."

"Thursday, 14th. These three days past have been very agreeable. The storm that lasted so long seems now to be entirely over. The change of weather has affected the recovery of all the valetudinarians. During the storm my appetite was quite lost. For several days I hardly tasted anything but water, gruel and pottage, which, however, was generally immediately vomited. Now, however, I have recovered my appetite and eat heartily almost anything, although I have a superior relish for oatmeal. I can hardly bear tea, and use a little coffee in the afternoon by a little compulsion. Indeed our most valuable sea store is oatmeal, and had we remembered to take plain eggs and rice we would have been much more comfortable than with our beef, ham and fish. I have not used any medicine as yet, except a little sea water, which has produced a capital effect."

"Sabbath, 16th. Yesterday a disagreeable affair occurred. In the course of the voyage several trifling articles had been pilfered. Suspicion fell on a young man who was yesterday publicly accused before all the passengers and crew assembled on deck. Proof was adduced against him of having pruloined one or two things, which afforded presumptive evidence respecting the rest. I felt considerably for him. He felt keenly himself. He immediately retired to bed, from which he has hardly removed since. I

113

believe all on board were secretly happy that they were not in his situation, whilst I fear few thought that they were equally guilty in the sight of God. At public worship I endeavored to improve the circumstance in some reflections on the 7th of Matthew, and endeavored to lead the attention of the people from the outward appearance of sin. I have more and more reason to adore that grace that has kept me from such conduct, for verily in my flesh dwelleth no good thing. Let this consideration always humble me and lead me to a more simple and implicit dependence on Him who hath said, 'My grace is sufficient for thee.' "

"Monday, November 25th. Today a particular account has been taken of our ages, avocations, luggage, etc. This our captain conducted with great ceremony. His character is somewhat difficult to portray. I have observed that he is a very inconstant man, greatly elated or depressed with the appearances of the moment. He is a very haughty man and unmercifully severe on his men, who in their turn most heartily detest him. His passionate temper could not be endured by equals, although the poor sailors are obliged to submit. His haughtiness is not manifested so much to the passengers, although I believe there are a few exceptions. Without all doubt he is a man who is in the gall of bitterness and bond of iniquity. He swears most shockingly, but sometimes admits it to be a bad practice, and, as is usual, throws the blame of it on the seafaring life."

"Friday, December 19th. This morning we had the most tremendous storm I ever witnessed. The peals of thunder and flashes of lightning were as awful and grand as nature usually produces. These were accompanied with sudden squalls and heavy rains. I rose at 7 in the morning and witnessed a phenomenon of which I had only heard, but never seen. It was a waterspout. There were thirteen of them seen at once around us. One of them began at the side of the vessel, and passed under it. It gave a violent shock to the ship, but being only just forming, it did no damage. This awful appearance reminded me of the Psalmist's expression in the 3rd Psalm. It seems to be formed by a whirlwind which carried up a vast quantity of water to the clouds in the form of a vast column of smoke arising from a great furnace. The one I observed lasted upwards of a quarter of an hour. In the course of the day the wind shifted in our favor, and has continued since.——"

"And so I see that thou wast able after all to read!"

Lisa dropped the diary with an exclamation of surprise. She had not heard Anderson come in, and now he stood above her, smiling, his dark, grave face illumined as she had seldom seen it.

It was very still in the room. Twilight was closing in, and a soft rainfall was thudding gently against the many-paned windows; but downstairs, the bride, Betsey Bayley, home for the day with her parents, was singing an old love-song, accompanying herself on the harpsichord; and the melody of it flooded the quiet chamber as if with light. Elizabeth had put on a dressing-gown of soft white wool which belonged to her hostess, and had wrapped about her the great patchwork quilt which lay at the foot of her bed; and rising unsteadily for the first time since her illness, had seated herself in the tall winged chair which stood by the shallow hearth, where a tumbling wood fire leapt and fell; the brass-tipped andirons on which it rested, and the huge brass warming pan standing beside it, shone in its mellow glow; and some of the glow rested, too, on the soft, fair curls falling about the girl's tired little face. Anderson came up to her silently, took her hands in both of his, and pressed them. She was the first to speak.

"If you are very sure," she faltered, "that there are no risks——"

"I am very sure," he said gently.

"For—for either of us?"

"I am very sure," he repeated.

"There is nothing I have not told you, nothing you do not know, about—about me, which might change your mind——"

"I know, as I have told thee before, that in time thy love for Basil Keith will be but a faint, fair memory, a sweet dream from which thou hast happily awakened, and that

115

thy love for me will come to be, as mine for thee, a wonderful and living reality."

"That has not happened."

"Not yet. But it will."

"I do not know. I know only that I am very tired, and weak—and a coward for what life, which has not yet been overkind, may hold next in store for me. I am afraid of this rushing torrent of life—and you are a safe bridge."

"It is true that thou art tired. But thou art neither weak, nor a coward. Thou art strong and brave, and has borne much. Nevertheless, it is always wiser to trust to the bridge, than to plunge into the torrent."

She gave a little sigh, that sounded to him like the distant fluttering of a tiny bird's wings, as it flies through the forests. Then she raised her face, laying her cheek against his, turning slowly until her lips rested on his——

"How soon?" he asked her a few minutes later.

He had kissed her as he might have kissed a child—or the image of a saint. She nestled more closely to him, so that he felt again the soft beating of her heart in her softer breast; and still he held her so gently and so reverently that she wondered how she could have shrunk so long from a love which, instead of fearing, she could have trusted completely.

"As soon as you like," she whispered. And raised her lips again.

## ELEVEN

THE NEXT FEW WEEKS were very happy ones for Lisa. She gained apace in health; and the graciousness which Mistress Johnson had shown her from the very night of the disastrous ball, had swiftly ripened to affection. Between the two, one of those rare and beautiful friendships which bind together women of disparate ages but kindred spirit sprang into being. They took profound enjoyment in each other's company; and thanks to Mistress Johnson, Lisa also saw not a little of Betsey Bayley, the Johnsons' newly married daughter, and of Phebe and Lucy, the wives of Hanes and David, the Johnsons' sons.

"Children tag at thy heels and men flock round thee like flies around a pot of honey," Mistress Johnson said teasingly to her guest, "but with friends among women it seems to me thou hast not been overmuch blessed in thy sour Scotch city. Well do I know the reason—a certain green-eyed monster called jealousy hath kept them all at bay. But that monster hath no cave here on the Oxbow; to sit and whisper about beaus and babies, and other such nonsense, with these girls of mine, and pick some flowers together; or do a little pretty senseless sewing, and drink a dish of tea, and thou wilt feel thyself grow better by leaps and bounds."

"Hast thou forgot that I came here to be a serving-maid?" asked Lisa, hesitant to accept so much kindness, yet conscious of how much she had missed the sweet and harmless gossip, the idling feminine intimacy, which she and Maisie once had shared, and which had never been offered her in Ryegate.

"Aye, that I have!" said Mistress Johnson sharply. "See to it that thou dost forget it too! Now run along, for I see Phebe waiting for thee in the garden. She hath in mind to give thee slips for a garden of thine own. She hath rare skill with roses, and her borders are as fragrant with clove pinks as my pantry is with spices. And she can teach thee how to plant sweet William and petunias and candytuft at little cost and less labor, and still make a brave showing."

So Lisa went out to meet Phebe, her fancy picturing a garden of her own. She could not have said which of her pastimes she enjoyed the most. The gardening hours that she spent with dainty, fragile Phebe, who looked like a flower herself, were delightful; but so were those during which she sat in David Johnson's southern parlor, reading aloud from one of his countless store of russet-colored books while Lucy sewed beside her. It was good to have the feel of leather in her hands again, the smell of it in her nostrils, to feast upon the printed pages; and when the prim and pretty little housewife had finished her "stint" for the day, it was good to wander across the street together to David's brick store, for this diversion, too, held out its own peculiar pleasures.

They were always greeted first by the faithful clerk, Timothy Tufts, who untwined his long legs from the rods of the tall stool where he sat perched, and laid down upon the high shelf of his secretary the quill with which he wrote so exquisitely, to blink and bleat his welcome to them; and next by David himself, who stood behind the high counter extending all across the back of the store, to which they literally had to "step up" because it was so raised above the rest of the room. He often had one of his own books tucked under his arm, reading snatches in it during the pauses in trade; or else he was carefully noting down his observations on the weather, the changes in which he never failed to register. He was a scholar by nature rather than a merchant, and all his avocations were intellectual; but he laid these aside willingly enough, and spread out lengths of shining calico for Lisa and Lucy to see, counseling Lisa that the one with flowered sprigs would well become her. Or else he teasingly told his wife, on whom he doted, and who was as demure as he was debonair, that she would ruin him yet with her fancy cookery, and make as if he would not let her have more eggs and butter to take home with her. Sometimes he was busy abovestairs, where the great bins stood, end to end, filled to the top with musty, sweet-smelling, powdery grains; and sometimes in the safe-room, where he kept his strong-boxes, which were separated from the main store by broad paneled walls. But he took his occupations in leisurely fashion, and looked the cultured gentleman no less when he was bending bare-armed above a bin, scooping out meal, or closeted with customers counting out clinking piles of money, than when he sat at the head of his candlelighted table, set with white, gold-banded china; and whether in his shop or in his house, he made his wife's companion feel at ease and at home.

At Betsey Bayley's house also, a scant half-mile away, Lisa was very welcome. Jim had found some excuse to ask if he might help with cider-making there; and Isaac

Bayley, winking one bright beady eye and twisting his large merry mouth quite out of shape to indicate his understanding of the case, guffawed, and slapped Jim on the shoulder, and said the mill could never run without him. So Jim for hours every day stood pressing the juice from apples gathered over all the countryside. But at candlelighting time he left his work and changed his clothes, and went into the paneled parlor where he knew Lisa would be waiting for him. It was the finest room that he had ever seen, he thought, and well he might. For on one side of the tall white mantel was a recessed bench, enclosed in graceful columns, which all the Bayleys had long called the "courting corner" and which now was offered to Jim and Lisa not only jestingly but generously. Indeed, Betsey, who was a very buxom, jovial girl, more like her vigorous father than her elegant mother, went much further: she said that any time they grew impatient they must remember the "marriage arch," with which the other side of the mantel was flanked, and under which every Bayley bride stood to be united with the good man of her choice. It was, she said, her pleasant, wholesome face twinkling with goodwill, entirely at their service!

One night when Jim had been sitting for a long time in the "courting corner" with his arm around Lisa's supple waist and his lips against her hair, his hand strayed up and tightened over her breasts, and his mouth closed down upon hers. And when he found she suffered this embrace without remonstrance or resistance, his breath came very hard, and he felt suffocated.

"Come," he said at last, hoarsely and impellingly, "come, let us go and stand together at least under the 'marriage arch.' Wilt thou do it?"

"Why not, if it will give thee pleasure?"

The room was dark within, but the shutters were unclosed, and a slender, sickle moon, cutting through the sapphire sky, shed some of its silver over the panels and columns. The arch was radiant. And Lisa, led into its light, became a figure tinged with mystic magic. The transparency of her skin, which had not yet regained its rosy color, the whiteness of her soft dress, the sweetness

119

of her docile mood, the pliancy of her lovely person, combined to make her seem ethereally unreal, for all the warmth and fragrance of her intimate presence.

"I scarce can believe thou art flesh and blood!" Jim whispered suddenly, dropping his arms and lifting his head, and gazing at her as if she were an apparition.

"What can I do to make you sure I am?" she asked so lightly that he felt a gauze-like quality even in her voice.

"I know not—but, meseems, that thou wouldst elude me—and escape me!"

"When I have let you hold me as you have—and kiss me as you have—when even now we stand together in this nuptial place, as if——"

"There is yet something——"

"My own laddie, there is nothing!"

Never before had she used a term of endearment in speaking to him. He thrilled at the sound of it as at the touch of her caress; and yet he sought past rapture to reassurance.

"Come out into the other room where there is candle-light," he said abruptly, "and let us sit with Betsey and Isaac and the others. I find it is uncanny after all to take our places in a marriage arch—methinks it were better not to do it in pretense. When next we stand together so, then it shall be in earnest!"

"As earnest as you wish," she answered blithely. "But that you shall be less uneasy now—well, let us join our hosts at roasting apples!"

Lisa's convalescence was so well established by the time the cider-making was done, that she might well have returned to Ryegate; but Mistress Johnson, seeing how much good she had derived from change of scene and company, was quick to urge that she should have still more before she went back to the settlement of which the sprightly lady persistently spoke as the "sour Scotch city."

"Thou hast never crossed the river yet since thy first journey here," she reminded the girl. "Let us go off upon a junket to Haverhill, thou and I—my good man here can bide with Lucy while we are away," she went on, dismissing, with a wave of her graceful hand, the doughty old Colonel who, it was rumored, found it easier to confront Indians than to control his wife. "We will go first to the Dow place, where Phebe's grandfather, General Moses Dow, and all his family will receive us; and afterwards we will go north through Tory Woods to the manor which Colonel Asa Porter hath built upon Horse Meadow. The Dow place is a very spacious one, and thou, with all thy love of beauty, wilt find it greatly to thy taste; but I must warn thee it is not overgay, though once there was no hospitality hereabouts as lavish as that which was there dispensed."

"What brought about the change?" asked Lisa, seeing that her hostess paused that she might ask the question.

"It was at first merely a matter of a highway—the house stood full upon this as 'twas first constructed. But a year or two since, the selectmen laid out a new road across the plain which is a part of the property, and discontinued the one that passed by the residence. For this they did award General Dow damages to the amount of twenty dollars; but he appealed from the award to the Court of Sessions, saying that the new road made necessary some six hundred rods of supplementary fence, and that it cut off eighty acres of pasture land from water. He made other complaints as well, chief among these that his dwelling place, once pleasant and delightsome, was isolated and gloomy now that all travel had been diverted from it. He was at length recompensed to the tune of no less than six hundred dollars, but that did not change his temper in the matter. Never hath he been the same man since. He hath been besought to enter the Congress at Washington, and duly elected—a great honor to come to any man. But he declined to serve on the grounds that he could not properly perform the duties of office. Such a thought would never have entered his head in his jocund years! And now that his daughter Mary hath been crossed in love, she is as grim as he, though belike the seclusion of their home suits her spirit well."

"How came it she was crossed in love?" asked Lisa, her interest really roused this time.

"Why, Joseph Bell, who lodged a time with the Dows

when first he came to practice law in Haverhill, so demeaned himself that he raised expectations on her part," Mistress Johnson explained, "though I am not convinced he did so purposely. I think it is more likely that she had reached an age when she so fondly hoped for some attachment that she could well persuade herself to believe in one. I do not think he trifled with her affections, or openly declared himself. Be all this as it may, one time when he was absent at court, it came to the Dows' ears that he was betrothed to a daughter of their old friend and neighbor, Colonel Asa Porter. When Bell returned, he found his goods and chattels hurled out in the yard, and Mistress Mary wailing of her grief for all to hear."

"How could she have so little pride?" exclaimed Lisa scornfully.

"I know thou canst not sympathize with her, nor can any maid to whom suitors have so freely flocked that she hath been distraught. But hath not some poet said there is no fury like a woman scorned?—Well, well, we will ride over and take our dinner with the Dows on Thursday, and hope 'twill not be flavored with the tears that Mary sheds; and later we will go on to the Porters' and tarry there awhile. If the visit to the Dow place does nothing else for thee, at least it will convince thee thou were right to snap up James e'er thou wert a day older!"

Elizabeth felt inclined, before the day in question was over, to agree with Mistress Johnson. The weather chanced to be dull and rainy, which rendered it even more gloomy than a fair one would have been; and from the first glimpse of the place to the last, it seemed to drip with woe. The dense growth of trees and underbrush between the highway and the house made the way thither almost impassable, and closed in about the erstwhile handsome residence in a way that made it as dreary as it was isolated. Moreover, the atmosphere of despondence and decadence had affected its occupants: The courtliness which must have once distinguished General Dow's behavior had been corroded; his wife was querulous in her garrulity; and their daughter Mary was indeed the embodiment of a blighted being, lugubrious of face and

122

costume. They greeted their guests with politeness and fed them excellently well, in a fine dining-room overlooking the valley, adorned with handsome furnishings and flanked with the largest fireplace Elizabeth had ever seen; but there was no real warmth in their welcome; and the bereft spinster, with her drooping mouth and brimming eyes and weeping-willow attitudes, had such an effect upon the laughter-loving girl that she vowed to Mistress Johnson, as they took their departure, that she would rather marry the first man they met than run the risk of being an old maid.

"Pray heaven thou never run a greater risk than that," the older lady exclaimed. "If thou canst hold thy impatient swain at arms' length until next spring, thou wilt do well indeed!—But it grieves me sore to see so fine a place as the Dows' going to rack and ruin, and Phebe can scarce be persuaded to set foot in it, she takes the decline of both family and homestead so much to heart. It would be better if it should pass into other hands and mayhap it will. I hear that enterprising young merchant, Henry Keyes, late come to Newbury from Vershire with his brothers, hankers after it; and since he is frugal no less than ambitious, doubtless in the end he will acquire it. Be that as it may, the manor to which we are now going is very different, as thou wilt shortly see."

"And in what way?"

"Why, Colonel Porter, like General Dow, is a graduate of Harvard College, and a man of learning and repute; and he is a still greater landowner, for it is said he hath more than a hundred thousand acres under his dominion. But he is much the better company, and wealthier than anyone hereabouts, for all he once buried a strong-box full of gold so deep in one of his meadows that he hath never been able to find it since. 'Twas during the war, when many of his belongings were confiscated, and he thought to save this treasure at least—as indeed he hath! But he and his wife are somewhat lonely in these days for all their riches, for there are many hereabouts who hold it still against them that they were sturdy Royalists, submitting to the laws of the New Republic only when they had no choice. Once when the feeling still ran very high Colonel Porter drove to Boston in his sleigh, which had the arms of England—the lion and the unicorn—painted on the side. He found himself the center of a jeering mob, which hurled not only insults but stones in his direction; and finding he must resort to drastic measures, he stopped at a paint shop and had the crest covered with a thick coat of plain color. He might have thought no more about it, for men set not so much store by signs and symbols as women, had not his wife Mehitable made a great to-do when he reached home and she saw what had happened. She was standing at the door to welcome him, and giving but one swift glance at the sleigh, she called her serving-woman to bring her soap and brushes. Then picking her way through the snow on her little high-heeled shoes, she fell upon the sleigh tooth and nail. Nor did she stop scrubbing, for all it was so freezing cold, until the old lion and unicorn reappeared again, fighting for the crown!"

"I like her spirit!" exclaimed Lisa, flicking Dobbin with her whip in her eagerness to reach more quickly the dwelling place of a lady of such high mettle.

"And so do I, my dear! Therefore I visit the Porters from time to time, though Thomas mutters that it is not fitting the wife of a Colonel in the Continental Army should be so intimate with Royalists. But I have not forgot, and tell him so, that I was born a Carleton, though I married a Johnson, and condescended somewhat in so doing! Nor that I am near kin to Sir Guy Carleton, Governor of Canada, who kept his state at Spencer Wood, when Thomas was hewing down logs for huts! Nor yet that once when there was great need, Asa Porter went on foot from Haverhill to Quebec, with a company of men, to fill a contract he had made to build a bridge for the British Government!—I hope I have some spirit myself!"

"Nay, you are a very shrinking sort of lady," Lisa said so gravely that Mistress Johnson turned a look of startled surprise upon her. Then she joined in her laugh, as the girl went on, "I call to mind some tale of a time when you were all alone upon the Oxbow, during a raid, and did load and fire all the guns that gave the tidings of alarm! Sure that was the act of a cowering woman, and no mistake!"

"Thou knowest thou wouldst have done the same, but let that pass. Look, we are entering Tory Woods! All this is Colonel Porter's land, and we shall soon be at his door."

The refinement of taste and abundance of comfort which marked the houses in which the Johnsons and Bayleys abode so harmoniously, the spacious and dignity of Moses Dow's establishment, had made a deep impression on the exiled girl; but she was still unprepared for the elegance and luxury of living which awaited her in the Horse Meadow manorhouse, which stood near a graceful bend in the river overlooking the fertile meadows of the big Oxbow, and, more distantly, the beautiful mountains of the Franconia range. Despite the informality of the visit she and Mistress Johnson were making and the mildness of the weather, Asa Porter came forward to greet his guests ceremoniously attired in a sable coat lined with scarlet broadcloth; and everything he did and wore seemed equally spectacular. Negro slaves were summoned to wait upon the traveling ladies. A feast of game from the woods, fish from the river, and sweetmeats from the South was set before them. They were installed in mammoth chambers fitted out with painted furniture of the very latest mode—yellow striped with bronze in Mistress Johnson's room, and gray with garlands of roses in Lisa's. Mounts from the stable of fine blooded horses, which Governor Wentworth had helped their host to choose, were urged upon them so enticingly, that it roused all Lisa's sense of loyalty to remain true to Dobbin! Although she did not accept one of the Colonel's fine steeds as a gift, she rode one blithely enough when she accompanied him while he made his rounds over his vast estate; and she went with him excitedly to the little balcony he had built on the top of his house, that he might watch his servants and see if they toiled unceasingly in the meadows.

One day, in jest, he handed her his field glass, and asked her to look through it and see if the woods and pastures of Ryegate were by any chance visible, and if

125

she could see James Anderson industriously engaged. And when, falling in with his mood, she turned the glass in every direction and answered that she could not, he inquired, still jestingly, if she believed that out of sight were out of mind, or if that were not included in her prodigious stock of proverbs.

"Nay," she said swiftly, suddenly arrested by something strange in his face, "it is to another maxim bearing a different meaning to which I have always subscribed: the one saying that absence makes the heart grow fonder."

"I see," he answered, with mild irony. "I can only hope then that after you leave Horse Meadow you may have fond thoughts of your visit here. For you have been as welcome as you are charming, and it is my hope that you will come again.—My good friend Peabody Ladd, who sometimes passes along this way, as I believe he does along yours, has spoken to me of you; but he had not half prepared me for all that I should find."

She did not ask him what he had found, and soon, vaguely uneasy, she made an excuse to go away from the balcony, leaving him still gazing through his glass. She knew him to be a man of high repute and a leader of great influence; more over, he was married to a lady of virtue and loveliness as well as spirit, and was old enough to be her father. Yet she felt instinctively that somehow she had unwittingly stirred his senses; felt, too, that he was a man through whose strong passions ran a vein of cruelty, and one who might take strange revenge when his desires were thwarted or his power flaunted; and she was troubled at what he might do now, without sound reason for fearing that he might do anything. But later in the day, she heard he had observed from his glass one of his negro maid-servants shirking her labors, and making free with the great black who worked beside her. And he had rushed down from his tower, and caused the wench to be tied to her companion, and whipped until the blood ran; and after she had been released, lacerated and quivering, he told the black to take her and do with her what he would——

That evening Lisa asked Mistress Johnson if she might share her room, giving as her excuse that she was again

126

the prey of those fits of the vapors which had so depressed her during her illness. And while the sprightly lady slept peacefully beside her, snoring gently and disdainfully, she lay wakeful and trembling, listening with dread and terror at every mysterious sound of the night.

"How well did Mistress Sutherland advise me," she whispered fervently to herself, "to beware of the sinful lusts of the flesh! Into what injustice and violence they lead even the noble and righteous!" But after giving voice to these sentiments, she dreamed, as she finally fell asleep, inconsistently and gloriously of Basil; and woke flushed to an ecstasy which she could not suppress for hours. When Mistress Johnson asked solicitously the next morning if her vapors had passed, she said tensely that they had not; and indeed there was so strained a look about her fair little high-cheeked face, that Mistress Johnson was not long in declaring that they must be off betimes to the Oxbow. Lisa agreed with almost feverish eagerness, and stayed so closely by her side that Mistress Johnson laughingly said she knew at last the meaning of the phrase to stick like a Burr! But for all that, their host contrived to find a way to have a word alone with the girl before she had gone, speaking to her with gravity and courtesy.

"Fret not your gentle heart about the negro wench," he said softly. "I have given her and her black a little cabin of their own, and she is as happy as if yesterday's lashings had never taken place, singing and rollicking about the place chipper as any lark. The black is a gentle enough fellow for all his size, else I would never have turned her over to him—and she is as carnal as he—it is the nature of these people. Now that she has a mate and master she has forgotten even the sting of the whip, much less that it drew blood—which is the way of women of every color and clime, though as yet you do not seem to know this, Mistress Burr."

Again he looked at her intently, as he had the day before, making her feel that no detail of her thought or person escaped him; and when, though she went red under his scrutiny and his insinuation, she did not answer him, he went on still softly, "Indian summer is a treacherous

127

time in the turn of a man's life as well as at the turn of a year; and you are the sweetest sight that has come to my eyes in many a long day. But I will not forget myself again, and it will make me very happy if you will believe that I will ever be your faithful friend, on whom I shall deem it an honor if you will call at need. Will you remember?"

"I will remember," she said, and found she could not draw her hand away when he bent over and kissed it. But she knew that she would never call upon him, and that it would be well if the glimpse she had of him standing in his sable and scarlet beside his doorstep, as she and Mistress Johnson rode away, should be the last she ever had of him.


TWELVE

THE VISIT TO HORSE MEADOW was the last one made in the vicinity of Newbury; but when at last Elizabeth's fully restored health gave Mistress Johnson no further excuse for keeping the girl at the Oxbow, she went to Ryegate and asked Judge Cameron, who still retained his guardianship over her, for permission to take the little Scotch lady to Boston to buy stuffs and silver for her dower chest. The leave was granted; and they made their journey by the pleasant way of the Grafton and Londonderry turnpikes. They stayed with a prosperous family of sea captains, to which Mistress Johnson was related through the Carletons, during their sojourn in the Massachusetts capital; and in the round of entertainment planned for their pleasure even theatrical performances and games of chance were included. Both of them took unbounded delight in the cultured society and sophisticated diversions which they were privileged to enjoy; and it was not without real regret that they abandoned these for the chillier company and more stilted occupations of the Connecticut Valley. When they returned from their trip, which was prolonged long beyond the time originally intended—or at least originally mentioned!—they found that Anderson had bought a little farm in "Scotch Hollow" at the crossroads leading to South Ryegate and Newbury Center, and was getting out the lumber for his cottage and barns; and he begged so hard that his betrothed would now come back to Ryegate, where he could see her more frequently, that she had not the heart to deny him.

"I have tried to be very patient," he said tenderly. "Heaven knows I have not begrudged thee the joy of thy junketing; and that thou shouldst make friends with such women as Mistress Johnson and her daughters pleases me as much as it doth thee. But now that all these French refugees are hanging about, and chattering with thee early and late in their own gibberish of which I understand no single syllable, I shall sleep more soundly at night when I know thou art out of their way!"

"Their gibberish, as you call it, is music in my ears," said Lisa a little wistfully. "It is a long time since I have heard French spoken, and 'tis a lovely language. Moreover, I have forgotten so much of this tongue, which I once spoke almost as well as my own, that practice in it is most welcome to me—there is no knowledge, Jim, that has not value, and for which a good use cannot be found sooner or later. Besides, I have a strong sympathy for these refugees, for I feel that in their exile we have a bond in common. And we have discovered mutual friends——"

"I have thought of all that," said Anderson gently, "else I should have spoken of the matter sooner; but this fellow Augustus St. Pot is a very jackanapes and his boon companions little better. I hear they left Hanes Johnson's latest ball so tipsy they mistook the moonlit road for a sheet of water, and would not venture across to David's house, where they had kindly been offered hospitality for the night because of their rank, until Augustus had secured a wide plank upon which they could tread in safety. Meet company for a modest maid in sooth! No doubt thou wilt no sooner be back in Ryegate than they will commence giving dancing-lessons there, for even Timothy Tufts, I hear, longs to transfer his writing-school thither. But for all that, when thou art safe at Mistress Whitelaw's, and I can keep my watchful eye on thee, I shall be happier!"

Lisa knew that he spoke half in jest; but, after all, the other half was in earnest and she did not gainsay him. He *had* been very patient; and though it cost her a pang to say good-bye to the Oxbow and all its pleasures and comforts, she did not betray to James how great a pang this was, and went cheerfully enough to stay with the Whitelaws, who were noted for their kindness and hospitality.

Anderson was working hard at his building, and was not able to see his future bride as frequently as he wished; but his impatience at their temporary separation was checked by the thought that he was building the home in which he was to keep her with him forever; and often, on a Sunday, when all work was of course laid aside, she went home with him after church to spend the day with his parents. Agnes Anderson was a simple and gentle woman, who never thought harshly of any living creature, and who felt a real admiration and affection for her son's sweetheart, which she revealed in countless tender and thoughtful ways; and James Anderson, the elder, though fearful that Lisa might prove a spendthrift, still felt a secret pride in his son's conquest of the maid whom almost every marriageable man had sought to make his own, and whose station in life had obviously been one of importance. Between them, the elder Andersons made her very welcome; and the word "daughter" fell so soon and so naturally from their lips, that long before she was married Lisa had begun to feel herself very much a member of their family.

While Anderson was occupied with his building, she was busy in a different way. It was considered proper for a bride to be able to show her wedding outfit, spun, woven and stitched by her own hands; and in this instance she had no quarrel with propriety. The work was a joy to her, and she sang under her breath as she did it. She was not slow to see, either, that her standing in the community as Anderson's affianced wife and Mistress Johnson's friend was very different from what it heretofore had been. Previously, it seemed to her, she had been perpetually and unconditionally condemned, or at least criticized; now she was—almost equally—perpetually and unconditionally approved. Mistress Whitelaw beamed upon all she did and helped her with her bridal preparations. General Whitelaw was, inevitably, away from home much of the time, for his work as land surveyor took him into more than forty towns, and his duties as town representative kept him at the capital during the sessions of the legislature. But his attitude, too, was one of such friendly goodwill that Lisa warmed to it instantly; and in his absence his wife found sprightly company in their guest, and one far more responsive than her unappreciative neighbors to the endless discourses she loved to hold on her husband, his peculiar characteristics, his vast abilities, and his incomparable achievements.

"Never was there so skelpin [1] a man!" she doted on exclaiming. "Hast thou marked, Lisa, that ever in the bitterest weather, he goes forth to spend both days and nights in the woods without so much as a covering for his hands? And he sleeps without a thought of shelter in the dead of winter! Yet years pass when he neither snuffles nor sniffles! And such a mind and memory as he has! At a moment's notice, or on no notice at all, he can describe to anyone who asks what manner of soil and lumber lie on the lands under his charge, and what they might be worth. Aweel, I miss him sore when he is gone, and such as he is not met with above once in a lifetime, as Thomas Johnson himself hath said; yet even when he is home 'tis little time I have in his company, as he must ever needs be in his office attending to sales and purchases, or writing lengthy letters to all and sundry who would confer with him, or drawing maps and yet more maps of this entire region. He hath it in his mind now to draft again the one he made long since of Vermont state—the first achieved by any man—now showing all the villages and roads, the meetinghouses and e'en the mills. 'Twill be a bonnie thing when 'tis done. But I would be well content if he would let all this and many other

---

[1] Lusty or vigorous.

matters wait, and sit idle by the fireside with me for awhile."

"Fie upon you, Mistress Whitelaw! Here is thy husband a man of such note that the mightiest in the land are quick to recognize his work and place dependence on him. Sure thou wouldst never be the one to hold him hamshackled!"

Mistress Whitelaw still protested that all she longed for was to have her good man for herself; but Lisa knew better. She saw the pride that lighted the woman's face every time she bade her husband Godspeed, as well as the deep and passionate joy with which she welcomed him back. Theirs was a partnership presenting an aspect of marriage with much the girl had hitherto never come in contact. She brooded over it, quietly, wondering with a glad hopefulness if she would ever send Jim away from her to do worthy work and watch for his return.

Her sense of contentment and well-being grew apace; it was reflected in her physical attributes no less than in her mental tranquillity. She grew rosy and rounded, and Wells Goodwin, now fully restored to health again, and making his first trip over the hills, after two long winters had passed, found a look of sweet repose in her face that he had never seen there before.

"Canst make satin slippers as well as leather brogans, Wells?" she asked, smiling after she had welcomed him warmly. "I bought none in Boston on purpose to give thee the chance to fashion what I shall wear on my wedding day."

"And thou art going shod in white satin?" he asked in astonishment. "No bride hath ever done that in Ryegate."

"Then I will lead that others may follow. 'Tis never too late to start a new fashion. See, I have fetched thee the stuff—wilt not love to stitch on anything so snowy fine?"

"It is no finer than the lass who will wear it. May she step into nothing but happiness in the shoes of my making!" Wells exclaimed, his blunt freckled face beaming with goodwill.

The service of Peabody Ladd, too, was bespoken for the marriage. Elizabeth would not hear of being wedded without music or that anyone but he should furnish it.

When she first spoke to him about it, he rallied her mockingly, but he did not gainsay her for all that.

"Hast thou given up all thought of Arcady?" he asked, balancing himself lightly on the edge of the table at which she stood, mixing and molding pies and puddings.

"Nay, I have found Arcady here."

"And a man who hath not quicksilver in his veins, but fire?"

"Aye, that also."

"And the fire in thine own burns hot at the thought of him and the touch of him?"

A color swept over her face and neck, such as Peabody had never seen there before. He thought, for an instant, that there were tears on her lashes. But the next, he was uncertain whether, after all, he might not have been mistaken, for she answered him steadily and calmly.

"It burns strong and true, which counts for far more," she said. "Art thou done with questions? If so, answer the one I asked of thee—wilt thou play for me on my wedding day?"

"Aye, that I will," he answered, grave for once, "but with music that will be gayer than my heart. For I have loved thee too—in mine own way."

"I know that, Peabody," she said gently, "and though thy way could never have been mine, thou hast ever been and ever will be, I trust, my true and blithe companion."

"God grant," he said soberly; and bending, he kissed her cheek before he left her, so softly and so swiftly that she felt as if a butterfly had brushed it.

He might have troubled her, had he so willed it. But all wished her joy and not woe in those days, and he did not ripple her peace. She was very happy, and her cup of joy seemed full when she heard that David Sutherland had come back from his travels. His return to Bath had been long delayed, for his fame was now so widespread that even after he had reached New York he had been importuned to go hither and yon, delivering addresses at special occasions, and he could not decline to do so. It was a task for which he had a special gift, as he had rare skill in adapting discourses to the requirements of every time and place; and he had made his way circuitously

133

back to New Hampshire by way of Philadelphia, Boston and Hartford. But now he was at home again, and Lisa and Jim rode over to Bath together as soon as the roads were broken through in the spring, to ask him to unite them in marriage.

"We will see if Jim values me at more than half a bushel of beans," Lisa said roguishly, referring to a fee of which the Priest had once told her. "Perhaps we can push him up to a full bushel, though there are times when I fear he hath inherited over many of his father's frugal ways."

"For thy sake 'tis to be hoped he hath," retorted Sutherland merrily, "for money slips through thy fingers like water off the back of a duck. Every time I hear of the surprising good fortune of some ne'er-do-weel hereabouts, the next thing I learn is that the 'little Scotch lady' hath listened to some sorry tale he had to tell.—Ah, well! At least James will not serve me like the groom at whose importunities I went some score of miles to marry, and who paid me with two half-dollar bills—the one a counterfeit, the other issued on a bank that had failed!"

Jim and Lisa both joined in the Priest's hearty reminiscent laugh.

"Nor do I fear your wedding will be as gloomy as the one I first performed in Ryegate, which—I will now confess—I thought but a dull place in my early days hereabouts," Sutherland went on. "It was the ceremony uniting Mary Brown and William Brock, and the company was numerous, but grave as if at a funeral. And although it was a wedding day it was not a feasting day, for I got no dinner, and came home very late to tea, and chilled to the marrow of my bones. That was before we had our own manse, and the woman with whom Mistress Sutherland and I were then lodging received me with very ill humor, because I kept her victuals waiting, commencing a taunting attack upon me without once inquiring what had detained me. I stood all unhungered on the threshold while she scolded me most unreasonably. This is a conduct practiced by many wives, Lisa, and if thou shouldst ever be guilty of it, I hope James here will wean thee of it, for 'tis most reprehensible. It is most difficult to effect a cure, but 'tis worth it in the end."

134

"I am sure I will come to thee for advice on that and other scores," Lisa said demurely. "Mistress Sutherland is a lady so uniform of temper and reasonable of behavior 'tis certain *thy* conjugal admonitions have been a good effect.—As to our wedding, I know thou wilt not find it gloomy, whatever else it may be. We are to be married in the orchard when the apple trees are all in bloom, pink and white, and for the ceremony shall stand on the flat rock beside the great boulder where I have so often sat to look at the mountains—and to pester Jim with my willfulness!" she added archly, slipping her hand into his and pressing it. "I seem to be doing so many things contrary to custom, that I thought I might add one more breach of convention to the others, and have the service out of doors instead of in church or parlor. Abigail and Marian Whitelaw will be my bridesmaids, and there will be a feast at the Whitelaws' house, and something in which thou canst drink the health of the bride!"

"In buttermilk only!" Sutherland said firmly. "Thou knowest my views, which are firmer than ever—but I will cast no gloom upon thy wedding feast," he added with a knowing twinkle in his eye.

Never had he seemed more gracious and beneficent to Jim and Lisa. They felt their being flooded with the glow of his loving-kindness as they went along their way again, talking tranquilly but joyfully of their own concerns.

"I have engaged old Nannie Crawford to come and live with us and do the heavy work," Jim told Lisa, "and have promised her a dollar a week if she does it well. —Is aught amiss with that?" he asked, noticing a strange shadow flicker across the girl's face.

"Nay, naught. 'Tis provident and thoughtful of thee to have so bespoken her," Lisa said quickly, "and I am very grateful. Only—I cannot help but remember—I thought for so long a time, my dear, that when I set up housekeeping, it would be Jeannie who would bear the brunt of it for me. I cannot cast her from my mind at such a time as this."

"But thou must," Anderson said firmly; and she saw that she had hurt him. "Jeannie is but a shade of the

135

past, buried in that mocking grave where thou thyself hast never lain."

"Ah, laddie—there are still times when I hear a voice telling me that the past is not, after all, quite dead!"

"It is a false voice," Anderson said almost sternly. Then, as if dismissing a closed subject, he went on with some abruptness, "I think thy housekeeping will rest lightly on thy shoulders. I have agreed with Nannie that she is to do all the washing. It is not my will that thou shouldst scrub the floors, nor lift heavy kettles beyond thy strength."

"Curly locks, curly locks, wilt thou be mine?" chanted the girl, trying to fall in with his mood.

"Thou shalt n'er wash the dishes nor e'en feed the swine;
    But sit on a cushion and sew a fine seam,
    And feast upon strawberries, sugar and cream!"

"Aye—that is exactly what I would have thee do!"

"And that is exactly what I shall do," she laughed, "but I have been busy enough with my outfit these last months, goodness knows! I must show thee my bridal gown, which is of finest white lawn, and which I have broidered from hem to waistline, besides making a little broidered cape to go with it. Likewise I have freshened with new trimmings the blue silk gown thou dost like so well, and have two new ones which will last me all my life, one corded black silk and the other of maroon brocade which will stand alone. Besides, I did slip in a light one which will not last at all, but which thou wilt find very good to look at none the less—rose-colored it is and very soft and frilly. Then there are homespun and calico dresses galore, and aprons and petticoats—and—and other garments which thou art not supposed to know anything about!"

"After having helped first my mother and then thee hang them on the line all these years? I may be dull witted, Lisa, but——"

They laughed together again, the moment of tension between them entirely past.

"My pile of sheets and towels is growing apace too," Lisa rattled on. "And I have nearly enough feathers for two beds. While thou hast been building with wood and with stone, I have been building with flax and with silk and wool."

"Wilt thou not walk over some afternoon now, soon, and see how that building of mine progresses? It is some time since thou hast seen it, and old Willie Neilson has warned me that I would do well to see thee suited if I would save remodeling. He came along the other day when I was hard at work, and said in his brusque blunt way, 'Jeamie, you're a fule, you're a fule.'—'Oh, I know all that now,' I said. 'Tell me something I don't know.' The old man went on, 'The birds first pair and then build their nest, and when finished it suits both. Now you will go on and build your house and make it exactly right, as ye think, and when ye get married and bring your wife home to it, she will look it over and find this wrong— and that wrong, and she will say, "Jeamie, take this out, Jeamie take this down," and of other prized handiwork, "Throw it away, I don't want it!" and so it will be with all your most cherished plans, whereas if ye consult your little Scotch lady first, ye will save all remodeling.' "

"Master Willie Neilson slanders me!" the girl exclaimed with mock indignation. "I shall be content in the house of thy building if it contains only a but and a ben.[1] However, I will gladly come and see thy handiwork."

They agreed upon the following day as being none too soon for her visit as they lingered over their farewells; and from noon onwards, Jim watched for Lisa's coming, his impatience, and then his anxiety, growing with every hour that she failed to appear. At dusk, he threw down his tools and was starting in search of her, when she came into sight, her blue cloak billowing about her tiny figure, a small white lamb clasped to her breast. She ran to him, and raised her face for his kiss.

"Wast thou frightened?" she murmured, with her lips against his. "I am so sorry! But as I came along the trail I saw a bear carrying off this little ewe. I followed after it, a long way, trying to think how I could make it give up its prey, without avail. At last I screamed as if I

[1] One inner and one outer room, after the manner of Scotch cottages in the Old Country.

were in a great fright—and the bear itself, at the sudden sound, took fright and fled. And see, I have the lamb all safe!"

"And meanwhile I have feared for the safety of my ewe lamb!"

"But she is safe too—and is to be safer than ever, with you, a few weeks hence.—Perchance Master Gray, to whom, I believe, this lamb belongs, will sell it to us and we will start our own flock with it. General White-law hath promised me a heifer calf as a bridal gift, and Judge Cameron says I may ride home with thee on Dobbin when we are wed, and keep him after that. And, Jim —I wish that thou wouldst seek out a yoke of oxen, the best that thou canst find, and a good stout cart to go with them, and let me know the charges. For after this I shall use the gold that comes to me from Scotland. The thought that it may help thee hath purified it of all dross, and I would not come to thee empty-handed."

"Hadst thou done so it would have mattered nothing to me so long as thou didst come! But the oxen I will gladly and thankfully get and, with thy approval, another hundred acres of land, since I can now secure it at fifty cents an acre. In years to come I greatly fear that it would cost us more, so in the end a purchase would be prudent now."

"Then why not buy two hundred acres?"

"I will, if thou art well disposed to help me with thy gold. And if this will buy comforts for thee which I could not earn, I shall be more than glad."

"I will have no comforts which thou wilt not share."

"Then I will share them with thee, Lisa! Indeed, I have prepared a few for our joint sharing. Come, let me show thee all that I have done."

He led her with pardonable pride towards the cottage he was building. Its location was most "sightly," as the set-tlers said, for hills, covered with the fresh verdure of spring, sloped down around it on every side; and it stood foursquare and firm upon its strong foundation of granite blocks, two wide slabs of stone, one set upon the other, serving as a doorstoop, a stout brick central chimney ris-ing above a shingled roof. The clapboards were on all the outside walls, and everything about it looked substantial. Inside its coziness was even more apparent. On one side of the front door was a good-sized parlor, on the other a good-sized dining-room; each was furnished with a fire-place, and back of each was a little "parlor-bedroom"; abovestairs were two larger bedrooms, and in the ell an ample kitchen with a "shed chamber" over it. Without possessing the spaciousness or the elegance of the Oxbow houses, it was built true to chaste and simple lines, and gave an immediate effect of compactness and solidity. Lisa had not seen it since it had progressed beyond its base; and there was heartfelt enthusiasm in the exclamations with which she now greeted each new attraction she discovered.

"It is the snuggest, sweetest, little house in all the world, I believe, laddie!" she exclaimed. "And thou didst let me believe thou hadst only a but and a ben for me! Why, this is ample and cozier, too, than any house in Ryegate—I feel as if I could not wait another day to come and live here!"

"Never fear, thou hast not many days to wait!"

"I fear nothing any more, laddie," she said gravely, "except that my indebtedness to thee may not be canceled."

She spoke the truth. She feared nothing, she dreaded nothing and her affection was a continued wellspring of graciousness and generosity. Having denied him so long, she seemed to feel at last that she could never repay him for all his gentleness and patience. In the complete absorption of bestowing all she could on one so worthy of her bounty, she was conscious of missing no other raptures, she forgot she had ever longed for them. James had no need now to urge her to hasten the date of their marriage. She watched for appleblossom time to come as eagerly as he.

Their wedding day dawned under a sky so benign and bland that it seemed as if the very heavens were smiling on their union. By noontime half of Haverhill and Newbury as well as all of Ryegate had foregathered on the hillside pasture facing the mountains, beside the orchard when the fluffy blossoms had burst into sudden rosy

139

bloom. The men who had served in the Continental Army —General Dow, General Bayley, General Whitelaw, Colonel Johnson—stood out in the brave array of their buff and blue uniforms—only Colonel Porter, of all the officers present, was not in full regalia, but in his scarlet and sable coat. Lucy Johnson was there, clinging to David's arm, Phebe in a dress garlanded with roses, Betsey already great with child, Mistress Abigail in stiff and shining brocade; and near her, in fringed leather, beaded moccasins and feathered headdresses, Molly Squaw and Indian Joe stood immobile and silent. Mistress Sutherland's expression was complacent—had it not been for her good counsel, the feckless lassie who was now so modest a bride might never have listened to reason; Agnes Anderson was simpering with satisfaction, and her husband's hard-bitten look had melted magically away; while Mistress Whitelaw's sweet face was shining with loving-kindness. But Wells Goodwin kept glancing down at the new shoes he had made for himself, as if the sight of them gave him little pleasure; and Peabody Ladd, for all he turned this way and that as he fiddled, betrayed the blurred look in his eyes. Little Jeffie Cameron kept bounding up and down in her mother's arms; and when she saw the bride coming towards the company, dressed all in white and leaning on the Judge's arm, followed by Abigail and Marian Whitelaw, she gave a shout of delight, and could scarcely be restrained from leaping off to stand beside the girl who took her place with such composure on the great flat rock beside the tall dark man, his splendid somber face aglow, who waited for her there, clad in the handsome "freedom suit" of well-fulled cloth, which had been set aside from his majority to grace the wedding day——

Later, when the Priest of Bath, appareled with ministerial dignity, had joined their hands together and spoken words of blessing as Jim placed the wide gold band on Lisa's finger, the great feast followed the simple ceremony; and after it was over the groom lifted the bride, as he had so often done before, on the pillion Dobbin carried behind his saddle, and rode away with her in the soft twilight across the silent hills. Ticklednake Pond,

140

cupped in the hollow of the hills, lay dark as a great green emerald at their feet; Blue Mountain towered above them like a huge blue sapphire; the forests which had first befriended them closed in around them. And when they left the woods behind them and reached cleared ground again, they saw that lights were shining from the windows of the new little house, that smoke curled from the square-built solid chimney, and that the paneled door stood open, showing fires lighted on the friendly hearthstones. Lisa slipped from her high seat into her husband's outstretched arms; and as he lifted her across the threshold, she put her arm around his neck and laid her cheek against his face.

"I did wrong to keep thee waiting so long, Jim," she whispered. "But, oh, I will make up for it now!"

# PART THREE

## *The Crossing*

### THIRTEEN

For a few months, complete contentment filled the crossroads cottage with a sweetness that was akin to sanctity. The marriage which, in Elizabeth's first forebodings, had seemed so dreadful a thing, held no more terrors, she found, than betrothal had done. James claimed her now, to be sure, in a new completeness; but it was with the same gentleness that he had always shown. No bride was ever led more tenderly into the nuptial chamber; and, as her husband had foretold, something from within his wife, warmer than gratitude and affection, leapt out to meet him almost at once. Face to face with his clean and vital passion, the young and ardent girl herself was kindled. The knowledge that she was to have a child, coming swiftly upon the consciousness that she rejoiced in being a wife, bore her upon swift wings to a higher and yet more glorious heaven.

She went, from this self-created paradise, to a purgatory dreadful beyond imagining: she gave birth to her first child prematurely, in a torment that lasted for forty-eight hours. When she was at last delivered, it was of a stillborn son.

For weeks after the cold and tiny form had been taken from her clinging fingers, she lay numb and suffering, her spirit lacerated no less than her body. So this hideous passion-fruit was maternity! Never, never would she taste of it again! She turned her face to the wall, refusing to see or speak to her husband. She had been grateful to

142

him, she had trusted him—and he had brought her to this. Her affection for him had had its basis in gratitude and trust, and these seemed buried with the child, killed in the torture she had endured, from which he had not saved her. In her distorted vision, desire and all that came of it appeared dreadful and disastrous, her own lot little better than that of the wretched mother whose suffering she had not assuaged and to whose succor she had gone too late.

No man, however compassionate, can form even the faintest conception of the agony of a woman's travail or of the extreme delicacy and sensitiveness of her emotions; and Anderson, loving Lisa completely, was hurt and grieved and resentful, and what was infinitely worse, he was intolerant of her hysteria. In his lack of understanding he was puzzled at the loss of her confidence. Her morbid state, natural enough under the circumstances, was a repellent mystery to him. He was too unimaginative to realize the depth of her suffering, too stoical to comprehend the abandonment of her grief for an infant which had never even drawn breath. His old silence fell upon him, his face grew dark and hard again, as it had been before Lisa had transfigured it with tenderness; and he went about, grim and stern, unable to express the depth of his own sorrow, searching for a way to end it and bring them both back to their short-lived happiness, and failing utterly to find it.

At last he reached a conclusion which seemed to him portentous: had the child lived, no matter how much anguish its birth had caused, this separation would not have happened; he and Lisa would have been more closely united than ever before. Feeling this, and rightly, he reasoned that the sooner she bore another, the sooner the damage would be repaired; that the condition to which abnormal difficulties and unskilled treatment had reduced her made this actually dangerous, did not occur to him; that she still shrank from his slightest touch seemed to him, in his pitiful ignorance, relatively unimportant.

He came into the room where she still lay prostrate one evening about candlelighting time, his mind full of his

143

purpose. Since her confinement he had been sleeping in the cramped little "shed-chamber" under the eaves; and the discomfort and loneliness he had endured for weeks had served to increase his longing for her. His stimulated senses acted as a spur to his obsession. Without preamble or warning he suddenly leaned over her, slipping one arm around her and kissing her full upon the mouth.

"Lisa," he whispered tensely, "Lisa!"

For an instant she was too startled to speak. She had fallen into a light doze and had not even been conscious of his presence until she felt his weight against her.

"What is it?" she asked, when, thoroughly roused, she had succeeded in twisting herself half free from his embrace. "You—you hurt me, Jim! And frightened me, coming in like that! What—what do you want?"

"Thou knowest," he said, still more tensely, reverting instinctively to a phrase which had so often touched her in the past. Then, as she gave no answer but a little smothered cry, he added with vehemence in his voice, "Lisa, I am anhungered for thee."

"And dost thou think only of thy hunger? Nothing of my pain?" she asked bitterly.

"Dost thou remember only thy pain when—when I come to thee—as thy husband?" he countered.

She turned wearily away from him, too far spent for argument or protestation. He misinterpreted her gesture. To his imperceptive vision, it appeared not one of debility, but one of insurrection.

"Thou wouldst not seek to deny me?" he asked almost roughly.

He had never spoken to her so before. In spite of her weakness, her resentment both of his proprietory assumption and his manner of expressing it, roused her to recklessness.

"Aye, that I would and will!" she exclaimed; and lifting herself on her pillow, she met his compelling gaze with a look of defiant rage.

Her anger proved contagious. Anderson suddenly seized her by her shoulder. Her nightgown had slipped away from it as she raised herself, and his fingers sank, relentlessly, into her delicate flesh.

144

"No, that thou shalt not!" he cried, gripping her powerfully. "What rebellious folly is this, Elizabeth Anderson? Art thou not my lawful wedded wife, pledged to submission and obedience? Wouldst try to flaunt my rights now, as thou didst once flaunt my courtship? Believe me, thou wilt not find it so easy! As to thy pain, is it not what all women are called on to endure, over and over, and which most do endure with a resignation thou wouldst do well to copy, for their lot will be thy lot also! Hast forgotten it is ordained by Scripture that thy conception shall be multiplied, that in sorrow thou shalt bring forth children, that thy desire shall be to thy husband, and that he shall rule over thee."

His dark and driving mood engulfed them both. He did not leave her again that night.

It was the first mistake that he had made since he had kissed her by force in the woods. It was to prove his bitterest. Elizabeth had once been ready to give him everything because he had bided his time, because he had been tender and patient before he was importunate; had he been tender and patient again, she would have been ready to give everything again. She was too buoyant a being to remain long under the shadow of a memory, however dreadful, too fervent to be long unresponsive to passion, too just to cherish a resentment not basically sound. But her second pregnancy began before her tear-dimmed vision had cleared, before her weary soul had found refreshment and healing, before her quivering senses had regained balance and repose; and though she never tried a second time to resist her husband, she was filled with hot resentment and bitter revulsion against him, with terror and hatred of the new life which was to take her into the valley of the shadow again.

This, Anderson assured himself, watching her intently and with a heavy heart which he strove in vain to make lighter, was not unusual for women in her condition—he had often heard old wives' tales to that effect. He knew that he had hurt and grieved her, but he did not dream he had wronged her also. He believed he had acted both righteously and beneficially, and though aware that she was suffering, felt his misery to be immeasurably greater

145

than hers. His pride and his purpose both impelled him to continue the claims which he had once enforced, unconscious that he himself was undermining the structure of the very relationship he strove to cement. But after his first primitive exultation in the subjugation of a rebellious spirit and an unyielding body, he took no joy in the intimacy which he had achieved with such violence. And in spite of the sense of the insatiable which inevitably accompanied his persistent possession of a woman as crushed as she was compliant, he shut his consciousness of present frustration resolutely away from him, looking eagerly forward to the fruition of the future, confident that after the child's arrival, these hideous intervening months would be forgotten by both Lisa and himself.

The unseasonable severity of a bleak and early winter had already been upon them when the stillborn baby had battled its way so disastrously into the world; and the child so savagely begotten and so sorrowfully conceived was already quick within its mother before the dreadful grip of snowless frigidity relaxed its hold upon the imprisoned valley. The rutted roads frozen into deep furrows, and the intensity of the cold rendered communication between settlements, and even between neighbors, almost as dangerous as it was difficult; and neither man nor beast ventured abroad unless driven by dire necessity. So for many months the outsiders who entered the crossroads cottage were few and far between; and since Lisa steadfastly declined to see such infrequent travelers as trespassed upon her hospitality, but left them, without apology or explanation, to the grim and grudging welcome of her husband and the fumbling ministrations of old Nannie, none guessed of the pass to which she had been brought. Indeed, this was not disclosed until Anderson, feeling that he could no longer stand the hostility of his own four walls, faced the biting wind and rode over one evening to see his parents. Then after a cheerless conversation with his father about the dearth of money and the ailments of stock, he answered his mother's affectionate inquiries for her daughter-in-law briefly and evasively. Finally, when she amiably announced her intention of coming to visit Lisa at the first possible moment after their long separation, Anderson reluctantly took her into his confidence.

"Thou wilt find Lisa much changed," he said with strained hesitation. "She is not overstrong and her spirits are low."

"Why, what can be amiss with her?" asked Agnes Anderson in quick solicitude. "I did hear that it went very hard with her when she was brought to bed with the poor dead weanie, but sure a lass as young and daft as she could na' long be ailing!"

"She is with child again," said Anderson bluntly, and turned away. Then as his mother gave him no answer save a startled exclamation, he asked angrily, "Is aught amiss in that? May no woman be in the family way oftener than once in two years, because thou never wert?"

"But, Jeamie, she is such a bit lassie," faltered his mother, "and hath been so unused to—to——"

"She is more used now," he said still more angrily; and flung himself out of the door without bidding his parents good night.

By the betrayal of her astonishment and concern, the gentle, well-meaning woman had done the young wife more harm than good. If he had been wholly at rest with his own conscience, Anderson would have experienced no annoyance at his mother's words. Now he felt criticism of his conduct was implied even when none was intended; he imagined that the entire countryside already knew that he had lain with his wife while she was still confined, that men were making ribald jests, and women counting months upon their fingers; and when a tardy thaw made services possible once more, and David Sutherland begged leave to ride home with him after meeting, a submerged streak of perversity in his nature leapt to sudden animation, and he bristled with self-defense.

"Didst see Lisa when she was in travail, James?" the Priest asked quietly, at last, after listening without comment to Anderson's outburst as they went on their way to the crossroads cottage. "Or hear the cries wrung from her in her anguish?"

"I was not with her," Anderson replied shortly, wincing in spite of himself at something in Sutherland's voice. "And I heard but little. Nannie bade me begone from the house when the pains began. For the most part I stayed in the barn."

"Next time stay by thy wife," said the Priest in a voice of stern authority. "Not only that thou mayest give her what poor succor and help lie in man's power when woman goes down into the valley of the shadow; but also that thou mayest witness with thine own eyes the excruciating agonies which accompany a human being's entrance into this transitory life."

"Yet there is scarce a woman in the settlements who hath not borne upwards of a dozen children," Anderson said defiantly.

"Aye, and scarce a man who hath not lost at least one wife in childbirth or from overmuch childbearing," said the Priest significantly. "Art minded to marry three or four times, James Anderson? Will any woman serve thy purpose as well as doth thy lovely Lisa, provided only that she be meek and fruitful?"

"Thou art unjust," said Anderson hotly. "Thou knowest my love for Lisa." Then he went on, still unrelentingly, "Besides, is it not written——"

The Priest interrupted him. "Aye, it is written," he said with a strange vehemence. "And in this instance at least, the words of the Scriptures have come to pass. But fear not, James, to comfort Lisa in so far as thou canst, lest the Laws and the Prophets be not fulfilled. And forgot not, neither, that thou art as pledged to cherish her as she is to obey thee."

Anderson, muttering something unintelligible, looked away.

"Thou didst speak of Nannie," David Sutherland went on somewhat more gently and persuasively. "Was she alone in her attendance on Lisa?"

"Why not?" asked Anderson in genuine surprise. "She hath experience and skill as a midwife. Had the cold not been so great and the roads so full of ruts, my mother would have gladly ridden over at need, or Mistress White-law. But at the time none could go abroad with comfort."

"With comfort!" exclaimed the Priest scathingly. "And she was how long in labor, thy wife?"

"It was a matter of two days and two nights," Anderson answered unwillingly.

"And thou talkest of comfort for some other woman! Another time, see that thy mother is by—and tell me not afterwards that the heat was so great she could not stir from the shade of her own elms, or that her kitchen was so full of haymakers whom she must feed that she could not leave them! Moreover, it might be well to bespeak, even in advance, the services of a physician."

"A physician!" exclaimed Anderson, his voice betraying still more astonishment than it had before, and one in which revulsion was now mingled.

"Aye—there are cases so critical that the services of a midwife are insufficient—as I once learned to my cost," David Sutherland said, with a bitter emphasis which was lost on Anderson. "Thereafter, when these occasions have arisen in my own family, I have summoned a doctor."

If Anderson's anxiety had been really roused, it would have conquered both his perversity and his aversion to Sutherland's suggestion; but he listened with confidence to Nannie's cackling assurances that it was only first labor which was prolonged or perilous, and that all would be "as right as rain" with Lisa this time. When summer finally came, it was with a sudden onrush, as if to make up for its disastrous lateness; and Anderson was out in the fields before sunup every day, in order to catch up with the farm work so retarded by the raw and windy spring. He had actually forgotten, under the grueling pressure of his own burdens, that his wife's hour was almost upon her, when he came in from the fields one noon to find that there was no dinner prepared and waiting for him; and he called for Nannie three times with increasing impatience, before she came towards him with a bustle of importance and a smirking expression which the agonies of another woman's parturition so often evoke on the part of a midwife.

"Nay, nay, I heard thee the first time," she said scoldingly, "though at the moment I deemed it best to stay where I was. Canst thou not make out for once on beans and milk and corn bread? At supper time I will have a goodlier meal spread out."

"Will it be all over by then?" asked Anderson, groping for release from the fear that suddenly gripped him.

"Na doot, na doot," Nannie said soothingly, though he thought evasively.

"And I can do naught to help?" he asked with hesitation, remembering the charges the Priest had laid upon him. "Would it be well that I should fetch my mother? Or go and sit with—my wife awhile?"

"As to thy mother, do as thou seest fit," Nannie responded, evidently torn between her desire to prove that she could cope with an important situation unaided, and her willingness to be relieved of some of the drudgery attendant upon it. "As for thy wife, leave her to me! She is better off without thy meddling and mollycoddling."

Anderson ate hurriedly and scantily, closing his ears, as best he could, to the stifled groans which, with an ominous and dreadful regularity, came to him. His thoughts reverted, involuntarily, to the times when he had heard "the abandoned girl" sobbing in the forest, how the sound of her weeping had baffled and intrigued him, how he had sought for her, and finally found her, and comforted her. Now he guessed, and guessed rightly, that Lisa was stuffing the bedclothing in her mouth to smother the sounds of her suffering while he was in the house, that if he tried to approach her she would repulse him, and that she would at least give freer vent to her anguish when he was gone. As he finally stood, still hesitant, with his hand upon the latch, he heard a cry of such irrepressible agony that it made him feel as if his heart were being twisted around a skewer within his breast; and with a sudden sense of desperate urgency, he made off at a gallop to fetch his mother.

As if in fulfillment of David Sutherland's prophecy, he found her half prostrated by the heat and half distracted by the task of lodging and boarding a crew of hired men. But she rallied to the sternness of his voice when he bade her prepare to go with him at once, and did not whimper at the furious pace with which he hastened back to the crossroads. His horse's hoofs clattered as he swung into the dooryard; and before either he or Agnes Anderson could dismount, the door of the cottage was torn open, and Nannie Crawford, her face blanched, sprang out to meet them.

"I have listened and listened for ye and still ye did not come!" she shrieked. "For all that I can do mother and child will both be lost this time! Ride, James Anderson, as thou hast never ridden before, in search of Dr. Samuel White of Jefferson Hill! And come thou here, Mistress Anderson, that I be not left alone in this house to listen for a death rattle!"

She threw her apron over her head and disappeared, still screaming. Agnes Anderson rushed after her. James, lashing his hard-ridden horse onwards again, tore off, cross-country, towards Jefferson Hill, inarticulate terror tearing at his throat. What if the physician were not at home? What if having been found, he could not save Lisa? The Priest's mocking words, which he had heeded so little when they were spoken, seemed to reverberate now in the ears of the distraught man. "Would any other woman serve thy purpose as well as does thy lovely Lisa, provided only she be meek and fruitful?" Lisa was the only woman the world had ever held for him, or ever could hold; and if he lost her, it would be through his own violent folly. He groaned, gritted his teeth, and rode on.

Samuel White was not at Jefferson Hill when he finally reached it, and Mistress White could not say where he had gone or when he would return. She spoke gently to the haggard-looking man who bespoke her help, but she could offer only the cold comfort of her hospitality, and the kindly, but ineffectual suggestion that her guest should await her husband's return. He had no choice but to do so, since otherwise he might have followed the physician vainly about, without ever finding him; and throughout a violent thunderstorm, which suddenly arose,

151

he sat staring steadily ahead of him, apparently so oblivious of the raging elements around him that his good hostess grew anxious and went and touched him lightly on the shoulder.

"Fear not for thy wife," she said consolingly. "A doctor is but an instrument in the hands of God, we know. But it would seem that my husband has been often chosen as such an instrument, for he hath wrought miracles, under God's guidance, in the past, and will do so again."

"How can he work miracles if he doth not come?"

"Be assured, he will come yet."

The intolerable night had already closed in upon them when the good physician came ambling up the hill which led to his house. He had ridden over fifty miles on his rounds since noon, had witnessed birth and death, sin and suffering, courage and cowardice, all in his day's work; his rosy and benign face, framed, as in a halo, with soft white hair, had settled into lines of deep fatigue, which lifted a little as he reflected on the prospect of repose which he had earned so well; and as he saw that a stranger awaited him, looming urgently up before him in the darkness, the lines deepened again. But he had turned his horse's head away from home once more before the frenzied words which came tumbling from Anderson's lips were half uttered; and they rode off together into the valley, silent, because the hour was too dreadful a one for words, each fearing to share with the other the hideous thought that dominated his mind.

But when they came to the crossroads cottage, the tortured writhing creature with blood and foam upon its livid lips, which once had been a lovely girl, was still alive.

## FOURTEEN

THE BABY GIRL, whose life had been bought at so terrible a price, was finally brought into the world by forceps, just before dawn. The compassionate surgeon who had been powerless to mitigate the horror of the rack on which perforce he stretched the mother, watched vigilantly lest his instruments of torture and deliverance should destroy the child; and thanks to the delicacy of his skill she was unharmed. She cried lustily while she was being bathed and dressed; but when she had been laid back in the bed again, she cuddled down contentedly, and soon was fast asleep.

It was evident, from the very hour of her birth, that she would not suffer from the moribund condition of Lisa, who lay with a heavy sweat pouring from her pallid forehead and drooping limbs, a ghastly embodiment of exhaustion, apparently bound to earth only because she was too far spent to die. Indeed, the baby, like a little vampire, seemed to drain the vitality, to the last drop, of the ravished woman to whom she owed her being. She tugged, hungrily and effectually, at her mother's bruised and swollen breasts, reeling away only when she had reached a point of satiation, her small pink face moist with warmth and exertion, her plump little body distended; and she slept almost continually, soundly and without wailing, in the hollow of her mother's limp arm. She was a beautiful child, as fair as she was vigorous, with her mother's blue eyes, and downy curls clustering over her round little head; and Samuel White, who took tremendous pride in her well-being and progress, always paused, when he came to the crossroads cottage, to chuck her under her small milky chin, to poke her well-covered little ribs, and to thrust out a great forefinger that she might close her wee fat finger tightly around it.

"Never have I seen so lusty an infant!" he exclaimed repeatedly, "or so pretty a one—bonnie, you would call her, would you not?" he asked, turning towards her mother. "But when I see you gaining in the same measure she does, I shall be still better satisfied!" he always ended, his piercing glance directed towards the recumbent form on the bed beside him.

"How can she gain?" Anderson asked him bitterly at last. He had been in his wife's room when the doctor arrived, looking down at her in silence and with a shudder which he could hardly control. Her blue-veined transpar-

153

ent eyelids had been closed, and her coverings, sweeping away from her alabastrine face and neck, had molded her motionless figure like a winding sheet. So far she had neither stirred nor spoken when he had approached her, and the mortuary stillness which enshrouded her chilled and appalled him more and more with every passing day. Now, as he followed the physician down the stairs, he burst out with sudden vehemence, "There is no life-blood left in her! And no wonder, since she hath been half slaughtered. Every time I think of those shambles——"

"They were a gruesome sight," agreed the doctor. "But do not think on them overmuch, since they will do no good—at least not now. You must be like me, and shut the thought of those shambles out of your mind. If a doctor dwelt on all the dreadful work that he must do he never could go on. But I hold fast to a hope it will not always be like this. Indeed, I have the strong belief that childbirth can in time be somewhat shorn of ghastliness. For instance, if some stupefacient vapor could be found, the sharpness of the pangs could be assuaged by breathing in the fumes; and if unconsciousness could be induced for a short time, even such murderous instruments as you saw me use, could be applied without torture."

"A vapor!" exclaimed Anderson incredulously. "A vapor which would produce unconsciousness!"

"Captain Samuel Morey of Orford has found one that will cause a ship to move without either oars or sails," the doctor said imperturbably. "I am well acquainted with him and I know this for a fact. Every Sunday morning when his good neighbors are gone to meeting, he leaves his fine house on the Ridge and takes his boat, the *Sally Anne,* out on the Connecticut River, where he makes his experiments unmolested by the curious and scoffing. No doubt some other man will bring his strange process to the public notice and get credit for it—Morey is a rugged soul, but a diffident one, and does not know how to push himself forward. For all that, I do not doubt he has made a portentous discovery, and one that may bring about great changes. And if navigation may be transformed by one vapor, discovered by a sailor, why should surgery not be transformed by another, discovered by a physician?"

"Pray heaven that it may!" said Anderson, using an expression that came so seldom to the lips of any Scot, and speaking so fervently that the doctor realized afresh how beset he was with brooding thoughts.

"But until it is—remember that a man who truly loves his wife, however hard resistance to her charms may be, should so constrain himself that she will not reënter her torture chamber too soon after she has left it, or too often."

"Too often!" interrupted Anderson fiercely. "Dost think I will let her go down to that hell again?"

In spite of the man's vehemence, the doctor turned away to suppress a smile. "I know you think now that you would not," he countered noncommittally. "But I must warn you, James, none can know better than a doctor that the spirit is willing but the flesh is weak! Many is the man I have heard speak as you do, to whose wife I have been called to minister again inside a year. But that at least I do not look for in this case," he added hastily, sensing that he was giving real offense. "I see you are as well aware as I that it will be a marvel if yonder little lady revives within so short a time from what she has endured already; and that if she should soon be called on to endure more, no miracle could save her. But, every symptom notwithstanding, it is my belief that all will yet be well with her. She has both courage and vitality in most uncommon measure, and that counts for much. We must see that she has nourishing food and abundant peace, and most of all the consciousness that fostering love surrounds her. For all the rest we can but trust to time."

He rode benignly and cheerfully away, leaving Anderson reflective but less despondent than he had been in months; and when next the good physician cantered into the dooryard of the crossroads cottage, the gloomy young giant came out to meet him with the air of one who is the bearer of good tidings.

"I have seen her smiling at the child, and heard her cooing to it when she did not know that anyone was by," he said excitedly. "And last night she emptied the bowl of broth Nannie took her, and ate to the last spoonful the jelly sent her by Mistress Whitelaw. Moreover, she has spoken to me several times—gravely but without hostility. We have talked together of diverse matters, but mostly of a name for the bairn. I think belike that we shall call her Sue."

"A sweet pretty name for a sweet pretty babe!" said the doctor with delight. "As to your wife, what did I tell you? We shall have her propped up on pillows in no time, and soon thereafter get her out of bed to have her mattress turned. But let me hasten to her—I cannot wait to see her for myself!"

He found her with her head raised on one arm, gazing down, with a look of radiance that gave an illusion of color to her ethereal face, at the child beside her. It was lying wide awake, its blue eyes solemnly fixed upon its mother's face; suddenly a look of dawning intelligence shone upon them, and it chuckled. Lisa leaned over, snatched it up ecstatically, and covered it with kisses. As she caught sight of the doctor, she turned to him rapturously, pressing the baby against her breast.

"Sue knows me!" she exclaimed joyously. "She smiled at me! Did you see her? Do weanies often smile, as young as that?"

"But seldom," said the doctor soberly and mendaciously. "Yet who can wonder that she smiles, seeing that she is bursting with content?" He poked her little ribs, according to his custom, and the infantile chuckle broadened into a beatific grin. "Well, well!" he said, beaming in his turn. "She is a jolly little girl, and no mistake! It pleases me to see you are so happy with her, and with such good cause.—And you yourself," he added, noting with satisfaction the golden curls neatly plaited for the first time, the gay patchwork quilt upon the well-made spool bed, the swept and garnished aspect of the chamber, through which the sunshine streamed, "I think that you are better, Mistress Anderson!"

"I think that I am well!" she answered most gaily, "thanks to the best of doctors in this whole wide world!

Whatever should befall me now, I still should feel with faith that you could cure me!"

A slight mist obscured the doctor's twinkling eyes, and reaching for a large bandana handkerchief, he blew his nose somewhat noisily upon it.

"Well, well!" he said again, speaking a little gruffly to hide his emotion. "Perhaps more patients have recovered through their faith than through their physicians' skill, though for myself I always say I have bad luck only when they have come down with their last illness! But so they do recover, and give me the credit, why should a poor quack quarrel with that?"

"May I get up tomorrow?" Lisa asked impetuously, "and see to my neglected household?—And if friends come now asking for me, may I bid them welcome, and show them this bonnie bairn of mine?"

The doctor held up his hands in mock horror. "Get up!" he echoed scoldingly, "I should say not! When I was last here you were still too far spent to speak to me, and now you talk of getting up! Next time I come it will be plenty soon to argue that. As for visitors, one now and then, for a matter of minutes, would do you no great harm—though if they stay too long, and I find they have tired you with idle chatter, I shall be very angry!" He scraped back his chair, his eyes twinkling again. "Eat all you can," he said encouragingly, "that is a greedy little wench of yours and you must keep pace with her. And if you will compose yourself with sleep whenever she does, I guarantee you will become plump and rosy too."

Lisa joined in his contagious laugh; and after a moment he went on more gravely, "If there should be some moments left when you are not asleep, or at meat, or entertaining guests, or cosseting this small stout suckling, and therefore have them free, remember there is one who yearns to spend them with you."

She did not answer at once; then in a voice from which the buoyancy had been swept away, though it betrayed no repugnance, she asked, "Do you mean my husband?"

"Yes," answered the doctor steadily. "He has learned a hard lesson in a hard school. You must be just to him,

157

Mistress Anderson. And if you can find it in your heart to be generous also——"

This time she did not answer at all, and the doctor, fearing to press his point, went away. But as he continued to watch her intently, during his subsequent visits, he felt that even without his word of admonition the fairness and bounty which were so obviously an intrinsic part of her nature would eventually have triumphed over any rankling memories she might cherish. Indeed, noticing the sweetness and deference which marked her attitude towards her husband, he guessed that she was making a painstaking effort, not only to do her full duty, but to act with loving-kindness; for he divined that her very strength of character made her disposition essentially imperious rather than docile. When, after a long convalescence, the perfect balance of her health was at last restored, he saw that she had also become blithe and winsome again; and that there was a new quality of enchantment in the elusive charm which had always made her so bewitching, and which now pervaded her like a soft and fragrant bloom.

"Well, I have lost my patient, and not because of a last illness either," he said at last, as he emerged from the cottage one day in early winter, and found Anderson, as usual, waiting to speak to him. "Yonder little lady has no more need of me. She is as sound as a bell and chipper as a lark again. I must not take the time from those who are suffering by passing the time of day with her—though it is certain I enjoy her jocund company, and praise be! I am not so busy now as in those days when I was the only doctor in Coos County."

"I am more beholden to thee than I know how to say," Anderson replied with the hesitation which nearly always marked his speech when he was deeply moved. "Well do I ken that but for thee she would be lying cold in her grave, instead of working and singing about the house. If some day chance should favor me so that I can show my gratitude I shall be more than glad. Meanwhile, fail not to let me know thy charges for all the skillful services thou hast so freely rendered."

"I have as yet not added my accounts—there is no

158

hurry," the doctor said easily, bending over to fasten his snowshoes. There were drifts in the roads already, and in winter it was not his custom to make his rounds on horseback. "My charges for the most part range from three to six shillings a visit, or thereabouts, when I go as far from Jefferson Hill as Ryegate; but I confess I have kept no track of the number of calls I have made here at the crossroads; and when I do reckon them up we will forget a few, partly for the pleasure I have had in making them, and partly for the fear your father should hear of the size of my bill, and think it without reason! I know how thrifty a soul he is, and can make some guess of how it must have irked him to see a doctor bobbing in and out of his son's house, so freely all these months!"

Samuel White stood up, the leather thongs of his snowshoes firmly tied about his feet and ankles, and began strapping his case of instruments and medicine to his back. "As to that other matter we spoke of once," he said casually, "do not reproach yourself if the time should come when all your best intentions are swept away, or believe that if they should be, they would be gone to pave hell. It is not good for man to live alone, the Bible says, and though I do not hold with all its teachings, I know that, good or not, it is uncommon hard, when he is married to such a woman as you are. Nor do I think it needful. Your wife is well already, and she will come to all the fullness of her strength, when that small stout suckling of hers has been weaned. Moreover, she has an understanding heart and a healthful zest for life herself— red blood, not cambric tea, goes coursing through her veins. For all she has been through, I would take my oath the memory of her agonies is dimmer now than yours, and that it would not trouble her overmuch, if perchance she should find herself with child again. Stretch out your arms to her some night, and see if you do not find her ready and glad to lie in them."

Having delivered himself of his sound and lusty advice, Samuel White trudged away through the snow up the Swamp Road, his figure looming like a bulwark of strength as long as it could be seen. There was something actually communicable about his vigor; nevertheless, Anderson saw him out of sight unheartened by his parting words. He, too, had been watching his wife searchingly since the birth of her child, his heart torn between thanksgiving, tenderness and longing; and as he saw the lines of anguish fade, little by little, from her face, he had seen, too, in time, that the baby was beginning to mean all he had hoped to her mother. Then, to his amazement, to his unacknowledged horror, he saw that she was meaning more—that she was meaning everything. She filled her mother's life. The horizon which had been painted black with suffering was flooded now with rosy glory. But it was a glory in which he had no share. For all of Lisa's sweetness to him, he knew that her every thought, like her every joy, was centered in the child. She did her housework with a tense rapidity that she might have more leisure to devote to the baby; her days were full to overflowing because of it, even her slumber time broken. She could not pause now for long hours alone with him, in which to share their every hope and fear. Besides, the dear habit of confidence was broken, shattered in those silent months when they had striven against each other. Now neither one could mend it. He knew she was as powerless to commune with him as he with her, and there was an element of irony in their estrangement which seemed to mock him. For Lisa had found fulfillment not in marriage, but in maternity. The experience, so dreaded, so resisted, and, at its inception, so terrible, had after all proved to be the greatest event in her life, the supreme compensation for all that she had lost, forfeited and sacrificed. Before long it had become, as it does to every woman who so visualizes it, a dominant force, rampant with power, insatiable.

If Anderson had recognized what, in the end, this evolution must mean to him, the bitterness which lay like iron upon his soul would, in part at least, have been lifted. But he felt that a stone wall rising between him and his wife could not have been a more insuperable barrier than the soft, suckling baby through whom he had thought to be so indivisibly knit to its mother. There were times when he almost hated the bairn. He did not guess that as soon as she was weaned her mother would be consumed with longing to have her empty breasts filled and throbbing again, or that, by the time the infant had become a toddler, her mother's vacant arms would be stretched out, starvingly, into space. His intuition, far less sensitive than Lisa's, gave him no enlightenment; and it was inconceivable to him that his wife, no less than he, should battle against desire or find the intensity of yearning almost uncontrollable.

He had put so strong a curb upon himself that every avenue of approach towards him seemed closed; her dignity precluded her from making an appeal which would be to his senses alone; and since she had once repulsed him, she could not entreat with him except with almost intolerable sacrifice of pride. But the increasing consciousness that her husband was too benumbed with bitterness to strive for reconciliation, and the determination that their separation should end, fortified Lisa in her purpose; and with a burning heart she bided her time, watching for the auspicious moment when she could unburden her soul to him.

Her opportunity came at last one evening when they were sitting by the fireside together, enveloped in the benignant warmth emanating from its embers. Old Nannie had gone to bed; little Sue was fast asleep in her cradle. There was no light in the room except that which rose and fell with the flickering flames; but Lisa felt, rather than saw, that her husband's gaze was resting on her intently; and laying aside her knitting, she rose and walked across to the place where he sat, silent and gloomy, in the huge and shabby chair where he was wont to rest after a hard day. She laid her hand lightly on his hair, and then as lightly sat down upon his knee.

"A penny for thy thoughts, Jim," she said whimsically, "unless in thy opinion, they are worth more. If so, I must dig into my crock of gold!"

He did not answer at once, nor did he return her caress. But as her hand descended to his cheek, stroking this softly before she put it around his neck, he said soberly, "When my thoughts are not on the stock and the land, and how I shall wrench a living from them, thou knowest they are always on thee."

161

"And were they on the stock and land just now?" she asked, leaning back against his shoulder.

"No," he said briefly.

"Jim, it is easier to wring cheese from a stone than words from thee, sometimes!" she cried in mock despair. "Why art thou so loath to talk with me?"

"I am not loath to talk to thee. Only, at the moment, I was thinking, as I often do, of a time I can never remember without shame. But I cannot speak of it, even to thee."

"Let us speak of it," she said quietly, "and afterwards thou wilt forget thy shame. Dost mean the time when—the time after our first baby died?"

"Aye," he said slowly and painfully.

"Of the night when thou didst tell me 'twas ordained by Scripture that a woman's conception should be multiplied, that her desire should be to her husband, and that he should rule over her?"

"Aye—but there is one part thou hast forgotten."

"Nay—I have not forgot it—'In sorrow shall she bring forth children—' I left it out because that part alone, it seems to me, were best forgot."

She raised her face until it rested in the hollow of his chin. "But all the rest," she murmured, "let us remember together. For thou wert right, as I would have granted hadst thou but bided thy time till I was not so crazed with grief and sick with suffering—but let that pass, and never think of it again. It is better to say the right thing at the wrong time than never to say it at all—much better than to say the wrong thing at the right time. Think only that thou wert right and I was wrong—as I do now admit most gladly."

"What seekest thou to say?" he asked gropingly, as if dazzled by a light which had shone so suddenly upon him that it bewildered him.

"Only what thou canst guess."

"I have guessed nothing."

"Not that—my desire is to my husband—and my wish—that he shall rule over me and my—oh, Jim, must I say it all?"

"To the very end, if I am to believe."

"And—and my hope that my conception may be multiplied," she whispered throbbingly.

There was a long silence, and still James Anderson did not move, though he thought his wife must feel the tightening of the muscles that lay beneath her arm, the beating of his heart against her own. At last he spoke, still very slowly.

"Then this time thou wilt come to me of thine own free will?"

"I have come," she said even lower than before. "Oh, Jim, wilt thou not take me?"

## FIFTEEEN

THE URGENCY OF THE IMPULSES which had driven Lisa to seek for a reconciliation, and the intensity of emotion in which Anderson's long repression had culminated, gave a fiery force to their reunion. Every instinct of maternity, every compulsion of virility, welded them together; and every circumstance of their joint lives seemed to enhance their mutual need.

When Sue was about two years old, she succumbed to an attack of spotted fever—a disease which was sweeping through the settlements, bringing death and destruction in its wake. Thanks to her natural sturdiness, and the devoted and intelligent care with which she was tended, she suffered little and rallied quickly; but before her recovery was assured, Lisa's fear of bereavement had mounted to terror, for almost every known case of the malady had been fatal; and she could not recapture her sense of security so far as her little daughter was concerned. Every time the bairn sneezed, she foresaw pneumonia; every time she had colic, her mother's mind leapt to cholera infantum. Anderson, who was fond of the child, but to whom she had never become the obsession that she was to Lisa, at last remonstrated with his wife for her perpetual and unwarranted anxiety regarding the welfare of the robust little girl.

"Thou knowest Dr. White hath always said he hath never seen so lusty a wean," he reminded her. "Do not fret over her and mollycoddle her so! She is no longer an infant in arms."

"Nay, and I have no infant in arms," Lisa answered in a tense voice; and Anderson, looking at her more closely, saw that her eyes were full of tears. "Oh, Jim—if we had two or three I might not be so sore afraid for little Sue, though every bairn has its own peculiar place in its mother's heart, and she is sure the sonsiest little lass that I ever saw. But if we lose her, we lose all we have. Sometimes I think that I shall never bear another child, as judgment upon me that I once rebelled against a woman's lot."

"Nay, but thou wilt," said Anderson comfortingly. "There is no judgment meted out to those whose repentance is as complete as thine has been," he added, with one of his rare smiles, and a look that made Lisa blush. "And there is no danger that thou wilt lost Sue—rather the danger is that we cannot keep her in clothes, she grows so fast, and that she will eat us out of house and home, she is so greedy: But even if we should—how canst thou say, Lisa, that we would then have lost everything, when we shall still have each other?"

"It—it is not the same," Lisa said quickly.

"Nay, it is not the same—it is far greater," he said, so gravely that she looked at him in swift astonishment. "As for me, I am as well content to have thee to myself this little while—thou wast so soon a mother after thou hadst become a wife, and then so long an invalid—and then all mother and not wife at all! This year, and this year only, hast thou been my very own." He paused and added more lightly, "And for thyself, art thou not glad to be without encumbrance, to have leisure for thy garden and thy needlework and such like?"

"I am tired of them," she said suddenly. "So many days go by, each are like the other— Jim, wilt thou not go and stay with thy parents, a few days, and give me leave to take Sue and visit Mistress Johnson? It is long since I have seen my Oxbow friends, and I wish——"

"Go visiting!" he exclaimed in bewilderment. "Without me!"

"If thou wilt come too, I shall be all the better pleased."

"Thou knowest I cannot leave the land and stock," he said shortly, "nor can I understand why thou shouldst wish to depart from thy home and husband."

It was not the first time he had detected signs of restlessness in his wife, and they disquieted him. His own life had lacked variety, his horizon had been singularly limited. He did not—indeed, he could not—visualize what it meant to a girl who had been brought up as Lisa had been—roaming freely over her father's country estate, moving in the pleasantest society of a great city, traveling unconfined through France and Italy—to stay season after season within the four walls of a cottage, managing a household, and caring for a child. When his day's work was over, a quiet hour beside the hearth, preceding a long night's sleep to refresh him for the labors of the next day, was all that he desired. That it would have meant refreshment to her, no matter how weary she was physically, to go to the simple and infrequent merrymakings which the countryside afforded, did not occur to him. He had taken her, of course, before their marriage—that was a recognized part of courtship; but a woman's home, and her children, were supposed to fill her existence after she had acquired them. That was the code of the settlement, and from it Anderson was conscious of no reason why he should depart. He went with her to church, with the utmost regularity; occasionally to his father's house; less often, to the Camerons, and Whitelaws'; he had never offered to go farther away than this, and was vaguely surprised and displeased now that she suggested it. He did not actually refuse her, but he countered her request, and, without appreciating the forbearance she showed in her lack of insistence, he was thankful when she changed the subject.

It did not arise again for some time, for Anderson's hopeful prophecies were fulfilled not long afterwards, and in the joyful preoccupation of preparing for the child of whose advent she had begun to despair, Lisa's restlessness was stilled. Though far too high-strung and slightly

165

built to escape abnormal difficulties in labor, she brought her second little girl into the world without the prolonged and terrible anguish which had endangered her life and reason at the time of her previous confinements; and when Anderson did not conceal his disappointment because the baby was not a boy, she sought to minimize the sufferings she had undergone in order that he might feel no compunction in requiring her to continue to endure them until she had borne a son. He was less touched by her sensibility towards him than a man of more subtlety would have been; indeed, he was hardly aware of it. But he was thankful to find that the fear of a second estrangement was unfounded; and there was no such resentment in his heart against the wee lassie whom Lisa had suggested calling Agnes after his mother, as there had been towards the elder sister whose very existence he felt had menaced his possession of the woman for whom his passion was still unassuaged.

The next year brought placidity and prosperity to the little farm at the crossroads; the land was fertile, the crops abundant; the herds throve and increased. Lisa was not only conscientious and compliant as a wife; as the mistress of the crossroads cottage she had begun to attain an established and respected position in the neighborhood for industry and efficiency, in which Anderson took a deep though unexpressed pride. No woman in the settlements, it was generally said, could turn off a greater day's work with so light a hand and so merry a manner; none showed herself more dutiful to her husband or devoted to her children. If Anderson had passed on to her the praises which were so often sung in his hearing, it would have given added zest to her zeal. Instead, mistrustful of fostering vanity, he cautioned her against extravagance and a too literal interpretation of the Biblical injunction that Christians should be "given to hospitality." He did not tell her that men said to him, "Thou are fortunate in thy helpmate, James—truly her price is beyond rubies!" He told her rather than he was beginning to hear that their house was called "The Poor Man's Tavern," without adding that he also heard this was because, " 'Twas well-known through more of the countryside than could be seen that no poor soul in need was ever turned away from it without food and shelter."

"Dost ever think, Lisa," he asked her, one morning when he saw a shabby journeyman who had taken refuge with them for the night trudging away carrying over his shoulder a bundle which bulged suspiciously, "how much this free-handedness of thine is costing us? I sometimes fear that we may want in our old age because of thy prodigality. Look to what comfort and security their prudent ways have brought my parents! In all the years they have been married, they have never yet bought a pound of sugar or meat or flour, and never have their annual cash expenditures exceeded thirty dollars! While, if I mistake not, thou hast given away that much outright during the last six months."

"Thou dost not mistake," she said merrily, "but I have saved it for thee in other ways. I can spin twice as much in a day as thy mother, and our bairns go clad as never hers did, and at trifling cost."

"Thou shouldst not make a boast of it," he said severely, "nor forget that now there will soon be another bairn to clothe and feed."

"I do not forget it," she said, "and I shall clothe and feed it, never fear!—Art thou not content, Jim," she asked, sensing that he was brooding over more than money, "that there is to be another wean?"

"I shall be well content if it be not another lass," he answered rather shortly.

She saw that he could not be reconciled even to the thought of another girl; and so she was not unprepared when he appeared to regard the birth of their third daughter almost in the light of an affront. He made no response to Lisa's laughing comment that they now had "Three Graces" abiding with them; and recognizing that he did not even understand the classical allusion, she concealed her surprise, stifled her involuntary consciousness of superior culture, and sympathized thoroughly with him in his sense of frustration, even though she did not share it, for each little girl had seemed to her even lovelier than the last. The discussion of a name had always interested him, and she hoped that this at least would do so now.

But when she confided to him her wishes concerning it, a little hesitatingly, he looked at her with indignation.

*"Jane!"* he exclaimed. "Thou wouldst call her Jane—after thy mother!"

"We named the last lass after thine," she said serenely.

"Hath my mother not shown thee every kindness always? Whilst thine——"

"She was still my mother, Jim," Lisa said quietly. "I have learned, in these last years, what that means. And she thought me guilty— She did not realize— Is there not a passage in Scripture which saith 'Father, forgive them, for they know not what they do'?—Moreover, she was completely under the dominion of my father——"

"As thou art under mine, I suppose thou wilt say next!"

"I shall not say it," said Lisa, flushing, but still forcing herself to speak gently. "Nor did I think of doing so."

"Not of saying it, perhaps! But the thought is in thy mind, every time I dissuade thee from scattering money to the four winds or from gadding about the countryside!"

She pressed her lips together. "The money is after all mine own, Jim," she reminded him a little sadly. "The—the price of my exile. My only comfort in it lies in the thought that it may make others happy.—And I have not been abroad overmuch lately. Only twice this last year as far as Newbury, seven miles away, each time taking both bairns with me."

"Wouldst leave them with a feeble old woman like Nannie, who hath scarce the strength to do her own work, let alone thine, and whose wits are beginning to wander?"

"Yet you thought her capable of caring for me unaided in my agony, and she would be doing so yet, if Priest Sutherland had not shamed you into getting me a doctor!"

She spoke scornfully at last, and her colloquialisms disappeared from her speech, as they always did when she was aroused.

"Shame on thee, Lisa, for saying so unjust a thing! I rode as if the deil himself were after me to get Dr. White as soon as I knew how it was with thee——"

"As soon as you knew! But how long did it take you to find out?"

He winced, knowing she had good cause to taunt him with his blindness. But his perversity would not permit him to acknowledge this, and he took refuge in another approach.

"Thou speakest always as if the bairns were the apple of thy eye," he said derisively, "yet it appears thou wouldst be glad enough to leave them any time for light company. It might be well for thee to think on what befell the Grays' lassie."

Lisa winced in her turn. Jean and John Gray, who were highly respected members of the community, had also been the parents of a lovely little girl, whom they had left one day in charge of her elder brothers and sisters when it seemed needful that they go to Haverhill. She had been suddenly seized with convulsions during their absence, and on their return they had found her dead. The shock had been a terrific one, from which Mistress Gray had never recovered.

"Call the wean what thou wilt," said Anderson, seeing that he had scored, and feeling the moment opportune to leave the room before Lisa collected herself and retaliated. "It concerns me but little. My interest will be more aroused when there is question of naming a boy— if such question ever arises. It seems thou canst not breed a male!"

"My first-born was a boy!" Lisa cried, goaded beyond endurance. "And little did you grieve because it came dead into the world! Your thoughts were all upon how soon you could get another!"

Anderson shut the door violently behind him, and went out into the yard, seething with rage, and leaving his wife trembling with anger as much as with weakness. It was their first real quarrel since her mutiny against him, and now she found it took all the will-power she could summon not to revolt again. Unbidden thoughts crowded upon her consciousness, recreating figures of a past she could not bury, peopling her imagination of a future she had forfeited but could not forget. If she had married Basil, there never would have been the dark and dreadful

169

year of strife, the memory of which still made her shudder; there never would have been the stern and inescapable rule of duty and docility; there never would have been this abnegation of all individuality, all freedom, all joyousness! Their life together would have been one of mutual delight, their children born of a spontaneous gladness. And many strong and beautiful boys would have sprung into life and being, for Basil would have given her sons. Was it her fault she could not "breed a male"? Had she not heard it said a hundred times over, that these were the legacy of overwhelming love, the love she could not bestow upon Jim, for all her striving, but which she would have so bountifully lavished upon Basil? Almost she resolved that if her husband ever again reproached her, though she went cheerfully down to her bed of pain, year after year, hoping to grant him his heart's desire, she would tell him this!

She never did. Returning strength brought with it self-command; and through it she was able to control her thoughts and subdue her anger. But she did not seek a second time for reconciliation; and, in his turn, Anderson made no overtures towards peace. Indeed, when the baby was baptized, in the new barn he had just finished building and which had not yet been put to use, he actually rebuked his wife in public because, when the bairn began to greet, she took it in her arms during the ceremony and comforted it.

"Is it not enough," he asked her harshly, "that thou shouldst once have been tried for heresy without bringing down the wrath of the church on thee again for indecorum?"

Half the assembled company must have heard the affront, for he did not even lower his voice as he spoke. Lisa bit her lip to keep from quivering, as much as to check the quick retort with which she almost choked; and only pride prevented her eyes from brimming over. She knew that their guests were hard-put to conceal their amazement at his rudeness, and that John Gray, always called "the peacemaker of Ryegate," because of his gentle ways and powers of conciliation, made open efforts to pour oil on the troubled waters; while James Mulliken, the young preacher, who in the absence of the Priest of Bath had been called in for the christening, protested that neither church nor minister would take action against so devout a Covenanter as Mistress Anderson, however far she might forget herself. But Anderson did not voice his regret, and, to do him justice, he did not guess how much a spoken apology would have meant to Lisa—she must, he reasoned, see that he was sorry, and that should be enough for any reasonable woman. Besides, he strove to make indirect amends for his discourtesy by offering to take her with him to Horse Meadow, where he wished to consult with Colonel Porter about the purchase of a horse: his mother, he said, had consented to come and mind Sue and Agnes; and they could take Janey with them on the pillion.

Since he had no glimmering of a reason why the manor-house was the only one throughout Coos to which she did not wish to go, he misinterpreted her hesitation about falling in with his suggestion, and put it down as lack of appreciation; and when the day arrived which had been set for the expedition, to which Lisa had finally agreed, he came in early from the barn and told her brusquely that he could not go, after all, because the colt was sick.

She expressed no disappointment of the change of plan, took off her black silk dress and Janey's broidered muslin without comment, and when they were clad in homespun and cotton again, went about her regular occupations. The ironic words which Asa Porter had whispered to her so long ago on his balcony, about the way with women of every color and clime, kept ringing in her ears; and the thought of them made her silent. She wondered whether he remembered as well as she did his penetrating implication that she had found neither her true mate nor her real master in Anderson. She could not help feeling that he did, and that if she had gone to his house, he would have sought means to remind her of this. In a way, she was glad to have escaped the satire to which the contemplated visit would have subjected her; but, on the other hand, the thought of Porter's sophistication and culture fascinated her, and she knew she would have found a tilt with him stimulating. Since her life was so barren of excite-

171

ment, she was inclined to regret, after all, that the encounter had not taken place.

As the day wore on, Anderson noticed a look of repression in her face which he set down to sullenness. But his intuition had failed him again. She was actually in the grip of a revulsion against his personal habits which sometimes overcame her, and which had been stimulated partly by her resurrected thoughts of Asa Porter's charm, and partly by the uncleanly condition in which her husband had entered the kitchen to tell her of the colt's sickness. During their courtship and betrothal he had striven never to come to her unwashed and unshaven. He had recognized and indulged her fastidiousness, even though he did not understand it, and had not failed to change his rough blue smock and leather breeches for clean linen and well-dyed wool whenever he could. Now he was becoming more and more careless about the niceties which meant so much to her and which seemed to him so unimportant. He always came in late and ravenous for his supper, and sat down to it, scarcely pausing to plunge his unkempt head and bearded face into a basin of cold water at the sink, after thrusting his hands into the bucket of softsoap that stood beside it. An hour later, he tumbled into bed, disregarding almost angrily any reference to the pot of steaming water hanging on the crane, to the huck towels and wooden tub placed near the fire.

The children, scrubbed from top to toe, their rosy faces shining with cleanliness, their yellow curls damp around neck and forehead, were put to sleep between sheets sweet from scalding, from blowing in wind and sun, from lying sprinkled with dried lavender, and rose leaves; and after they were settled for the night, their mother bathed too, slipping her simple nightgown over the smooth, fragrant flesh of her slim body, dusted with cornstarch, brushing her golden hair until it shone and shimmered, and then braiding it into a crown. The intimate contact with sweating and begrimed humanity, in the person of her husband, filled her with physical disgust and repugnance amounting to nausea. It enveloped her like an unclean garment which she could not take off; the robe of Nessus, she thought, could hardly have been

172

more painful. But when she tried to tell Anderson this he laughed at her squeamishness, calling it absurd, telling her to overcome it. She might do what she pleased with the children, and he did not interfere with her own practices, though in his opinion they consumed her time and reduced her strength. He would be grateful, he told her, if she would allow him the same freedom. Eventually she ceased to refer to the fact that he shaved only on Sundays, and bathed less often still, and he concluded that she no longer minded it; but there were times when she found him actually revolting to her.

Elizabeth had too valiant a spirit to succumb to either antipathy or self-pity; and she was never long enough idle to become the prey of introspection. At the same time, she consciously struggled against an inner turmoil which she could not subdue and for which she had no outlet. The hungry maternity which had once driven her into Anderson's arms did not help her now, for its clamor was quieted. The three little girls were all healthy and hearty, and it was inconceivable that disease or disaster should rob her of them. Even the utmost solicitude could not deepen into a fear so groundless. And since it had been her yearning for children which had stimulated her feeling for Anderson, there was nothing to stir it now that this was stilled. During the first months of their marriage, it had been but the reflection of his own passion, mirrored in the deep waters of his desire; it had never been a wellspring gushing from her own heart. And though afterwards her being had been merged with his, the fusion had been one of submission and conquest rather than of union, illumined by false fire, and fanned into flame by primitive instincts which had possessed no radiance and which left no afterglow.

The more desperately conscious Elizabeth became of this, the more unremittingly she strove to be patient, to be dutiful, to be long-suffering. But she was naturally impetuous, strong-willed and proud; and she had never recaptured her lost reliance on Anderson as a confidant and companion. With their common interests confined within the four walls of their cottage, it was doubly hard for her even to create conversation which gave the illusion of communion. It was hardly necessary that she should tell him that the bread was baked, that the floor was scrubbed, that the baby was beginning to walk; these things he could see for himself; and hesitant at expressing her inmost thoughts, sometimes imagining and sometimes knowing him to be out of sympathy with them, she had eventually ceased to give voice to them. She talked, indeed, but it was with an effort where once it had been a relief; she touched only the surface where once she had dug deeply. He resented this, was hurt by it, and showed that he was resentful and hurt, but he could not remedy it. He could not see that his own silence and lack of understanding made it impossible to her to reach the soul which she had once clasped in her two hands.

## SIXTEEN

Matters were at this pass between them when the strange phenomenon known as the "famine year" fell on the little farm at the crossroads, as it did on the rest of the valley, bringing desolation and suffering to the happiest hearts, searing theirs with a deeper bitterness and unconfessed terror. Spring had come warm and early, full of unusual promise; but it broke its pledges of fruitfulness, as Anderson had broken his of cherishing. The snow on the mountaintops did not melt away, but lay there, hard and cold and white, through June; returning, after its tardy and reluctant departure, intermittently through July and August. Moreover, it was not only the hills that were blanketed: in May the pastures were buried five inches deep, a foot the following month; and their malign covering melted only after it had frozen all that lay beneath it. The building of a brick house in Bath was abandoned by the masons in midsummer because the mortar stiffened in the open air. Night after night the mercury fell below freezing; the gardens were destroyed, and there were no potatoes to lay away for the winter. The wheat did not fill and corn was saved for seed only by the building of bonfires in the fields; and night after night Anderson took his turn at keeping these flames alive, returning cold and exhausted to face his day's work, wondering, as he milked his thinning cows, on what they were to be fed through the oncoming winter.

It was not long before he began to wonder on what he was to feed his wife and children. There was no money in the valley, and even the Scotch gold and his own savings were of little avail when no provisions were to be had without making a journey to obtain them, when the comparatively wealthy boiled and ate weeds of all descriptions, if they could find any spared by the common blight of cold. Mercifully, almost miraculously, the oat crop was spared. The little mill at Boltonville ran day and night, grinding the oats brought by men who had never tasted them before, and who now tardily blessed the Scotch settlers for introducing oatmeal into their midst; and Anderson, coming late into the kitchen one night with a bag of these ground oats for the supper that had perforce been delayed until his arrival, because there was nothing else in the house to eat, found Sue lying listless in her mother's arms, already faint with hunger.

"We must be very good, mustn't we, mother?" she was saying. "If we are to die of hunger, when winter comes, we will be sent to hell unless we have been patient through the affliction which the Lord hath sent upon us. So Nannie says."

There was no patience in the eyes Elizabeth raised to her husband's over the little girl's drooping head. She never complained, to be sure. She worked unceasingly and fought valiantly, making the little they had do much, denying her own hunger and hiding her own fear. That she should feel resignation through it all was too much to ask of her brave and rebellious spirit. The child was fed, of course, and tucked away at last under her warm, gay, patchwork quilt beside her little sisters, comfortable and happy. Nannie's porridge bowl and Jim's were filled again and again with the smoking hot food. But when the old woman was nodding in the corner again, and the man had gone out to do his neglected chores, his wife

175

set back the iron kettle which still held some of the steaming oats, to save them for the morning, after taking out only a scant cupful for herself.

When at last Anderson had caught her at this more than once, and remonstrated with her for it, she turned on him with a fierce fury, the bitterest he had seen her display since she had been accused of heresy.

"Would you have me starve the bairns to feed myself? Or you? I can at least give you food!" she exclaimed, and he wondered whether she was reproaching him, or herself, because she could now give him nothing else. "Or poor old Nannie," she went on scathingly, "whose age and feebleness are at best so great that she is not strong enough, in your opinion, even when sufficiently fed, to care for two healthy children if their mother leaves them for an hour? If I die, call me a suicide if you will, and bury me here at these crossroads, as ye did poor Mary Dunn, beyond the forks in Dow village at Barnet line!"

The taunt was a bitter one. Mary Dunn had been a lovely girl who had come from Maine to visit her aunt and uncle, True and Daniel Wormwood. She was devoted to them and their family, especially to their little twins, John and Janet; and she often came to spend the day at the Anderson cottage, bringing with her the two bonnie bairns to play with Sue and Agnes and help keep Janey amused. She was a grave, gentle girl, who wore her dark hair smoothly parted away from her white brow, and who dressed with nunlike simplicity; but she had intelligence as well as refinement, a broader outlook than most of the settlers, and a sympathetic spirit. Her friendship, the first ever spontaneously offered to Lisa by any person of her own sex in Ryegate, meant even more to the exile than Mistress Johnson's had done, for in this companionship there was nothing of condescension. Besides, the two young women were of almost exactly the same age, and shared, to a great degree, the same ideals, interests and tastes. Anderson, who had been at first inclined to regard Mary's frequent presence in his house as something of an intrusion, was gradually disarmed by her candor and sweetness; and when she became betrothed to Hugh Folger, the attractive and engaging young man whose slight but arresting resemblance to Basil had first struck Lisa at the Johnsons' ball, and whose brother William had married one of Anderson's sisters, he was almost as much pleased as his wife at the thought that Mary was to be kin to them.

One evening he was just closing the barn doors for the night, when he saw Mary ride into the yard; and he was vaguely surprised that she did not lift her head or wave her hand when he called out a greeting to her. But he thought no more about it until he went into the house, and found that preparations for supper had been arrested midway, that the children were all crowded into the kitchen with Nannie, and that except for the distant sound of smothered but passionate weeping, a strange stillness reigned in the little cottage where usually there was so much wholesome bustle. He gathered, from the confused chatter with which Sue and Agnes finally answered his curt questions, after the first brief but stubborn silence characteristic of all children, that Mary had apparently come in, beside herself with grief, and that Lisa had drawn her swiftly away to a quiet place where she could unburden her heart. They were locked, he soon discovered, in the parlor-bedroom which he and Lisa shared: Mary's abandonment to sorrow and Lisa's exclamations of compassion were both audible when he went to the door and listened. And shaken as he seldom had been by the sense of some violent calamity, he went back to the kitchen, marshaled the two elder children through their supper and tumbled them into bed. Then, taking the hungry baby in his lap, he sat down in a rocker, comforting it as best he could, while he waited for his wife to come and explain the mysterious tragedy which had taken place.

It was very late when she came swiftly into the room, untying her bodice as she hastened forward. And when she had caught up Janey and laid the bairn against her breast, she sank down on her husband's knees in such visible exhaustion and with so blanched a face, that he thought she was going to swoon.

"What is it?" he asked, putting his arm around her to

177

steady and support her. His voice, which had so long been harsh, was tender with solicitude. "What is it, Lisa?"

"She is asleep at last—asleep on our bed. I thought she never would be calm again!"

"But Mary is always calm," he protested in bewilderment. "That is why she is so beautiful. What hath happened to disturb her?"

"Hugh Folger had gone suddenly insane! He is fastened like a wild beast, with a chain about his middle, in a cage behind his parents' house. Mary was summoned to see him there this afternoon."

Elizabeth brought out the terrible tidings with a cry of anguish. The fate of the mentally afflicted was a horrible one in the settlements; even the most skilled physicians did not know how to minister to them, and they almost never recovered; there were no asylums where they could be confined for safekeeping and humane treatment; and they dragged out a hideous lifetime of fettered and incarcerated existence. The sight of their sufferings was almost unbearable to their helpless relatives, and even the thought of it unendurable to those who loved them best. Anderson gave an exclamation of horror.

"But why was she at least not spared—why was she summoned———"

"She would not believe when Dr. White told her. She said she could not unless she saw. She trusted in God's goodness and thought he would not punish her for some crime she had not committed, when Hugh was more than life to her!"

Lisa was sobbing convulsively, her head against Anderson's shoulder, her child clasped to her breast. But she was not thinking, her husband knew, of either Janey or himself. She was thinking partly of the bereft and distracted girl whom she had just lulled to a brief but merciful slumber, and partly of that other girl who had once reasoned as little, trusted as blindly, and loved as deeply as Mary Dunn.

The consciousness that his wife still dwelt on her own bereavement hardened Anderson's heart. He kept his steadying arm around her; but some of the compassion was gone from his voice as he bade her control herself, and said that Mary should not question the inscrutable ways of Providence: If Hugh had meant more than life to her, as she declared, he might well have meant more to her than her Maker; and if that had been so——"

"If that was so, and I think it was, she will not survive this shock!" exclaimed Elizabeth passionately.

"Maids do not die of broken hearts," Anderson answered with conviction. "Least of all maids as pure and modest as Mary. She is not wild of impulse and ungovernable of spirit."

He regretted the implied censure and comparison almost as soon as it was uttered; and he repented it still more deeply when Elizabeth came back from the bedroom, where she had gone to lay her baby in its cradle, saying, with a face whiter than ever, that Mary had disappeared! They went breathlessly out into the night together to search for her and give the alarm that she was lost. But morning came and no trace of her had been found; and when Elizabeth, driven by the dependence of Janey upon her, went back to the cottage, she found Nannie sitting with her apron over her head and moaning.

"Never will we see her again in life!" she wailed. "I knew that she was fey[1] the instant she opened the door in the gloaming! There was the look of death in her eyes! And all night long, beside me in the wall, I heard the tick-tock-tick of the ghosties' clock.[2] She's shrouded already, be she shriven or na'!"

Old Nannie spoke the truth. The sun was hardly high in the heavens when a white shape was seen floating on Ticklenaked Pond, and before noon the drowned body of Mary Dunn had been recovered and laid upon a bier. True Wormwood, beside herself with grief, sent for Elizabeth to come and dispose the dead girl for her burial; and when the soft dark hair had been plaited away from the white brow for the last time, and the slender figure

[1] Doomed to die.

[2] There is an old Scotch superstition that a steady ticking sound in the wall presages death.

robed in the snowy garments which were to have adorned it on Mary's wedding day, Elizabeth called in her husband, who had taken her over to the Wormwood farm on his pillion, to look at the lifeless form and face, and spoke to him with such intensity that he was stunned.

"Take your hand and lay it over Mary's heart," his wife commanded, in a voice so strange that he was startled into doing what she bade him. He could feel the coldness of the body through all its coverings; and he was appalled to find how still a breast could be that did not throb with heartbeats. He recoiled from the touch, and was aware that Elizabeth was looking at him with concentrated antipathy. "Do you say now, James Anderson," she went on relentlessly, "that Mary's heart is not broken? That pure and modest maidens do not die for love? Mark that they do—or, living, learn that life is worse than death!"

If she had not so taunted him, her plea that the suicide should be buried in hallowed ground might possibly have been granted; but in the face of Anderson's stubborn refusal to intercede with the church, superstition and prejudice prevailed, and Mary Dunn was denied a last resting-place in the old churchyard. Elizabeth had passionately implored her husband to use his influence with the elders. He had refused, claiming that they were within their rights; and when, touching upon ground long untrodden, she begged him to forgive her cruel words, which she knew had cut him more deeply than any he had ever uttered to her, and besought him to do it for her sake, he made no reply. She had turned away from him then without speaking another syllable; and when the pitiful funeral took place, she had walked beside the rude coffin at the head of the pathetically small procession that accompanied it over the hills, scattering flowers upon it as it was lowered to its shallow grave, but not shedding a tear. And afterwards she had gone and stood motionless for hours beside the cage where Hugh Folger crouched and snarled and rattled at his chains.

Elizabeth had never spoken of the tragic episode again until she made her wild reference to it in the time of famine. But Anderson realized then that he had dealt her a blow from which she had not recovered, and that if she had ever loved him before, she surely did not love him now. The grueling conviction made him increasingly silent and bitter. He sought no more to reason with her.

## SEVENTEEN

THE LOSS OF A FRIEND as dearly loved as Mary Dunn would have been a terrible shock to Elizabeth Anderson, even if it had not been attended by the twin tragedies of suicide and insanity; and the "famine year," following in the full force of its deprivation and desolation, sapped her strength and embittered her soul. But though she grew pinched and wasted from malnutrition, she went her way with her teeth set and her head held high; and firmly resolving that, if she were to starve, she would do so with spirit still unsubdued, she began to teach little Sue the Highland fling, sensing that in the gambols of the lovely child she would find distraction and delight.

She was not mistaken. From the very first, Sue proved an apt pupil. She was so quick and graceful that as she posed and pranced and pirouetted, she seemed to become the personification of the blithe spirit of the Highlander interpreted through motion. And there was something communicable about her gaiety: Agnes imitated her with a mimicry as merry as it was clever; and soon the two little sisters were dancing together, while Janey bounced up and down in her high-chair and gurgled ecstatically as she watched them. Even Anderson's somber face lighted as he saw his little daughters skipping skillfully up and down the cleared floor of the parlor, their arms intertwined, their feet flashing; and though the settlement was at first inclined to look askance upon such frivolity, and never fully understood how Lisa could find alleviation for hunger and sorrow in diversion, its judgment was on the whole lenient.

"Jeamie Anderson's weans have been taught the Highland fling by their mother"—so the word went around from neighbor to neighbor. "They caper about after supper when the work is done and the house tidy for the night—Mistress Anderson is an excellent housekeeper, say what ye will. She plays for the bairns to dance, and even shows them how to step through the figures. But when the fling is over, the jig tune gives way to a hymn, and the little ones kneel down in their places and pray with their mother sweetly and earnestly before they start to bed. No light-minded woman would set such store by family worship, or show so devout an example to her children!"

Lisa was "stepping through the figures" herself one evening in early spring, with a merry little girl dancing on either side of her, and a still smaller one patting her hands in time to their singing, when the tune of the music they were making was suddenly caught up outside the window, and another voice merged with theirs. Before Lisa could disengage herself and run to open the door, this was flung open with a jocund greeting; and Peabody Ladd, with a bundle strapped to his back and his strange instrument slung over his shoulder, stepped across the threshold.

"I have been hearing of these antics all the way north from Hanover!" he cried, "where, by the way, I have just seen again that strange etching on the windowpane of which I told thee once—dost thou remember? It is still as clear as ever!—Well, well, this is a pretty sight and no mistake! Lisa, thou'rt lovelier than ever!"

He lifted her off her feet, and swung her in the air, kissing her on both cheeks as he set her down again.

"And lighter," he exclaimed, "though thou wert always like thistledown! Come, let me see if you great lassies are not heavier than your mother!"

He tossed up each of the little girls in turn, imitating the squeals of delight they made as he tickled them, and pulling their flying curls.

"Much heavier!" he declared emphatically, when Janey, cooing with bliss, had been put gently back on the floor, and Sue and Agnes had both snuggled up to him, clamoring that he should swing them again. "I have always thought thou wert a fairy princess, Lisa, and now I am sure of it! Art living on fairy food?"

"Aye," she said jestingly, "and it suits me well!—Oh, Peabody, but I am glad to see thee! Thou hast been away so long! And since thou went——"

"I know," he said with swift gravity. "I have just heard —I have been far away, to that part of New Spain which is called Florida, singing as I went. It is always summer in that region, and there are fountains and flowers and fruits on every side. The sands on the shores are very white, and the stars seem very close to the earth."

"Arcady, Peabody?" asked Lisa, jesting again.

"It might have been," he said meaningly, "but was not —quite.—Where is Jim, Lisa?"

"He is at Boltonville," Sue answered for her mother, breaking in impetuously. "He hath gone to fetch our oats. Often he comes home very late. The mill runs all night, and he must wait his turn.—Toss us again, Peabody Ladd!"

"Thy oats! Hath it come to that!"

He gazed at Lisa fixedly for a moment over the children's heads. Then, putting Sue gently aside, he laid his strange instrument on a chair, stripped off his outer wrappings, and kneeling down, began unstrapping the pack he had worn.

"I heard in Boston how it was with ye in the valley," he said hurriedly and huskily. "I have ridden from there in three days. The fish was packed in ice before I left—it should still be fresh. I knew the streams hereabouts were still frozen and thought that it might seem a tasty bit. These chickens are new killed.—The ham I got in the South by way of a fancy—the Virginians boast so unceasingly of their curing, I was minded to show thee what it was like. And here is bacon too, white flour, beans, rice and tea, and sweetmeats for the lassies— sugar and spice and all things nice! 'Twill serve for a day or two—by then the carrier I have entrusted with further supplies will be here, and not long afterwards the sloop from Hartford with tubs and barrels of provisions. —Lisa, my love, do not look at me like that!"

He stretched out his hands to her. Before he could stop

183

her, she had seized them convulsively and was kissing them, her hot, quick tears falling on them as she held them against her lips.

"It was not for myself I minded," she sobbed stranglingly, "but I had given out so much gold here and there that there was none left to send away for provender! And it was bitter to see my own weans want because I had bestowed lavishly on others! I nursed Janey as long as I could, but I had to wean her because—because—and the bairns are all so little, and—and—I taught them to dance, to dance so that——"

"Lisa, dost think I do not understand? Come, dry thy eyes, and lift thy head, or I shall be driven to take thee in my arms, bairns and all!"

He spoke lightly enough, but there was a catch in his voice, and she was conscious of a fiery fiber of feeling running through it. She sat up quickly, struggling for self-mastery; and as she smoothed her hair and wiped the tears off her cheeks, Peabody went on talking in his easy lilting way.

"Are there not embers enough still on the kitchen hearth to roast the fish and bake some biscuits tonight?" he asked. "We could have a feast fit for a king if there are! And then, when the bairns are fed and sleeping, we could sit and talk together for a while as we used to do, till Jim comes home. After that, perhaps, I had best be on my way again."

"Be on thy way!" she exclaimed, "when thou hast ridden near two hundred miles in three days! Thou knowest, Peabody Ladd, there is ever a bed for thee in this house!"

"As for any wandering tramp? I know it is called 'The Poor Man's Tavern.'"

"As for the best and truest of friends! Cease the idle chatter to which thou art still so prone, and let us cook the fish that thou hast brought. The sweetmeats will suffice the bairns tonight. They have had an egg each and milk, besides their porridge, already. A few fowls still survive, and we have one cow left, though we know not how long we can keep her, since we have naught but a little hay to feed her."

184

Elizabeth raked the coals, beat some flour into batter, and set the fish and biscuits to cooking. Then persuasively she took the fascinated children away from Peabody and tucked them into trundle-bed and cradle, each with a sugarplum in her hand and another in her mouth. When she returned from the parlor-bedroom, she found that Peabody had spread the table by the fire, giving it, in some subtle way, an air of festivity for all its simplicity. He looked up from his task with a laugh.

"Some are born with silver spoons in their mouths," he said, "and some to lay silver spoons on the table!—Where is thy retinue? Will it not be serving us?"

"Nannie goes early to bed. She does not feel so hungry thus and she is very weak."

He winced. "Shall we wake her and feed her, Lisa?"

"After the fish and biscuits are cooked I will take some to her room. But I will not go to her before then unless I hear her stirring.—There is still a little cider which Betsey Bayley hath sent me. Wilt fetch it from the cellar?"

They had not long to wait before the meal was ready. Then they sat down facing each other, the savory fish smoking between them, the biscuits light and fluffy on their plates.

"Wilt thou say grace or shall I?" Lisa asked, looking across at the musician. "Peabody, I—I can think of nothing but the parable of the loaves and fishes. Nor do I feel it a sacrilege to say that thou hast had compassion on me, and that if these be blessed and broken——"

"Let us bless them together."

He was tremendously moved, stripped of all shallowness, shaken past all levity. But he was nearly as hungry as she, for in his haste to reach her he had hardly eaten throughout his journey, and he had ridden night and day. So after the hallowed and tremulous moment of grace-saying was past, he fell avidly on his food, thankful that his voraciousness checked his emotion. Lisa was now so used to scanty fare that she could eat but little at a time, though she had to check herself as she took the first morsels lest Peabody should see how ravenous she had become. So they had soon finished, and when Lisa

185

had wakened and fed Nannie, and the remnants of the feast had been put away, she and Peabody seated themselves on either side of the hearthstone, and he took up his guitar, fingering it while she talked to him, but playing so softly that his music seemed only to support her voice.

There was deep comfort for her in telling him all that had happened in his absence, even though much of the news was ill news. "Poor Mary's has not been the only death," she said. "Indian Joe and Molly Squaw have lost Toomalik, and in a horrible way. It has cost them not only their son's life, but their friendship with old John and Sally Squaw, the only Indians hereabouts with whom they were on terms of amity."

"I remember that all came from the St. Francis tribe," said Peabody, still strumming. "How did it happen, Lisa, that Toomalik's death divided them?"

"Because he first killed their son, Pial," she answered swiftly. "I found Joe here, squatting on the threshold, one day, when—when I had been to put flowers on Mary's grave. He did not even grunt when I came up to him, and I knew he was in trouble. At last I coaxed him to come in by the fire, but for a long time he rocked back and forth upon his haunches without speaking. Then at last he jerked the tidings out: it seems that Toomalik and Pial and other young Indians had gone to Haverhill in search of fire water. They found it and drank of it in great abundance—there must have been an orgy. On the way home Pial laid his hands upon a girl both he and Toomalik coveted—a gay young squaw named Maya. She laughed and slipped away, then sidled up to Toomalik and whispered to him. Afterwards, still laughing, she escaped. But Toomalik strode up to Pial, and drove his knife into his friend's throat!"

"It is not the first time a worthless wench has come between friends tried and true," Peabody said. He went on plucking at his strings, but his music was fitful and melancholy, and he sighed. "And Pial died—at once?"

"He lunged forward—staggered a few steps—and fell dead to the ground. Toomalik picked up the body and carried it to old John and Sally Squaw himself. And then he sat with them all night, joining in their wails and lamentations. He knew that John would be his executioner, for he was nearest in blood of the slain youth. But for all that they mourned together by the same camp fire!"

Peabody shuddered. "A gruesome wake, indeed! And Joe told thee of all this himself?"

"Aye. He used to flaunt the courts—dost not remember his bravado when Toomalik killed Lewa? But now they were too strong for him, so he begged that I would go with him and Molly—when justice was done."

"Surely thou didst not go!"

"Oh—but I did! Could I refuse—when they have done so much for me? But 'twas a dreadful sight—and all the winter I have dreamed on it——"

Peabody put his arm around her shoulder. "Tell me of it. 'Twill relieve thee and thou wilt cease to dream."

"We took our places in the Newbury Courthouse," Lisa whispered, "Joe and Molly and I together; and Old John, leaning upon his gun, stood staring at us through his bloodshot eyes. We had not long to wait. Toomalik came at the appointed time, unbound and all alone. He sat down on the floor and bent his head and crossed himself. 'Twas plain that he was saying prayers the priests in Canada had taught him. Hast ever noticed, Peabody, the hold the Catholic faith hath on men, even the worst of them and those who stray farthest from it? Toomalik was a fornicator and twice a murderer and much besides that—yet could he have had a Jesuit at his side and a crucifix in his hand he would have died the easier. And I—I would have fetched him both could I have found them in this Puritan and Covenanter country, where no minister, not even the Priest of Bath, would come to him!" she broke in fiercely. "Yet how was I to know beforehand that he craved them, or find them had I known?"

"Thou couldst not," said Peabody soothingly. "Do not reproach thyself, Lisa, for what thou couldst not do. At least thou didst stand by old Joe and Molly Squaw, and that itself was not a coward's act."

"When Toomalik had prayed," Lisa went on, almost as if she had not heard, "he lifted his head and cried,

'*Mach bence!*' [1] Then old John raised his gun and fired—I had never heard a shot like that or seen a man crumple where he stood. Afterwards we took—him—home to the cave. And there were gruesome rites—and then we buried him— I cannot talk of it, Peabody, even to thee! Two deaths since thy departure for the sunshine of New Spain—two deaths so different and yet both for love!"

"I know. There is no need that thou shouldst talk of it further," Peabody murmured. "Thou hast told me enough. Come, let us speak of other things! There must have been some trusty friend whose company hath cheered thee in my absence. How fares it with the Priest of Bath?"

"Well—so well that he hath now a chaise, and when the roads are good Mistress Sutherland rides abroad with him wherever he goes. He comes not to Ryegate as often as he used."

"And goest thou never to Horse Meadow or to the Oxbow?"

"Never to Horse Meadow; seldom to the Oxbow."

"And why?"

Lisa hesitated, disinclined to say anything that might be interpreted as critical of her husband, and yet yearning to speak freely to her old friend. Loyalty prevailed over longing.

"Few convenient occasions have arisen," she said briefly, pressing her lips together in a way that precluded further discussion, though Peabody immediately guessed the cause of her reticence.

"And Wells? Comes not Wells here to make brogans for the bairns?"

"Wells?" Lisa said, lifting her head in surprise. "Hast thou not heard?—But, nay, thou hast been too long gone. He went to war—to fight in a war with my country—for I feel ever that it *is* my country. In that at least I am like Asa Porter. I know not rightly what the trouble is, but it hath to do with ships and sailors. Wells came to see me ere he left, and begged that in so far as I could, I would befriend his mother. Thou knowest, dost thou not, that

[1] Kill me quickly."

188

she hath been bedridden these many years? I go to see her when I can, but 'tis a long walk and the hills are very steep; and I must carry Janey like a papoose when I go, and take the other bairns by either hand. Mistress Goodwin is a sweet woman, and grateful for my visits as I am glad to make them. I only grieve I cannot go to see her oftener."

"If I am hereabouts awhile," said Peabody carelessly. "I will take thee—thee and the bairns, if thou wilt go with me."

"Why not?" asked Lisa as carelessly. "I shall be thankful, Peabody, for the ride."

Peabody looked at her searchingly. He guessed, correctly enough, that though Anderson had been vaguely jealous of him in his courtship days, he was the type of man who believed that a woman, however lovely, was immune from admiration once she was married. But that Lisa herself should show such small discernment revealed how apathetic she had become.

"It is somewhat strange," she went on, "that Wells chose to enlist as a bugler. Never, as thou knowest, hath he cared much for music of any sort, except that which thou and I used to make together. But he began to yearn for it in this still place, and lament that thou wert not here to give him lessons. I think it was the sound of fife and drum, as much as any patriotic purpose, that sent him off to fight a foe towards whom he hath no real ill-will. There were only some half dozen others who went from hereabouts. Indeed, he scarce understood what the quarrel with the British was, no more than I do. We have no newspapers since *The Orange Nightingale and Newbury Morning Star,* which Nathan Coverly brought out, ceased to exist—though there have been two publishing ventures in Haverhill, both the *Coos Courier* and the *Advertiser,* were short-lived. If thou canst tell me what this hard feeling was about, I should be glad to know."

"Well, as I have heard, these compatriots of thine—if thou must still call them such—made no bones of impressing our seamen, replenishing their crews from those of American merchantmen," Peabody explained. "We suffered it a time in patience, then took action. On land

189

there have been no great conflicts, though doughty old Tippecanoe held his own in Ohio; but on the water, our victories have challenged the supremacy of England's navy. In less than one short hour the frigate *Constitution* so crippled the frigate *Guerrière* that she had not a spar left standing. And on Lake Erie, Commodore Perry not only won a battle, but coined a phrase, by which no doubt he will the longer be remembered. 'We have met the enemy and they are ours,' was the message he sent to the authorities."

"It is as terse and telling as Cæsars own!" Lisa exclaimed. "But how comes it that you know so much of all this, Peabody, when you have been in New Spain?"

"Why, many Indians fled there after General Jackson won the Battle of the Horseshoe on the Tallapoosa River," answered Peabody, "and they brought tidings. And, as I wandered north, I heard yet more, coming along my way. 'Twas in the South and West that patriots felt the most zeal—New Englanders, so I have gathered, first viewed the war with little favor, though now the prowess of Yankee ships hath made them puffed with pride. But all is over now in any case. A treaty hath been signed at Ghent some three months since—too late to stop the Battle of New Orleans, which was fought two weeks after peace was declared!"

He rose, stretched his long arms over his head, and reached out his hand to her. "Wells should soon be coming home now, bugle and all," he said, "and I am here already. And winter is almost over—sap will soon be running in the trees, and green things growing in the garden and crops in the fields. Springtime is here, Lisa, and better days!—Dost know, we have talked half the night? Come, let us go out and look at the stars together before we sleep! The sight of them, shining so steadfastly and enduringly, ever gives me new courage."

She fetched her cloak, threw it around her, and went out with him on the stoop. The night was very clear, the moon shining brightly, and the sky so strewn with stars that the firmament itself was hardly visible. An element of magic seemed to permeate the profundity. Lisa seized Peabody's hand and clung to it.

"Something is going to happen!" she gasped. "This is not a night like other nights! I have felt it from the moment I saw the food you brought me, and now I know it! This is a night of miracles!—Oh, Peabody—look—look!"

A streak of lucid matter had shot suddenly out of the west above the horizon. As Lisa cried out, a similar streak, springing from the east, rose to meet it. The silver strips mounted swiftly and simultaneously, their sides, jagged along the edges, scintillating as they ascended; but as they met at the zenith of the heavens, the vivid vibration ceased, and they were unified in a smooth broad arch of incandescence, curving high above the glowing moon, and linking earth and sky together with a radiant band.

"It is a celestial sign!" Peabody exclaimed. "Have we not read that God set his bow in the sky, in token of covenant, in the days of Noah? Lisa—Lisa—it must have been one like this, of molten silver, surpassing any iridescence ever seen! This shining circle is a portent that deliverance, more powerful than I can bring thee, is at hand. Wait only a little longer! Wait with a hopeful and a quiet heart!"

"I believe—I believe—that thou dost speak the truth!" she faltered. "I know not how it can come or whence— but I feel with thee that it is coming! Oh, Peabody—my soul doth magnify the Lord, for he hath done wonderful things!"

With fingers interlocked, they stood spellbound, gazing raptly at the celestial marvel, shining in still splendor above them. For a long time its glory remained undimmed, its supreme station unchanged. Then slowly, almost imperceptibly, the intensity of its white fire began to fade; the arch itself receded, declining towards the south; the scintillating streams of silver disappeared. As the last shimmering spark vanished from view, Peabody threw back his hand and laid his forefinger against his lips.

"Hark!" he said excitedly. "Someone is coming!"

Lisa leaned forward. She half expected, as he did, to see a phantom figure on the road before them. It seemed

191

a night when ghosts might leave their graves, to wander in the radiance of the silver arch; and now that this was gone, that they might lose their way. If Mary Dunn, enshrouded in ethereal draperies, had glided towards them from among the shadowy trees, the sight of her would scarce have startled Lisa, straining her eyes to follow Peabody's pointing finger. But as she caught sight of a dark figure, instead of a white one, coming towards them, she held her breath—would it be the shade of Toomalik in fringed leggings and feathered headdress, or of Wells, his fingers on a spectral bugle that made no sound? Or would it be an apparition not of death but of deliverance, such as Peabody had foretold? There was a moment of terrible intensity. Then she gave a hysterical laugh which ended in a sob.

"It is Jim," she said convulsively, "bringing back the oats from the mill. He hath waited all night for his turn—waited, I know, without impatience or complaint! Look—it is almost morning!"

## EIGHTEEN

THERE WAS GENUINE CORDIALITY in the welcome which Anderson gave to Ladd, that went deeper even than his heartfelt thankfulness for the provisions with which an empty larder had been so amply stocked. The "famine year" had taken heavy toll through other ways than hunger: it had sapped men's spirits as well as their strength; and to a man naturally silent and introspective it had been disastrously depressing. Anderson was longing for companionship almost as much as Lisa was; but he was both too constrained and too proud to grope his way towards it of his own initiative. Peabody, however, was so prodigal of good cheer that the most reticent nature expanded in the warmth of his geniality; and he had not been at the crossroads cottage twenty-four hours before the bane which rested on it began to lift.

Both Ladd and Lisa asked Anderson whether he had

seen the silver bow in the sky; he answered, with some surprise, that he had not, though he added that his eyes had been on the ground rather than on the heavens, and that he had been nearly blind with weariness to boot as he rode home from Boltonville. He did not scoff at their story, and indeed, the strong sense of mysticism so indigenously Scotch, made him feel, scarcely less than they did, that the phenomenon had been portentous. He would have been glad, rather than otherwise, if they had discussed it with him further. But since they thought it was beneficient in significance to Lisa rather than to him, they did not speak of it again when he was present.

Almost as if awaiting the fulfillment of a prophecy which he was expectant of seeing come to pass, Peabody made himself at home in the "shed-chamber" over the kitchen, declining to occupy the spare bedroom which he insisted must be kept free for "worthier guests." It was seldom that his roving spirit permitted him to abide long at peace in any place. But for once his restlessness was quiescent, and he was well content. Finding that Lisa was teaching her children not only prayers and dances, but other lessons as well, he volunteered to help her; and with shabby textbooks spread out on the kitchen table, and Sue and Agnes sitting between them, they taught the little girls their "Three R's," while Janey played on the clean floor, and old Nannie spun peacefully in the corner, and the sun streamed over the rows of flowering plants that stood in the window.

"It hath been voted in Town Meeting that parents shall send in half a cord of wood ready-cut for the fire for each child they send to school," Lisa told Ladd, "and with this law we have complied; so both lassies are entitled to attend. Moreover, John Page—'Lame John' as everyone doth call him—is a forceful and able teacher, for all he goes on crutches—he hath been known to use one of them for a rod under provocation! But the schoolhouse itself is old and rickety, stuck up on a side hill between two roads among the rocks on the edge of the woods; its furnishings are crude and meager, and it is badly crowded; and the books in use are so few in number, and so great in diversity, that it is a wonder any man can teach or any child learn at such a disadvantage! Moreover, half of Lame John's time must be taken in mending and making quills! As long as I can better this instruction, I shall keep my daughters at home!"

She lifted her little head proudly as she spoke, and Ladd's quick mind leapt to the thought of the learned tutors under whom she must herself have had her schooling. But she said no more, and he did not wish to force her confidence. So he answered casually enough, and they bent again to their joint task, after Lisa had gone to the brick oven to see that all was well with the bread and pies which were baking there and which gave forth such a sweet scent.

The frost was coming slowly out of the ground and the roads were deep with mud; but sometimes they went for a walk in Scanty Lane in spite of the bad going, taking the bairns with them; and sometimes they all piled on Peabody's great white horse, Troubadour, and rode up hill and down dale towards Hickory Village, to visit Mistress Goodwin. The cottage in which she lived stood perched on the top of a high crest of land rising above a deep declivity, through which a broad brook curved its way; so that to reach it there was first one long slope to descend and then another to mount. The children of the neighborhood loved to coast on "Goodwin's Hills," for the impetus which precipitancy gave them sent them down one hill and up another, so that they had but a short way to walk before they could turn their sled around, and reverse their headlong dive into the snow. Sue and Agnes had almost the same thrill in going over the ground on Troubadour. As he galloped towards the brook, they shouted "Down, down, down!" in joyful unison; and as his hoofs clattered over the rickety wooden planks which spanned the brook, they began to cry "Up, up, up!" with even greater zest. They knew that when they reached the cottage Miss Lucretia, who cared for her helpless mother so gently, would set out barley-sugar candy and peppermints for them to eat, and make new dresses for their dolls, and let them "listen for the sea" in the pink shell that stood on the parlor mantel; for while their own mother and Peabody Ladd sat talking with the cripple, the sweet little spinster cosseted the children with the pitiful tenderness of the barren woman whose maternal instincts have been sacrificed to her sense of duty. So the days when books were set aside and Troubadour taken from his stable were times of great rejoicing at the crossroads cottage.

"What pleasure thou hast given my bairns!" Lisa exclaimed gratefully one day, as they started for Hickory Village. "There are fresh roses in their cheeks and a new sparkle in their eyes since thou hast come to abide with us. How can I ever thank thee?"

"I need not other thanks than this," Peabody answered, turning to look at her as she sat, wrapped in her scarlet cloak, on the pillion with Janey in her arms. He had Agnes on his lap, and Sue before him on his saddle, and both were shouting to him to be off. "They would have taken well to gypsying," he added jestingly, "had their father been a rolling stone instead of a moss-gatherer! And well I know how joyous a Romany I should have been with three such bonnie lassies to light my camp fires for me!

> "One could dance and one could sing,
>    And one could play on the violin——"

"Peabody! Cease thy old idle chatter!"

"May I not even chatter, so long as I never tease?"

"Nay—it makes me sad——"

"Sad! Art thou sad today?"

"A little!"

"And why?"

"Partly because you stir my fancies, instead of fiddling them away, as once you did. And partly because you remind me, in speaking of how well content you would have been with three lassies, of how ill content Jim is that he has not a son and how—how much I wish that I could give him one. And partly because—nothing has come of the portent we saw together in the heavens."

"It is not I that stir thy fancies, but the first breath of spring in the air," Peabody answered. "The pussy-willows are out already——

"Oh, who will sing
A song of spring?
Pussy-will-oh!

Blood runs in our veins, as sap in the trees, differently now than at any other season—even such blood as thou callest quicksilver, Lisa! As to the son thou hast not yet borne, be thankful thou dost not bring him into the world in time of famine. Thou wilt have a son yet—I believe before another year hath passed. And that thou wilt have many I do also believe. Thou wert meant to be a fruitful vine as well as man's delight. And for the portent— wait yet a little while and see. I woke this very morning feeling that e'er many days had passed——"

"Why doth not Troubadour gallop, Peabody Ladd?" cried Sue, beating her little heels against the horse's sides. "We shall not reach the Goodwin cottage at dinner time!"

Miss Lucretia had, indeed, already wheeled her mother up to their simply spread table before Troubadour clattered into the Goodwin yard. But she set swiftly about amplifying the frugal meal; and later, when the lassies were nodding, their little stomachs well stuffed, she begged that she might lay them down for their naps and watch them sleep, while Ladd and Lisa kept her mother company. They saw her leave the room with the baby against her flat breast, and the two little girls clinging to the thin hand that was free; and then they sat down on either side of Mistress Goodwin's wheel-chair, and Peabody took up his guitar.

That each family should include at least one invalid was more or less taken for granted in the settlements: Maidens crossed in love almost inevitably "went into a decline," and, indeed, were rather encouraged to do so as an evidence of delicate sensibilities; and what an affair of the heart could not accomplish, "galloping consumption," treated by air-tight rooms and alcohol, often did. An operation or an accident was nearly always disastrous in its consequences; and a condition of permanent helplessness often resulted from these, or from an attack of rheumatic fever. One of the many Johnson households numbered three cripples, one on crutches, one confined to a wheel-chair, and one bed-ridden; but so long as there was not a case of insanity, with all its attendant horrors, to be dealt with, nobody complained, least of all the invalids themselves; and Mistress Goodwin's condition would probably have commanded only rather casual commiseration had not the contributing circumstances been such as to elicit unusual sympathy.

She had been an arrestingly striking girl, with glossy black ringlets, snapping black eyes, cheeks as red as roses, and a fleet step and erect carriage which bespoke both spirit and strength; and all the swains in the settlements had tagged at her swift heels. As is so common in such cases, she had married the worst of the lot, giving even the most faithful and devoted of her suitors, Daniel Heath of Piermont, the go-by for an irresponsible and dissipated youth named Moses Goodwin. He had deserted her when her youngest son, George, was an infant in arms, and had disappeared, leaving no trace behind him. Under almost overwhelming difficulties, she had run her farm and taken care of her ten children herself; and when at last she had crumpled up in a little heap one day when they were all past the age of helplessness, and it was found she could not stand again, the compassion of the countryside went out to her. Wells, her first-born son, had always been the apple of her eye and her main source of support; for though only twelve years old at the time of his father's desertion, he had immediately taken hold of the helm with his mother; and even after he had learned his trade of shoemaking and had begun to ply it throughout Coos, he had directed and helped in the farmwork done by his younger brothers, and achieved not a little road-surveying besides.

Yet Tryphena Goodwin had seen him go off to war without a murmur of complaint for herself or an expression of fear for his safety; and the only intimations of what his absence was costing her were made indirectly: she asked that the infrequent letters, which had ceased altogether since the receipt of the news that he had been wounded at Lundy's Lane, should never be moved from the little table that stood beside her chair during the day and beside her bed at night; and she insisted that both bed and chair should be placed facing the southern windows through which she could look out and see the hill dipping down towards the broad brook, and the crest of the other rising beyond it. And there she sat or slept, her red cheeks parchment-white now, but her hair still glossy and her eyes still bright, gay-spoken and indomitable as ever.

The sun was shining full upon her as her fingers flashed with her knitting needles, while Peabody strummed and Lisa hummed on either side of her. They had caught up some of the songs which Lisa had sung at the Johnsons' dance, and the cripple had joined in the merriment with which they gave these together now. As they lapsed into intermittent silence, she looked down searchingly at Lisa, who was sitting with her small hands clasped over one swinging knee, her slim body bent back, her golden head held high. At last Tryphena spoke to her affectionately.

"It pleaseth me to see thee blithe," she said. "These have been hard days for all, these times of famine which are passing at last—for we shall have a warm spring and an early one—I feel it in my bones! But that thou hast sung through it all shows something of thy mettle."

"I have not always sung," said Lisa sincerely. "There have been times when I have wept—but I have done that in shame and in secret. And since Peabody hath come back, I have found it easier to practice what I always preach, and not lay more at the heart than I can kick off at the heel!"

"And the other proverb to which thou hast always held—about the safe bridge? Art faithful to that too—since Peabody came back?"

Lisa flushed under the cripple's searching gaze. But Peabody answered for her.

"Aye, that she is," he said; and casting allusion aside, he added impetuously, "Lisa knoweth, and so do I, how to measure the worth of a man.—I brought a knapsack of dainties up the valley from Boston in three days —once; but Jim hath ridden throughout the winter to the mill at Boltonville, and come back at dawn with a bag of oats for which he hath waited night after night. The inference is plain."

"Peabody makes light of everything, including his own good deeds," said Lisa quickly. "I was near spent, for all Jim's perseverance, when Peabody came rollicking in with his flour and fish. Why make comparisons between men's actions, both so different, since both are good?"

"There is no need. Yet I am well content to know— how steadfast is thy heart."

"Lisa's heart is in the Highlands," said Peabody teasingly. "Did we not sing that song? Why, then we must!"

"Thou shalt do no such thing!" exlaimed the cripple sharply. "Her faithfulness is not confined to proverbs —any more than mine." Tryphena Goodwin had suddenly spoken with great feeling, and now she leaned forward and laid her hand on the younger woman's shoulder. "Dost mind the Biblical verse," she asked, "concerning the Apostle who had fought the good fight and finished the course and *kept the faith?* If thou canst do that all thy life, Elizabeth Anderson, nothing can harm or hurt thee. It is only those who turn their backs in battle, or sink down on the race track, or lose the beauty of their belief, for whom life is ever too hard. Think of Mary Dunn, who killed herself, in the name of love! If she had loved enough, she would have kept the faith that Hugh would be restored to her. And now she lies in an unhallowed grave, and he is cured—and bereft!"

"I shall fight on," she continued, after a moment with increasing tensity, "and finish my course—aye, though I do it in this chair, though still I believe that some day I shall leave it. And I shall see my boy again, whom all count lost, as plain as I see you two here beside me. I know that he hath not been taken from me—those whom the Lord loveth he chasteneth, but not beyond the measure of their strength. And that alone would be beyond the measure of mine—if I should never look into his eyes again!"

Her outburst had exhausted her. She let her knitting slip to the floor, and leaned back, her eyes closed, her lips working, her delicate face transparent. Ladd and Lisa looked at each other for a moment too moved to speak, and soon they saw that Mistress Goodwin was recovering her self-command. One hand was still on Lisa's shoulder, and now she stretched out the other and laid it on Peabody's.

"Ye are good children both," she said gently, "and never will do each other harm. I know it, as James Anderson knows it, and as mine own Wells knows it. He hath spoken of ye to me many times. Come, let us have another song—a song such as he would enjoy if he were with us."

"It was the 'White Cockade' that Wells loved best of all my songs," said Lisa chokingly.

"Why sayest thou 'loved'? Be very sure he loves it still! So I would have ye sing it—for me—and for him."

Lisa sat still, her hands, which had been clasped across her swinging knee, fluttering to her breast. As she glanced at Peabody, she saw that his eyes, as well as hers, were full of tears. But as he struck his strings, she raised her voice.

"My love was born in Aberdeen—" she sang, trying to sing with the same verve with which she had sung in the Johnsons' ballroom——

> "The bonniest lad that e'er was seen,
>   But now he makes our hearts fu' sad—
>   He takes the field wi' his white cockade!
>
> "I'll sell my rock, my reel, my tow,
>   My guid gray mare and hawkit cow,
>   To buy myself a tartan plaid,
>   To follow the boy——"

"Stop! *Stop!* STOP!"

Mistress Goodwin had not taken her hands from their shoulders. Now, as she called out to them, she suddenly bore heavily upon them, straining forward in her chair.

"Listen!" she cried breathlessly, "Someone else is playing the 'White Cockade'—someone else is standing on the top of yonder hill! Can ye not hear! Can ye not see!— *Wells, my son, has come home!*"

Their looks leapt forward to follow hers. Dimly, in the distance, they made out against the sunny sky the blurred figure of a man. Dimly, in the distance, they heard the blurred note of a bugle. And as they looked and listened they felt the woman leaning on their shoulders raising herself up from them through the pressure of her hands. Then they were aware she was standing upright between them, her body straight, her face illumined.

"I am going forth to meet him!" she exclaimed. And as if no longer conscious of their presence, she walked swiftly past them and went out the door.


## NINETEEN

THE DOUBLE MIRACLE of Wells Goodwin's return and Tryphena Goodwin's recovery shook the entire countryside. It was far more than a nine days' wonder. Whenever men and women met together, they talked of little else, and the throng of visitors at the hilltop cottage was so great that the house could not contain them. Wells, whose bashfulness made him naturally reticent, and whose freckled face became as red as his hair when forced to talk about himself, was called upon to tell, again and again, the story of his wounds and his wanderings; to state authoritatively whether Perry or Jackson was the greater hero of the war; and to describe it minutely and for hours on end to eager listeners who up to that time had regarded it with inattention or aversion.

Meanwhile, the only child of doting parents would not have been coaxed as often as Tryphena to show how well she could walk; and Ladd and Lisa were importuned for a description of the marvel of her cure as they had witnessed it. A service was held in the church at Ryegate Center, with the Priest of Bath in the pulpit to preach the sermon of thanksgiving, and Mistress Goodwin, dressed in black silk as lustrous as her hair, walking up the aisle on Wells's arm for all to see.

Moreover, there was a celebration in honor of the mother and son at almost every house within a radius of ten miles. Sap was flowing freely in the trees, and sugar parties were the order of the day; but as the spring advanced there were variations in the form the festivities took; and the "sociable" at the crossroads cottage, where Lisa and her lassies danced for the entertainment of the company, while Peabody played for them, and all sang together dressed in "plaidies," was one of the merriest of all. There was scarce a guest, before the evening was over, who was not joining in a reel or in a song; and it was very late before all had departed.

But when the last visitor had gone, and Jim and Peabody had helped Lisa put the house to rights again, Ladd urged his hostess, as he nearly always did, "to go out and look at the stars" for a moment before she bade him good night.

"Wilt not come with us, Jim?" she asked, with her hand upon the latch. The merriment of the evening had mellowed his mood, and it was long since she had seen him appear so happy.

"Nay, I am for sleep, not for stargazing," he answered, but agreeably enough. "And do not linger long thyself. Thou must be very tired."

"I am never tired when I have been dancing," she answered truthfully. "It puts wings on my spirits as well as on my heels."

"Thy spirit is ever winged," he said, "but so long as it doth not altogether take flight, I shall not complain."

She was wearing her blue silk dress with a bertha of white lace, and her rustling skirt sprang out full and bright on either side of her tight bodice. Anderson's eyes rested on her lingeringly for a moment before he turned and left them, and Peabody spoke to her teasingly as the door closed behind her husband.

"He would have liked to span thy waist with his two hands," Ladd said, "and press them close together until he felt that winged spirit as well as that slim form confined within his grasp. And yet he cannot. Why dost thou never go up to him and invite a caress?"

"Wouldst have me forward, Peabody?"

"With thine own husband, yes. He is so tongue-tied he can say but little, so diffident he knows not how to make advances. But thou art all the world to him, Lisa!"

"The world—and also the flesh—and perhaps even the devil!" she answered mockingly. "Dost really think my waist is small enough to be so spanned?"

"I know full well it is," he said tensely, "though I have never made the proof, worse luck!"

The words were hardly out of his mouth when he suddenly locked his long flexible fingers about her, tightening them until he crushed her so that she cried out she could not breathe. For a long moment he held her relentlessly. Then, releasing her as suddenly as he had seized her, he shoved her gently away from him with a little push.

"There is even an inch to spare!" he said laughingly and lightly. "Lisa—Lisa—how small thou art—and how soft and sweet! But thy winged spirit escapes me too, even as it escapes Jim. And without the spirit what is the letter worth?" Then without apparent rhyme or reason he added more seriously, "Now that Wells is home again, and thou art certain of a friend to cheer thee at need, I think I had best be on my way!"

"Be on thy way!" she exclaimed with unconcealed distress. "Oh, Peabody, why—and where?"

"If thou canst not guess why I shall be tempted to tell thee," he said almost harshly. "As to where—I have never been to Canada as yet; and I have always longed to see the white birches on the Isle of Orleans, and the Shrine of St. Anne de Beaupré, and the closed convent of the Ursulines, where a lamp lighted in memory of a lost love hath burned now for more than one hundred years.—It should be lovely in Quebec come springtime."

"I do not wonder at thy longing to be gone," she said wistfully. "But I shall miss thee."

"Aye. And I shall miss thee. But not more than can be borne. If I linger here yet longer, we shall miss each other too much."

"I had somehow thought," she said hesitatingly, without making any direct answer to him, "that thou wert waiting—to discover the meaning of the silver circle."

"It had been my own thought. But thou wilt tell me when next I come this way—if thou art here. If thou art not, then I shall know in any case."

"If I am here!" she cried. "And where else could I be, in heaven's name?"

"I know not. But I feel the chance is even that I may never see thee again after tonight. Were it not for that, I should not have dared to try—just once—to see if my hands would go about thy waist."

She leaned against the door frame, looking at him in bewilderment.

"Is there no one," he asked abruptly, "that might come from thy home in Scotland and fetch thee back there?"

"None."

"Thou'rt very sure?"

"I am very sure."

He drew his hand across his forehead. "I am not so certain. There is something imminent—and if it is not that I know not what it can be. I do not wish to pry into a past of which thou hast never spoken——"

"My past is dead."

"Dost thou not believe in resurrection?"

She was so startled that she could not answer him at once. And when she did, she spoke with hesitation.

"I believe our Lord arose," she said haltingly. "Naught else." There was a finality in her words which made it impossible, Peabody knew, to penetrate past them. "Indeed I am not certain any more—the silver circle was for me. Since we saw it, there hath already been one marvel in our midst. How can we tell it was not that which it presaged?"

"Because it was revealed to thee, and to none other. Tryphena Goodwin did not see it. I have asked her. Why should a sign be set in the sky for her, but shown to thee?"

"I know not. It is very strange. Then thou'rt still sure——"

"As sure as that we are standing here. As sure as that I must say good-bye. As sure as that I shall pray to find thee here on my return."

He opened the door, and waited for her to enter the house. When she turned to say good night to him, she saw that he was no longer beside her.

204

There was an emptiness in the cottage the next day, which even the children were quick to feel. Janey toddled about expectantly, poking into corners and raising her head every time she heard a sound; and every time she found that it had not been made by Peabody Ladd, the beaming smile faded from her chubby little face. Sue and Agnes would not settle to their lessons; Nannie was cross and broke her thread as she spun; and Anderson was so plainly vexed at Peabody's precipitate departure that he showed himself more surly than he had done in weeks. He was going to Newbury, he said curtly, on business. Yet when Lisa, for the first time in over a year, asked if he would not take her with him, he gave her a grudging answer.

"I am to have a long day; the roads are very bad, and there is no telling what time I shall return."

"I do not mind that."

"Hadst not planned, today, to do anything necessary in the house?"

"Aye—but I can do those same things better and with more speed tomorrow if I can leave them for today."

"Nay—thou wouldst be tired out. And Mistress Johnson may not be at home—in which case, where couldst thou stay while I am busy?"

"Why, in the store with thee, if it should chance that Lucy and Phebe and Betsey are all abroad also."

He disregarded the sarcasm. "It would be dull for thee, waiting," he said with finality.

"Canst thou never learn, Jim, that it can be dull for me here?"

He went out of the room without replying. Fifteen minutes later she saw him ride away, and took up her work again, angrily ashamed at the bitterness of her disappointment.

It was a fair morning, warm and sweet, and an irresistible longing to be away from the house and outdoors in the sunshine and fresh air had swept over her. Part of her restlessness, she knew, was caused by her envious thoughts of Peabody Ladd, riding his untrammeled way to the rushing St. Lawrence on Troubadour. But part of it seemed to strike deeper than that. She sat half listening to little Sue's slowly spelled sentences, her hands lying limp in her lap, her eyes looking dreamily into space, her thoughts wandering. It was not until she realized that Sue was tugging at her gown that she forced herself to answer a question which she was half conscious had been asked of her already.

"What didst thou say?" she asked, trying hard to speak gently. "Is aught amiss?"

"Mother, Indian Joe is in the yard."

"Why, run then and bid him welcome, and ask him to come in!"

"But he is not alone. He hath a stranger with him. I have told thee twice."

Lisa straightened herself swiftly in her chair, and then sprang to her feet. Through the sunny windows she could see the Indian gliding across the yard, with the stealthy silent motion peculiar to him, and to which she was now so well accustomed. But there was on his stolid face an expression of indignation she had never seen there before, and he was drawing along by the hand an unresisting being so strangely clad that Lisa could not be sure whether it was man or woman. It wore long floating robes, of colors and fabric alike startlingly unfamiliar; and its head was wound about with a folded and pleated turban. Its face was slightly bent and half concealed by the fantastic headdress and the gorgeous draperies; but it seemed dark and alien even in obscurity. As Lisa flung open the door, the children crowding closer beside her, a shiver of prescience shot through her and she caught at the jamb to steady herself.

"Good morning, Joe, and welcome!" she cried, trying to free herself from the feeling that her words were strangling her. "Wilt thou not come in—thou and thy— friend?"

Joe stopped in his tracks, and glared malignantly at the robed figure which paused quietly and stood motionless beside him.

"This no Joe's friend," he said, spitting out his words venomously, "this bad man, heap big liar. Him say him Indian. *Indian!* Humph! Hah! Him no Indian, no even

French Indian, no even Canadian Indian. Him tell Joe, good American Indian, *him* Indian! Humph! Hah!"

The turbaned head was slowly raised, and Lisa, looking breathlessly towards the draped figure, was conscious of a respectful but unflinching gaze leveled at her from a pair of very dark and singularly compelling eyes.

"If the Mem Sahib will permit me to speak," the alleged impostor who had so aroused Joe's wrath remarked, speaking in perfectly enunciated English, "her humble servant, Hazar Mir Khan, will explain his intrusion upon her."

"Missie no let him speak," Joe muttered vehemently, "him bad man! Him walk along road, dressed skirts all same paleface squaw. Him say, 'Where I find Mistress Anderson house?' Joe say nothing. Bad man follow on just same, keep on saying, 'Where I find Mistress Anderson house?' Then bad man show Joe letter, say must bring letter Mistress Anderson. Joe think, Joe think hard, Joe think some more, then bimeby Joe say, 'Allight you come along with me!' We come over hills from Wells River, Joe talk bad man, tell bad man Joe American Indian scout, shake hands George Washington. Bad man say he Indian too! Bad——"

"I am from Bombay," the turbaned man said quietly. "The natives of my country are called Indians, Mem Sahib. I meant no offense in saying what I did to this guide."

"From *Bombay!* And how came you from Bombay——"

The East Indian bowed. "I went from Bombay to England with the great Sahib, my master," he replied, still speaking very quietly, "when my master returned to his native country from the Orient. I have been in England with him for some years. Lately, very suddenly, he left England again—this time to come to America. I was not told why, but I came with him—I never leave the great Sahib, my master."

"And—and how is it that you come to my house?"

"At the command of my master, Mem Sahib. We came yesterday from Hanover, arriving last night at Wells River, and took lodgings at the Franconia Tavern there, kept by Master Barstow. When I had done all that was needful for my master's comfort, he sent me to search for the Mem Sahib's house. Master Barstow told me the way as well as he could. But on the hills I became confused—the roads are not straight, like the roads in England. I was therefore thankful to meet with the skillful guide, whose anger I grieve to have aroused."

The East Indian bowed again, lifted his head and looked at her expectantly. The scout continued to regard him with animosity.

"On the other side of the world, Joe," Lisa said, conscious less of the effort she was making to speak than that she was speaking to gain time, "there is a country called India—a country where the people call themselves Indians. They are different from our Indians, but this man, whose name is Hazar Mir Khan, spoke the truth to you. He is not a bad man. He is a good man, faithful to his master—an—an Englishman. The great English generals command the Indians in India as—as George Washington has commanded Indians here. It is the law of the land."

"Why all same Englishman not stay India, why come Wells River?" asked Joe, still suspiciously.

"I—I am not sure yet. But Hazar Mir Khan will tell us. He will tell us the name of the great Englishman whom he serves."

"My master said you would know without telling," the East Indian said still serenely.

If an arrow had been shot through Lisa's heart, the pain which suddenly pierced it could not have been more swift and deadly. The effort with which she spoke now was almost superhuman.

"But—but you are going to give me the letter?" she asked tremulously.

Hazar Mir Khan took an envelope from the folds of his robe, made a deep obeisance, and handed it to her. It seemed to burn her fingers as she touched it. Somehow she forced herself to speak again.

"I must not keep you standing here while I read it," she said. "I pray you, come into the house with me—you two Indians who must be friends with each other."

She turned, leaning against the wall, as she walked. Without another word, the two men followed her into the kitchen, and stood quietly near her. Elizabeth broke the seal of the letter, unfolding the single sheet slowly. It was not like her mother, Sue thought, watching her curiously, as she had watched the whole strange scene, to do anything so slowly; it was not like her either to grow so white—as white as a dead baby that Sue had seen once, lying in its coffin at a neighbor's house—or to catch hold of the deal table and grip it hard at its edge, as if she could not stand without support—her mother, who was so straight and strong! And still she was silent, so silent that Sue herself dared not speak nor Agnes either, in their sudden fear of some unknown peril. Janey stopped playing and looked up from the floor in bewilderment, and old Nannie, cowering in her corner, stopped spinning, while the new, tall clock ticked loudly, and struck the hour, and ticked again.

It was a long time before Lisa looked at the little daughter who was watching her so intently. When she did, she lifted the hands she had been clenching and unclenching over the table edge, and which were still trembling, and carried them to her breast, the strange letter still held in them; after she took them down, Sue saw that they were empty. And her mother was speaking gently, as if nothing were the matter, smiling, for all her lips were so pale.

"Wilt go into the yard and catch Dobbin for mother," she asked, "while I change my gown? I must ride to Wells River."

"With father away?"

The smile flickered out. Her mother was glancing at Janey, who had begun to play again, at Agnes who had crept up to Joe and was fingering his feathers, at old Nannie who had silently resumed her knitting. Then she nodded, and spoke more sternly.

"Aye—there is urgent need that I should go with these two brave Indians who have come to fetch me. Thou art mother's great girl now—thou canst mind the weans, canst thou not, till I come back?"

The child's troubled heart swelled suddenly with pride.

"That I can. And the house. And all. And—I will study my lesson alone." She flung her arms around her mother's neck, hugging her close; and darted out in pursuit of the grazing horse.

Ten minutes later, Elizabeth rode out of the yard and down the rough road over the hill, without looking back, without haste, without hesitation. The Indians followed her on foot. None stopped her on her way. As she neared Wells River, she drew the note once more from its warm hiding place, reining in Dobbin as she did so. When she had read it she put it back, carefully, and went on her way, saying over and over to herself, in a whisper, the words which it contained.

"My own beloved Beth—
I have leared that you are still living, and have crossed the seas to find you. Come at once to the Franconia Tavern, where I am waiting for you.
Forever and ever yours,
BASIL."

## TWENTY

A FAIR DAY, MISTRESS ANDERSON, and fair tidings that bring you to town! To think that the news of your marriage should never, until he reached this town to visit you, have come to your brother's ears! He was entirely amazed when he heard it from me. *'Mistress Burr!'* I said when he came up to the bar and asked if you did not live hereabouts, and I could not help but let out a great roar of laughter, 'Why, she hath been Mistress Anderson these eight years, man, and hath three fine children to boot, for all she lost her first!' I directed him how to reach your farm, but he had a fancy to see you first here, and sent this heathen servant of his out to find you. I see he did not fail his master in his search. Your brother awaits you in his chamber—the best I have—facing the stair landing. Shall I show you the way?"

"I thank you, Master Barstow. I can find it, I know, myself. But if not, the strange servant, as you see, still walks beside me. He will not fail to direct me."

The innkeeper cast a glance, half contemptuous, half shrinking, at the silent, turbaned figure standing, with folded arms, at the woman's side. "I see," he said shortly. Then changing the subject abruptly, he went on, "Ere you leave, be sure to come into the shop—a shipment of books hath come in from Philadelphia."

"I will not fail."

"Likewise one of ardent spirits.—You are sure, Mistress, that it is not needful I should accompany you?"

Elizabeth declined the tavernkeeper's assistance a second time, and mounted the stairs, the Hindu at her side. It passed through her head, as trivial things will do in moments of great emotion, that all the unsatisfied curiosity which her appearance in Ryegate had wakened, more than ten years before, and which, though never killed, had been lulled, was already stirred from its sleep and crying aloud again. Every word of Master Barstow's speech had invited an explanation. Well, she had none to give. . . . On the other hand, she had, immediately before her, a thousand to demand. Her brain suddenly swam, her feet seemed weighted. She could hardly drag them across the hall, they were so heavy, hardly see the wall before her, she was so dizzy. Blindly, she forced herself ahead, and knocked at the door of the front chamber, which was Master Barstow's special pride, and in which he lodged his most distinguished guests. The Hindu, having bowed almost to the ground as she reached the threshold, sank down upon the floor, crossing his legs under him and his arms above his chest. It was plain to her that he would not stir from the spot until his master summoned him.

Even before she was greeted with a quiet "Come in," she had somewhat recovered herself. This was no time for cowardice—if she were to play the part of a poltroon it were better she had stayed at home! She managed to enter with her head held high and her eyes shining. Then she closed the door firmly behind her, and waited, her back against it, for the man who stood on the opposite side of the room, his arms folded, gazing towards her, to speak to her.

It was Basil, Basil beyond any shadow of doubt or fear of mistake—he had the same handsome, clean-cut face she remembered so poignantly, the same long, lithe figure, the same blue eyes and fair hair and skin as beautiful as her own. But, at the same time, it was a Basil subtly changed by more than years: the old expression of merriment was gone and supplanted by a new dignity, the old joyous curve of the lips was suppressed, the nonchalant ease of carriage straightened. He was no longer in uniform, the gorgeous trappings of scarlet and gold in which she had always visualized him, but in civilian clothes of an elegance of cut and fineness of fabric such as she had never seen, even in the days when she lived in Glasgow— garments dark in color, somber, for all their elegance. As she studied him, her heart, which had leapt with a sudden ecstasy of forgotten joy at the very sight of him, contracted suddenly—Basil her lover, would have had her in his arms before now. This man, who had become a stranger to her, was appraising her, as she was him.

She did not guess how easily she could afford such appraisal. The years between sixteen and thirty are apt to enrich a woman's loveliness physically as well as spiritually rather than to steal it; and Elizabeth had just turned twenty-eight. The girl from whom Basil Keith had parted had been bonnie; the woman who had come to him at the tavern at Wells River was beautiful, as she stood, almost defiantly, with her back to the door, the sun shining on the golden hair under the loosened bonnet, the scarlet cloak falling about her in graceful folds, one small hand holding her riding-whip, her dignity as unmistakable as her loveliness.

"So you came?" he said at last very quietly. "That means you still love me. If you hadn't, you wouldn't have run the risk."

"The risk?" she asked with shaking lips. What she had expected the manner of his greeting to be, she did not know. But certainly she had not expected this calm

212

scrutiny, this judgment passed upon her feelings and her actions without the least display of either passion or reproach. It unnerved her more than anything else could have done.

"Will you not sit down?" he asked courteously. "You misunderstood my use of the word 'risk'! There is nothing, of course, to fear. But I must talk to you.

"You will tell me——"

"You wish me to explain, many things, of course. And, equally, I wish to do so. But I must see you comfortable first, not standing, trembling, at my door, with your hand on the latch."

He poured out a glass of wine from the small decanter standing on a low table, and came nearer her. "I think you need this, too," he said, extending it. "You have had—rather a severe shock; and you have risen above it with—rather remarkable courage. As an old soldier, I am a good judge of such things. It would please me if you would accept from me this much hospitality—a seat, and some refreshment. I wish to make you welcome in my quarters, which, so far as possible, I have made ready for the honor of your visit." Still she did not move, and he crossed the space which lay between them to where she stood. "And my hand is welcome," he added, offering it to her.

Still trembling violently, she put hers into it. The warm pressure that he gave was subtly reassuring. But almost unconsciously she looked away from him and glanced swiftly about her. The tavern guest-room must indeed have been subtly transformed. She had never been in it before, but Master Barstow, for all his pride in his inn and his love of fine furnishings, could never have decorated it as it was now adorned; and left to himself, he never would have caused it to be so swept and garnished. The brasses on the hearthstone and the candlesticks on the lowboy had been polished until they shone like burnished gold; the crystal flagon and goblets glistened in the sunshine slanting in from clear-paned windows hung with India muslin; there were bowls of roses scattered about, and among them, delicate ornaments of porcelain and silver, a snuffbox inlaid with jewels, a carved and

213

painted fan. Enormous trunks and coffers, studded and bound with metal, stood in every corner of the room, their raised lids giving hints of treasure within. Flung over the back of a great winged chair was an embroidered crimson scarf, and on the canopied bed lay a smooth coverlet of brocade; while all about were other gorgeous stuffs in colors and fabrics she had never before beheld, and spirals of perfume rose in delicate smoke from a tiny enameled censer. The austerity of the New England chamber had been so softened, its atmosphere had been so mellowed, that it had assumed an air of luxurious, almost voluptuous, beauty.

"You have made it very lovely," she said breathlessly.

"That was my intention," he said, pressing her fingers again. "I hope you will be at ease in it.—Surely you do not feel that you must listen to my story standing?"

"No—o—o."

"You are going to listen to it, are you not, now that you have come?"

"Yes."

He lifted her up, as nonchalantly and yet as tenderly as if she had been a child, and carried her to the great chair standing by the hearth, near the gleaming fire which burned there. Not until she had drained the glass of wine which he held to her lips did he release her. Then, laying her gently back, and leaning against the mantel, his arms folded again, he faced her.

"It isn't a long story," he said. "I wrote to you often, while I was in the Indies, telling you not only of my love, but of all the wonders that I saw there, of the great adventures that I shared—it is no small thing to have been in Java and Singapore with Raffles, to have seen the British Empire grow great and glorious under his guiding hand —some day I shall speak of all this to you again—not once but many times. For the moment, however, let it pass, since there is so much that concerns us more closely. As you know, I received no answer to my letters. When I returned to England——"

"My father of course destroyed them——"

"Of course. As I was saying, when I returned——"

"How long were you in the Indies?"

"Three years."

"So you never received any of my letters, either!"

"Your letters! You did write to me, then!"

"Over and over again. I addressed them to the barracks, to your home. I found, here in the colony, the more trusty messengers that I could. I tried the usual postal channels also, of course——"

"I am glad that you wrote—even though I never got them. They may never have reached Scotland—or, reaching there, never have been forwarded, or, being forwarded, never reached the Indies. I do not need to be told how uncertain is the condition of the mails. Or they may have been lost, not through carelessness, but through willful interception. Your father had enough power for that. But, of course, perhaps they were only lost. A Junior Officer in His Majesty's service is not of great importance. When he goes to foreign parts he never expects that personal despatches will reach him promptly, if at all. But I cannot see why, after I returned——"

"When three years had passed—I ceased to write."

"Oh, then I do understand," he said with a faint irony in his voice, but still with no reproach. "However, though you had ceased to write, I went, immediately upon my return, to your father's house. I was told that you were dead."

Basil paused. Elizabeth, with a little sobbing breath, hid her face. "So then I went to the cemetery where a tombstone stands, bearing your name, and—" she looked up swiftly—"and gave way to my grief. Not once, but over and over again. I resigned my Captain's commission, which I was so proud of having won, and I stayed on in Glasgow, that I might be near your grave. I stayed for over a year."

"A year!"

"Yes. When I left it was because the death of a relative called me to England. Not a near relative. Not another death of the kind to wring my heart. But a death, which for lack of nearer kin, meant wealth, and ease, a fine estate, a—a title—for me. It would, of course, have meant all that to you also—if you had not died."

He paused to look, still with that faint satiric smile on

215

his lips, at the rough homespun gown, the coarse, heavy shoes, the plain linen collar fastened by a simple brooch, which the woman before him was wearing. "You would hardly have been dressed like this," he said, at last, "if—if you had not died.

"I took up my title, and went to live in my new domain," he went on, as she did not answer, "but everything that came to me meant very little, of course—since it had come too late. But I tried, though there was little joy in the trying, to live my life as you would have me live it—if you had not died. To keep my honor unstained for your sake. To be as faithful to you in death as I would have been in life. There had been no other woman before you. There has been no other since."

Their eyes met, and, for an instant, his held hers. "I must ask you to believe that that is true," he said.

"I do believe it," she whispered, "I—I know it."

"At last, after many years, I received a strange message, a message from a man unknown to me, who sent me word that he was dying, and that his wife, dead already, had convinced him that his soul and hers would be damned to everlasting torment unless he could confess a grievous sin to me on his deathbed. I had tried, for your sake, to show charity, always, in all ways. I traveled a long distance, and reached the man's bedside an hour before he died. It was your father's steward, Andrew MacPherson. He told me—the truth."

"Did you—forgive him?"

"Have you?"

The woman facing Basil Keith suddenly covered her face with her hands.

"I think I shall let you answer that for yourself," he said as she sat silent and trembling. "I am a man, you know, not a saint—and I had been treacherously robbed of the woman I loved. Not only that. I learned that she had been made to suffer far more than if she had died. That is, I felt that she had. Was I wrong?"

"You know that you were not wrong."

"That knowledge was bitter bread to a man who loved as I loved you, Beth. Nevertheless, for your sake, since he was dying, I allowed him to think that I forgave him, and he died in peace. The next day I started for America.

"The directions he gave me for reaching Ryegate were not very explicit. There had been no time for that, and it is a place little known in England. However, I made my way as best I could."

"What did you do?"

"I took passage on a good ship called the *Washington Noyes* and the ocean passage was swift and smooth. It lasted a scant eight weeks, and, had it not been for my impatience, I would have had much pleasure in it. The whales, dolphins, flying fish and waterspouts I saw were most diverting. My fellow passengers, moreover, were congenial and affable."

"And so, after a good voyage, you came safely to land——?"

"Yes. At last we cast anchor at Staten Island, and landed next day on the New York quarantine ground. But there my joy at arriving was dampened by finding that yellow fever was raging in the city, that it was being abandoned by its inhabitants, and it was so dangerous for Europeans to enter it that we were forbidden to do so. During two days' detention, I chafed and fretted. Then I found means to elude the authorities, and did so."

"You went into that plague-stricken city!"

"I have been in plague-stricken cities without half so cogent a cause before," he said carelessly. "If you could once see cholera in India!—Well, in New York I found there was hardly anyone at work on the wharves whom I could question, and when I got from the wharves to the streets the first sight that met my eyes was a death cart carrying away a poor wretch newly expired. Moreover, the window shutters were closed, betokening the absence of householders. Hence, I was in something of a dilemma: I was in the midst of pestilence, my luggage was still on board the ship, lying in a most dangerous place, and I was without a single acquaintance to direct me, for those to whom my letters of introduction were addressed had all fled the city. But in the midst of my perplexities, a fortunate chance led me to the home of a hospitable Scot named Thosburn, who constrained me to lodge at his house, and who, when I left him, loaded me with abundant provision for my next voyage."

"Which took you——"

"To Hartford, the principal city of Connecticut, on a sloop, which left New York on a Friday, four days after I arrived there, and took four long days more to reach the capital of Connecticut! At Hartford I found I could go no farther by water myself, though I could send my goods by this means. So I transferred bag and baggage to a boat bound for Newbury. I myself was forced to tarry still three days more, for no coach left going northwards until Saturday, and Hanover was still three days' journey distant. But in Hanover——"

"In Hanover—" she echoed tremulously.

"You stayed there once, yourself, Beth, did you not?"

"How did you know?" she whispered.

"Because I found there etched upon the windowpane in my tavern chamber two hearts interlocked, with lovers' knots around them and the twining letters B.K.— E.B. Was it not you who drew them there, my dear?"

"Yes."

"With the hope that some day I might find them and that they would lead me to you?"

"With the prayer that they might; and meanwhile as the testimony——"

"Of eternal love? Your prayers were answered. The rest of the journey was easy. I came up the valley with a singing heart. But as to the testimony—you know—when I reached here last evening, what I was told——"

Silence hung over the room, a silence heavy with the suppressed emotion surging up from two souls. It was a look—a look from Elizabeth's agonized eyes into those of the man who stood watching her—that finally broke it.

"I am sorry if I have hurt you by telling you this story crudely," he said. "God knows you have been hurt enough already. But it is hard for me to soften it, to clothe the naked facts with eloquence. I have had a shock, too. It never occurred to me, you see—that you would not have waited, too. I could not, of course, go to your husband's house, or let myself be known in this place for what I was—for what I am—your lover. Neither could I leave

218

without seeing you, if that could be brought to pass. All night long I thought—I tried to think—of what was best to do. I could find no other solution than to proclaim myself your relative, to ask you to meet me here. I knew that if you had ceased to love me, you would refuse to come."

"And now that I have come, now that you have told me this story—what are you going to do next?"

She had struggled to her feet. The room was swaying about her, and she put out her hand, blindly, to steady herself. Basil Keith's folded arms shot out suddenly, and caught her.

"Do next?" he echoed, laughing a little soft, triumphant laugh, as he drew her against his breast. "Why, keep you, of course, beloved."

## TWENTY-ONE

MY BETH—MY OWN DARLING—my priceless treasure——"

It was Basil, the boy-lover again, who was murmuring to her, as he pressed his lips against her hair, her throat, her closed eyelids—not the dangerously quiet, courteous stranger who had stood with folded arms. "Do you know how beautiful you are? You have grown ten times more lovely, these ten years—I saw that, the minute you entered the room; those hideous clothes you wear cannot hide you from me, even though you meant they should. Beth—Beth—is it nothing to you that I have been faithful to you—that I have lived starving—in purgatory?—Open your eyes, heart's desire, and give me your lips yourself.—Why, then, if you will not——"

"Wait—I—I will give them to you."

She would hardly have been human had she done less. But what the granting of that kiss would mean to her she did not guess until it was too late to recall her gift. It drained from her the last remnants of strength and resistance; it swept her, still quivering, into a realm of rapture which she had never known; it held her there, conquered—and triumphant.

When Basil at last raised his head, and saw how it was with her, he was frightened; and carrying her to the big chair by the hearth he laid her down there a second time, kneeling beside her.

"Forgive me, Beth," he whispered, laying his head in her lap, "I did not mean to hurt you so. But—it has been a long time."

"You did not hurt me," she whispered back, "or, if you have, I do not feel it. For you have glorified me." And she bent over him.

He kissed her again, but more gently this time, soon drawing his face, as wet as hers, away of his own accord. "You are more spent than you know, sweetheart," he said. "You must drink another glass of wine—and this time we will drink together—to our reunion."

"Our reunion!"

"Surely. Are we not reunited?"

Again he leaned over and unstopped the crystal decanter. The wine flowed out with a rich gurgling sound. He filled two goblets, touched one with his lips, and handed it to her. Then having raised his own high in the air, he waited until he saw her raise hers too, before he drained his.

"I wish you could have drunk as deep as I, instead of making mere pretense," he said, watching her shrewdly, "but never mind. Another day you will.—Meanwhile, when you are rested, we will talk."

"What do we need to say?"

He laughed again, that soft, beautiful laugh. "There seems to be scant need for speech," he acknowledged. "Now that we have kissed each other. But there are details to be arranged. Remember I have told our curious landlord that you are my sister. Under all circumstances, that will not explain why you should remain with me forever——"

Elizabeth sat up, pressing her hands against her heart.

"You—you do not mean that I shall go home again—at all?"

"Did you mean to go —while you were kissing me?"

"It was not that I did not mean to go—but that, for the moment, I forgot all else in your kiss. You know that."

"Then I must kiss you again."

"Oh, no—not until we have talked, as you said."

"That shall be as you wish."

He waited, with no sign of impatience, until she had collected herself. "My husband loves me," she said at last. "You have told me your story. Now you must listen to mine. You must hear that, too."

"Your story will not alter my purpose. Nevertheless, since you prefer—by all means, tell it to me."

She began, haltingly, but gaining assurance as she went on. Warming to her tale, she did it more than justice. She dwelt much on what had happened before her marriage, little, in her loyalty, on what had happened since. In extolling her husband's virtues, she scanted her mention of his shortcomings. James Anderson could hardly have asked for a kinder historian. Once Basil interrupted her.

"Are you telling me everything, or only what will sound well in the telling?"

She paused, confused. Before she could reply, Basil asked her a second question.

"There are few men who fail a maid when they are trying to win her against great odds. But after they have done that—has this patient loving-kindness never failed you, in eight years of marriage?"

"Sometimes. But only because he has not always understood. Only because I have in some ways misjudged him, and failed him, too. This has now and then caused him to withdraw himself from me."

"You have answered me. Go on."

She tried to regain the ground she knew she had lost. But she saw that it was useless. Basil shook his head, smiling, when she had finished.

"Do you think he has loved you more than I have?"

"No—oh, no!"

"Do you love him?"

She bent her head, and answered in a whisper. But she could not lie to him. The one word which her lips formed was what he had known it must be.

"Have you ever?"

"Not—not in the sense you mean."

"In what sense then?"

"There has been—a sense of obligation—" she said, speaking very low.

"Of obligation! You were obliged——"

"The obligation was first one of gratitude," she interrupted swiftly. "I cannot suffer you to be unjust—to labor under false impressions. I was a stranger in a strange land, an exiled and abandoned girl, and every hand was set against me—save only one. And the time came, though he was very patient, when he claimed more from me than friendship. I could not send him empty away, when he had given me so much."

"The only obligation then was one of gratitude?"

A quick and painful color flooded her face and neck.

"Nay," she said in a low voice, "later—my husband did oblige me to—to submit to his will. Not when we first were married—he was so tender then, so gentle, and so loving that the way was not overhard for me. But after my first poor baby died—I had been two long days and anguishd nights in travail—after that—in my weakness and my sorrow, I longed only for solitude—I dreaded further suffering, and I rebelled against authority."

"There was question of *authority,* at such a time!"

"Aye—I will confess those days and nights seemed very dark for me—but the child I conceived in such sorrow and bore in such agony has been the very light of my life, the compensation for—for all that I have missed in other ways. So much so that——"

"So much so that?" echoed Basil searchingly.

"The fear that I would lose her, and so lose everything, was more than I could bear," Beth whispered. "And so—and so—it was I who craved another.—Do you know how hard you make it for me, Basil, when you force me to tell you this?"

"Do you know how hard you make it for me, when, to wring the truth from you, I am forced to listen to such a story?" he retorted. "A strange and terrible story—coming from the lips of a beloved woman—of how she yielded to another man—first through gratitude—and then

222

through compulsion—and then through desperation! Throughout it, I can find but one ray of comfort—you have not loved him in the sense I mean, for love to me has meant not recompense, but response; not violence, but adoration; not recklessness, but ecstasy.—Is this not what love has meant to you, Beth?"

"Yes."

"And—do you love me?"

"Basil—do you need to ask me that?"

"Tell me."

He had to repeat the command; but when she obeyed it, it was without evasion or circumlocution.

"I love you with all my heart and soul and mind and body. I always have. I always shall."

He did not make the mistake of taking her in his arms again. But, kneeling once more beside her, he carried both her hands to his lips, and held them there for a long time. Then he rose, standing very close to her.

"After your kiss—even after the look on your face when you entered this room—" he said huskily, "I did not need that confession, beloved. But now you have made it—how can you expect me to let you go?"

She turned her head away from him without answering.

"You have broken the pledge you made me in the barracks. But have you forgotten it, too?"

Elizabeth winced, as if he had struck her.

"Have you, Beth?"

"No."

"Admit then that I have claims prior to James Anderson's! I believe, in any case, that he has forfeited his, though you will not acknowledge it. But let us suppose, since you are bent on argument, that he has not. The promise you made to me, the night before I left for the Indies, is, in Scotland, considered to be as binding as a marriage—in fact, it is recognized as a marriage vow, if it has been heard by witnesses. Maisie and her husband were at no time far from us. Are you sure—could you swear—that they did not hear you—me—either or both of us—make it?"

"No," she said through white lips.

"Neither am I. You are my wife and not Anderson's. I do not blame you for yielding to him and I never shall. But that he has a husband's rights I deny altogether."

"Even if that were so, you are forgetting something else."

"I think not. Do you mean your children?"

She nodded, her wet eyes overflowing.

"You love them very much?"

"Oh, Basil, *yes!*"

"That was one of the details of which I thought—what plan we should make for them. You will, of course, wish to take them with you."

"You would take—my *husband's children?*"

"I would take *Anderson's* children since they are also yours. It may be difficult to bring about. But it can be accomplished. If not in one way, then in another. You know the motto of the great Napoleon—'If it is possible, it can be done; if it is impossible, it must be done.'"

"But—Jim loves them too."

"And so should I. But leave them behind, if that would ease your conscience."

"I—I could not do that."

The heavy silence of an hour before fell over the room again. Again it was Basil who broke it.

"You will be able to give them in England all that you cannot here," he mused, almost as if thinking aloud. "Remember that you will be Lady Keith, the mistress of vast wealth and of great position. This means opportunities for culture and comfort, ease, travel, pleasure. You love your children—naturally. It should mean much to make all this possible for them, to see them make fine marriages later on. It would mean much to any mother— especially to a mother who herself has known privation. What hope have you of such advantages for them here in this wilderness?"

"I have not any," she said in a smothered voice. "But——"

He interrupted her with a sudden question.

"Are they girls or boys?"

"They are all girls."

Again he smiled quietly and triumphantly.

"What good fortune!" he said lightly. "It would be possible, perhaps, to make another man's son my heir. But it could never be my wish, above all since——" He looked at her, still smiling, and she felt herself flushing from head to foot at the implication of his smile. But he did not, as she half hoped, half feared, finish his sentence or clarify his meaning with another kiss. "I shall cherish these fair daughters of yours, never fear," he went on earnestly, as if he had not noticed the burning blush. "And it will be easy to say that they are children of another marriage, which happily is true. Have you ever noticed, Beth, how much more disarming the truth is than a lie?"

"Yet you are asking me to live a lie all the rest of my life."

"What lie?"

"Pretending to be your wife——"

"There will be no pretense to that. You will find that a reality—very soon—almost before you are aware of it."

For the first time a stab of terror pierced her. Grief and joy, doubt and certainty, shrinking and desire—all these had already flooded her soul in the brief time which already seemed like an eternity since she had entered the room. But not fear. Fear in connection with Basil Keith, the boy-lover who had been faithful to her through so many years, the conqueror who had come to claim her through so many battles—the being, whatever form he took, most dear to her in all the world, was unthinkable! Yet it was there——

"It is not easy, is it," the even cultured voice—so different from any voice she had heard these many years—went on smoothly, "for a girl of your background and breeding to live as you have done since you came to Ryegate? To be cold and hungry often—even sometimes dirty, I suppose? To hear no music save that which your itinerant friend of whom you speak has brought you, crude scrapings at best, to read few books, save when you are at Mistress Johnson's, whom you have not now visited in a long time, to meet fewer people with whom you have anything in common? To work early and late, to eat scanty fare, to wear coarse clothes? To see nothing

225

beyond this crude valley? Think of England in spring-time, Beth, of the green leaves coming out in oak forests, of Keith Manor standing in all its stateliness, of tapestries and marbles and paintings and velvet hangings——"

As he spoke, the shut-in years of her life on the little crossroads farm reared up before her in their stark monotony. The contrast, between the reality which existed and the possibility which he offered, was violent in its vividness. He had meant, of course, that what he said should be freighted with power; but never having experienced, or even imagined, the extent of the loneliness and barrenness of her existence, he could not guess how great that power would be. She struggled against it as she would have against an iron bar laid across her heart.

"Think how it would be," he went on softly but mercilessly, "if instead of laboring unceasingly in your crossroads cottage, you were sauntering with me through a rose garden in the sunshine! Or sitting beside me through the gloaming on a terrace overlooking green lawns and copses! Or nestled close to me in a great chair drawn up before a greater fireside in a paneled library! Or lying in my arms, as the moonlight streamed in through the casements of the chamber where the masters of Keith have always taken their brides——"

She made a pitiful little sound that was half a gasp and half a moan. But he went on as if he had not heard it.

"Which reminds me," he said tenderly. "I have brought with me the jewels which every master of Keith has given, for generations, to his bride; besides those which I chose for my own bride, throughout the Indies, before I knew I should be Lord of Keith. I had not much to spend—a Junior Officer. But I spent all I had."

He went over to one of the great coffers, took from it a small silver casket, set with amethysts and topazes, and placed it in her hands. Almost unconsciously she raised the lid. Coiled under the cover, like a small milky-white snake, lay a folded rope of lustrous pearls. Basil lifted them out, shook them to their full length, and flung them around her neck.

"These are the pearls I gathered one by one!" he cried.

226

"Look in the little mirror set in the casket-lid and see how well they become you! And this is the ancient ring of betrothal. Come, let me try it on your hand! We must find a place among the gems encrusting it for the little stone with which you etched your message of true love on the windowpane. And here is a shining brooch set with sapphires which match your eyes, to fasten over your heart!"

With swift, sinuous fingers he picked out a sparkling star-shaped ornament from amidst the other gems, and pinned it triumphantly on her bodice. Then, so quickly that she could not forestall him, he bent over her again, and kissed her, impetuously, hotly, in the hollow of her breasts.

For an instant she was too startled to withstand him, too dazzled by the sweet stab of joy that pierced her as she felt his face against her bosom, to draw away from him. Then, conscious how far his searching mouth was straying in its quest, how hard and insistent it had become, she shook herself free from the sense of intoxication that was flooding her senses.

"Basil, you forget yourself," she said, forcing herself to speak sternly.

"I do not forget myself," he answered instantly and without apology. "I seek only to wake your memories—of a past when you would never have repulsed me; to clarify your vision—of a future when you will not do it either.—This brooch becomes you well, Elizabeth—a Rajah's favorite wife once wore it so.—Those pearls possess more luster than I thought, when I first saw them matched and strung together in Ceylon. When we visit that enchanted isle together, we must add to the string—it might well have two strands instead of one. It is a long time since you have looked beyond this valley, Beth! But we will see the wonders of the East together yet!"

Elizabeth freed herself suddenly, closing the jewel-box with shaking fingers. "Basil, be still!" she said, trying to steady her voice and to speak sternly. "You are trying to tempt me—with the embraces you know I find it hard to deny you, with jewels so beautiful that any woman could not help but covet them, with your talk—of pleasures

227

and palaces, which do not matter, which ought not to matter. Your love should be too great to stoop as low as that. I will not stay and listen to you."

As she spoke, she walked across the room and tried to lift the latch of the door. It stuck. Instantly she felt Basil's hand close over hers.

"I locked that long ago," he said quietly, "and the key is where you will not find it. A love that has been long denied does not chance further denial. And as to stooping low—is it worse to reveal passion than to arouse it? Is it worse to bestow jewels than to covet them?"

He waited a moment for the answer he knew she was too shaken to give him. Then he went on relentlessly.

"As to the pleasures and palaces which do not matter —or ought not to matter, as you were truthful enough to put it later—let me tell you some things that do," he said. "Your life has been hard enough here up to now. But little by little you have accustomed yourself to it, little by little your memories of me have faded, the poignancy of your love for me has become, little by little, less piercing. Now these memories are awake again. They will cry aloud to you forever. Think what it will mean to you, after today, to go back to James Anderson! Every time he kisses you, all the rest of your life, you will remember that kiss we exchanged, a little while ago, in this room— and wear out your soul in longing for another like it! Every night as you lie beside him, you will remember that you denied me, you will think of me alone, and hunger and thirst to be with me! When your next child is born—your long-awaited boy—you will curse the hour of its birth, because it is his, and not mine! You will remember that the last of a long and honorable line must see his name buried with him because you would not be the mother of his son.—Think of all this, and tell me whether it does not matter!"

Her head was still turned from him, she was still leaning against the door. "You are very cruel," she said at last; and, as she said it, he knew, in spite of her averted face, that she was weeping.

"I would rather be kind. But you will not let me. Have I said anything that is not true?"

She began to sob, stranglingly, convulsively. Basil put his arms around her, and drew her hands away from her face.

"Answer me," he ordered.

Still sobbing, she strained away from him. But he held her fast and she was forced to answer him.

"You know that what you have said is true," she whispered. "It is all true. My God! do you think I do not know it? But you must let me go, Basil, for all that."

"Why?"

"You know why."

"If I did, I should let you go. But I can see nothing that compels me to give you up—a second time. If you can convince me that I should, I will."

"You will not let yourself be convinced."

"Try."

She tried, only to find herself smitten dumb. She had told him the story of her exile from start to finish. It had left him unmoved. She had pleaded her husband's cause. He refused to admit that her husband had a cause—even to admit that James Anderson was her husband. She had shown him that she could not desert her children, and he had almost forestalled her by telling her that there was no need that she should give them up. He had, it seemed, unlimited confidence in himself, unlimited power over her. The strength of the man, the hardness of his determination, loomed up before her like a mountain of granite. She would only dash herself to pieces against it. And, most of all, she knew that the secret of his strength and his determination lay in the certain knowledge he possessed of her love for him, of her longing to yield to him —a love that cried within her, that he could hear as plainly as if she had given voice to it, urging her to go to him——

"You see," he said at last, as if she had been speaking, "it is quite useless. Why do you struggle against me, Beth? Against my arms? Against my love? Against our life together?"

He was holding her so closely to him now that she could not free herself. But this time she answered him as if oblivious of his embrace.

"I will not go with you. I did wrong to come to you at all, wronger still to kiss you—to let you know I cared. I am not sorry. I know I ought to be. But it has meant—much to me to see you again, to know—that you still love me. And now—I must go home, and you must go away. In England you may forget that you ever found me. And I will remember you—always—always—always."

He thought, for a moment, that she was going to try to sink on her knees before him, weeping and praying—to God—or himself—as if it did not matter much which. That she was, as a matter of fact, deep in prayer, he could not doubt; but it was with an uplifted and no longer a hidden face, in exaltation, not in abasement. It has been granted her, after many years, to have at last the knowledge that he still loved her, the sight of his face, the touch of his hands and lips; that was so much more of joy than she had known since her exile that she was giving thanks for it. This was no supplication. It was, in very truth, a thank-offering. She was asking for nothing, all the rest of her life, but the unsullied memory of this. That, for her, would suffice. But it did not suffice her lover.

"Beth," he said softly, "Beth—my darling—don't—don't. You mustn't pray like that. You mustn't—look like that—I can't bear it. I don't want to hurt you, to make you do anything that you will regret. I only want you to trust me and come to me. I promise you you will never be sorry."

"That, she said swiftly, "was what my husband said, too, before we were married. And God knows how sorry I have been."

"And yet you refuse deliverance—when God offers it to you?"

"'Tis not God who makes you say what you have said to me. It is your own heart speaking."

"And do you think, then, that you cannot trust my heart? I remember when you did, entirely; and you remember, too, that your trust was not abused."

Elizabeth hesitated. She was very tired, weary, it seemed to her, past all endurance. Her brain was growing numb with fatigue. How would she force it to give her the words with which to reply?

"I did trust it before, Basil," she answered, "and I trusted it rightly. I have trusted it, unconsciously, all these years, I think. Do not force me, then, to stop trusting it now. Let me go."

"Do you think there is no end to my patience, Beth?"

"You have been patient for more than ten years. Can you not, then, be patient a little longer?"

"Do you mean—can I not wait for a heavenly reunion?"

There was a biting sarcasm in his question. If she had taunted him, she could hardly have aroused deeper resentment and anger. But she did not, in her own exalted mood, see this in time.

"Yes," she said softly, "why not? I am sure, my darling, now that I have seen you this once, that I can. Can you not do as much?"

"Are you a woman made of flesh and blood that you can ask me such a thing?" he said hotly, his arms tightening about her. "You know that I cannot! You know that you will never leave this room until you are mine, body and soul!"

His voice had risen triumphantly. Through his pæan of exultation, neither he nor Beth heard or heeded the sound of knocking, which had kept thudding persistently against it, gently at first, then with increasing vehemence. Now there rang out the battering sound of a heavy blow, falling on solid wood; the noise of creaking hinges and rattling bolts; the thump of a falling body. Then came a splintering crash, as the door fell heavily to the floor inside the room.

On the threshold stood James Anderson.


## TWENTY-TWO

MASTER BURR?" HE ASKED COURTEOUSLY, disregarding the wreckage at his feet as if it had not lain there. "James

Anderson of Ryegate—at your service. I am sorry I was put to battering down your door, and to treating your servant somewhat harshly. I fear he is unconscious from a blow I have struck him, but he strove to prevent me from so much as knocking, and when I persisted, reinforced his arguments with a knife. I have told Master Barstow's hired man to look after him.—And my lack of manners takes nothing from the warmth of my welcome to my wife's brother," he added, holding out his hand.

Keith had released Beth and had sprung towards the door as it crashed; but he had fallen back again as Anderson confronted him. Now he took the proffered hand almost mechanically. In the tense atmosphere with which the room that Anderson had so ruthlessly invaded was supercharged, the banality of a reply would have been impossible.

"I knew, from Master Barstow, that you were within," Anderson went on calmly. "So, when I had no answer, I feared there might be somewhat amiss—a sudden sickness or the like—rumors of plague in the ports have been current hereabouts. I am glad to see that, after all, everything is well."

He paused for a moment, without apparent design or effect, and turned towards his wife, shifting, as if unconsciously, into the familiar form of speech which still came most naturally to him. "Did I frighten thee with my rough ways, Lisa?" he asked gently. "I am sorry. A crashing door hath, once before, given thee a shock, as I remember. But then, the cases are hardly the same, for now we have cause only for rejoicing, whilst the other time—why dost thou tremble so? Thou art shaking like an aspen leaf."

He put his arm across her shoulder, and smoothed back her tumbled hair, apparently oblivious of its disorder, of the loosened string of her bodice, of the great rope of pearls still hanging around her neck and the sapphires on her heaving breast.

"Mistress Johnson and thy other friends in Newbury sent fond messages to thee," he went on. "I am sorry I did not take thee with me, as thou didst ask. They all scolded me roundly, and said, as thou hast done, that

232

now the bairns are older it will do them and thee both good, if thou art away from them, now and then. I admit myself in the wrong—another time, thou must go."

"Another time!" Lisa repeated breathlessly.

"Yes, and that right soon—Well, I was so delayed in my transactions, that I stopped here, since I could not get home for dinner or supper either for that matter, to talk to Master Barstow of that colt we have thought of selling, thou knowest, the brown one. He offered me a fair price. And then, he told me thy good news. Of course, I hastened to add my greetings to thine. Will not—" he paused, smiling, but speaking with more formality again, "I am sorry," he said, looking across at Keith above Elizabeth's head, "but I do not know how to address you. You must tell me your baptismal name. I cannot call Lisa's brother Master Burr."

"You know," said Elizabeth suddenly, "that I have no brother. You know that this is—Basil Keith."

She thrust her hand into the bosom of her gown, and drawing out the warm, crumbled bit of paper that had lain there, handed it to her husband.

"You are sure this is for me to see?" he asked.

"Please."

"And you are also willing, Master Keith?"

"That is for Beth to decide."

Basil Keith's tone, as he spoke for the first time, was not discourteous, but it was edged with a slight arrogance. Anderson appeared to take no notice of it.

"Yea," he answered levelly. "And she saith, 'Please.' "

He read it through slowly, refolded it, and handed it back to her without a word. When he did speak, he used almost the same words that her lover had done when she entered the room.

"And you came? That means you love him still."

"It could hardly mean anything else," said Basil, almost insolently.

"You are right. And, without doubt you also love her, since you have sought her out—by what strange means I do not yet understand—and have found her, after all these years. Shall we not sit down, while we talk? There would seem to be need of some adjustment here."

Again that strange, unconscious repetition! Elizabeth caught her breath at the weirdness of it. Were the composure and confidence of the man of the world so contagious that the woodchopper could, in one brief moment, contract them? Or did composure and self-confidence come to every man, whatever his condition, when he was fighting against heavy odds for his mate? She relived, swiftly, that strange night when Anderson had found her in the woods, the unnatural eloquence which had come to him then—shut it from her, and spoke, hurriedly.

"Andrew confessed. He sent for Basil on his deathbed, and told him what had been done to me. The next day Basil started for Ryegate. He has come into great riches—lands—a title—he seeks to have me share them with him. All these years he has been faithful to me—to my memory—for he believed, until very late, that I was dead. And now he claims the pledge I made him in the barracks—the pledge of which I have told you. He says I am his wife—probably by Scottish law, if not, at least in the sight of God."

"It is strange," said Anderson thoughtfully, "that men talk never about marriage in the sight of God except when there is no such sacrament in the sight of man. As to the Scottish law—are you so certain that anyone heard your pledge except him to whom you made it?"

"No," said Elizabeth quickly.

"And you?" asked her husband, looking at Keith.

"I am not sure that it was *not* overheard. It is likely that we were. I can find out, on my return to England."

"You can doubtless find someone who will say he overheard," said Anderson dryly. "There are ever those who are ready to bear false witness against their neighbors—especially for the sake of those who covet their neighbors' wives."

"I must remind you, without desire to be discourteous, that I did not cross the seas in order to listen to Scripture."

"And why did you cross them? Knew you, when you started, that Lisa was married to another?"

"No."

"And, had you known, would you still have started?"

"Yes."

"I am sorry. It seems a strange finish to a love so great as yours to journey to the ends of the earth for a bad purpose."

"A bad purpose?" repeated Basil ironically.

"Is it not a bad purpose for a man to make of the woman he loves a self-confessed adulteress?"

Anderson still spoke calmly, almost impersonally. But as Basil saw Lisa shrink away, with a smothered gasp of horror, from her husband's encircling arm, he retorted with mounting vehemence.

"You have no right to brand Beth with such a name. She has resisted me, and has refused to leave you."

"I have not branded Lisa. It is you would have done that had I not come when I did. And that she hath resisted you, and refused to leave me, I need not to be told either. I know her better than you seem to do. But you mistook me; and you are scarce consistent. If you truly believed that she was bound to you, and not to me, you would have understood more fully what I meant."

"And what did you mean, for God's sake?"

"I meant you would have spared her the knowledge that she had, for years, been living in sin with another man."

Too late Basil saw the trap which had been laid for him. He struggled to free himself from it with a taunt.

"At least you are not too blind to see why she came to me!"

"She could scarce have done less than that. She hath always loved you. That hath been no secret between us, and is no surprise to me. Besides, she hath not been happy, and hath been seeking for escape. This she will not have told you, though doubtless you have guessed it. And it hath been my fault, all mine."

He turned away from the other man, and laying his hand over his wife's, spoke to her as if they had been alone.

"Lisa," he said gently, "wilt thou tell me the whole truth as to what thou wouldst do?"

"I—I cannot."

"Perhaps I can help thee. Is it thy—thy desire to go away with Basil Keith?"

"Yes," she whispered, so low that he could hardly hear her.

"Dost thou feel—that his claim is greater than mine?"

She shook her head. "It is very great," she answered. "It is the claim of true love. But—but it is not like thine. If I had felt myself bound to him, I would not have married thee. I am thy wife—not his, for all that barracks' pledge—thy wife in very fact, the mother of thy children."

"And still thou wilt go with him?"

"Nay—I have refused to go with him, as he hath told thee. But—I long to go."

"And thy bairns?"

"He would take them, too."

"Thou canst love a man who would rob another of both his wife and children?"

Her head dropped lower still.

"Tell me, Lisa."

"Aye," she answered at last, with a great effort, "I can love him, whatever he does and whatever he is. Through this life and the life to come. I have loved him all these years. I have never deceived thee as to that. I shall love him, God knows, into eternity."

For a long moment the two men looked at each other in silence. Then Anderson lifted his hand from Lisa's, and turned his head.

"It appears that I have won," said Keith conclusively. "Will you strive to keep her after that?"

"No," Anderson answered slowly. "I shall not strive to keep her. She is free to go."

He crossed to the threshold, where the splintered door still lay, and stood for an instant motionless beside it, his head bent. Then leaning over, and raising it, he set it up again as best he could. When it was once more in place, he turned and looked levelly towards his wife.

"I will bring the children here in the morning," he said, "and such things of thine and theirs as will be needed for the journey. If any question me, I shall say that thy brother hath come to fetch thee back to the Old Country to see thy father, who is dying, and that thou hast been too shattered by these tidings to return to thy home tonight. More than this never need be told. There shall be no reproach cast on thy name—by me."

"Thou art leaving me—*like this?*"

Lisa had sprung suddenly to his side and caught at his arm. He freed himself gently.

"Dost think I cannot see what this man—whom thou lovest—can give thee, Lisa?" he asked sadly. "Compared to what I—whom thou dost not love—can give? Nay— what he can give thy children also? Shall I make thee beat thy head against the prison bars of exile when thou canst live in the freedom of the homeland? Didst think my love so poor a thing that it would make a jailer of me? Oft it hath failed thee, that I know, and more than once I have wronged thee in the name of love—though not as deeply as Basil Keith would have done had I not forced my way into this room. For all its failings, my love has been a thing good and not evil."

"Neither hath his love been evil, Jim."

"I know that, Lisa. He hath suffered—even as I have done—and hath yielded to temptation—even as I have done. But his love hath been good indeed, until today, and great as well—greater than it is given to most women to possess. Therefore my heart is sore that thou shouldst lose it. Hadst thou chosen it would have been thine to keep forever."

"*Lose it?*" she faltered, uncomprehendingly.

"The maid whom Basil Keith loved," went on Anderson deliberately, "was very brave. She shrank from nothing because it was hard or bitter or cruel. She shed no tears, even in deep sorrow, where any man might see her. She faced the world with a gay voice and smiling lips. Strong in the knowledge of her own righteousness, she ministered to the fallen in their affliction, and softened the hard hearts of the judges who strove to condemn her. Such strength and courage, Lisa, come only from a soul at peace with itself. From this day forth thy soul will never be at peace. Thou wilt shrink from thine own conscience, and shrinking, become a coward, forfeiting a brave man's love."

She shrank, visibly, now.

"The maid whom Basil Keith loved was very fair," Anderson went on. "And thou art fairer today than ever before, I think, Lisa. But there is only one kind of beauty which in a woman does not fade. That, too, comes from within, lending light to her eyes and warmth to her hands. When this beauty of the spirit is gone, Basil Keith will cease to love thee. The fairness which is only of the flesh is a mockery, both to the woman who possesses it, and to the man who possesses her."

"May we not cry quits," Keith broke in almost curtly, "without more moral platitudes and false dismal prophecies? Beth's mind is made up. No oratory can serve to change it."

"Since the die is cast," said Anderson, "You can scarce object if I speak."

He spoke serenely, with the serenity that is an attribute of power. Involuntarily, Lisa's tormented mind reverted to the night when she had seen him first, standing in a roughhewn doorway, his somber figure silhouetted against the glow of a great fire. She remembered how instantly she had become aware of a revelation of dignity and strength. The same revelation overwhelmed her now.

"Thy lover hath condoned one inconstancy, Lisa," Anderson said cogently. "He will no doubt condone a second. Indeed, it should be easier to forgive disloyalty to me than to himself. But will he forget it? Will he trust the fidelity of a woman proven fickle? Will he not see, in my dark fate today, a shadow cast upon his own fair fortune? I think he will, and when his faith is gone, his love will be gone also."

Anderson leaned over, and laid his lips against the bright head of the woman standing beside him.

"The maid whom Basil Keith loved was pure in heart," he said softly. "Her chastity hath been his beacon-light! Dost think a sullied memory would have held him all these years?"

He asked the question impellingly; and still he did not

wait for her quivering lips to form an answer before he went relentlessly on.

"He loves thee still. But what he gives thee soon will not be love, long denied, but lust, quick and easy to sate. Surfeit breeds indifference, Lisa, and this, after love, is bitter bread, salted with tears and eaten in exile—exile harder than any thou hast known. It is bitterest of all if a woman still loves the man who offers nothing sweeter."

She raised her eyes at last, and gazed steadily toward Basil Keith. "What he is saying is true," she said, in a low voice. "Can you deny it?"

"I can, indeed. I do deny it, utterly. He is trying to frighten you, Beth, to trick you, so that you will stay with him."

His voice still carried conviction, but strangely, subtly, it had ceased to carry authority. Lisa shook her head.

"No," she said slowly. "He is leaving me free to go. He is only showing me the path I will tread if I do. It was you who frightened me—with force. It was you who tried to trick me into staying—with you."

Very quietly she took off the pearls that still hung around her neck, unfastened the glistening brooch at her breast and laid it down. Her fingers trembled as she retied the string of her bodice. But when all was in place again her lips had ceased to quiver.

"Beth!" Basil said hoarsely. "Beth—listen to me!"

"I have listened to you," she answered, disregarding the deep entreaty of the voice from which all arrogance had now been swept away. "And I do not love you the more for what you have said, nor the less for what has happened in this room. My love at least is steadfast! And never shall my loyalty again be challenged, as twice, in different ways, it has been challenged here!"

"Forgive me that I ever challenged it! And believe me that my love is steadfast too!"

"I do believe it, Basil, with all my soul! Help me to hold fast to my belief!"

An immense stillness seemed suddenly to engulf the room. At last, still silently, Elizabeth turned and looked at her husband. Again Anderson held out his hand to Basil Keith.

"It appears, after all, that I have won," he said. "I will wait for Lisa outside. Ye twain will wish to say farewell to each other alone."

# EPILOGUE

## *The Country Beyond*

S NOW HAD BEEN FALLING ALL DAY, gently and silently at first, then with a whirl and a rush, beating against windows and doors, drifting in gusts down wide chimneys. By night it had become a blizzard, the flakes freezing to ice as they fell, the wind howling and moaning, the great drifts rendering the hidden roads almost impassable. Elizabeth Anderson, knitting beside the hearth, piled fresh logs upon it, drew her shawl more closely about her shoulders, and finally put on again the heavy woolen apron which she had discarded after the day's work was done.

It was very quiet in the pleasant, spotless kitchen, where flowers bloomed in the windows, and shining kettles hung on the clean white walls. The ticking of the brass-faced clock, the clicking of her needles, the purring of a contented kitten, dozing, its paws tucked under its breast, at her feet, were the only sounds; and these were comfortable and homelike and could hardly be heard above the raging of the storm outside. This, however, was so violent, that a knock at the door, loud enough to have reverberated through the little crossroads cottage under ordinary circumstances, was repeated three times before Elizabeth heard it and sprang to answer it, letting in, with a sheet of snow, the muffled figure of the Priest of Bath.

"Well, well, my lassie," he cried heartily, as he shook himself free of his heavy wrappings, disclosing a form still stout and stalwart, though his hair was as white as the snow with which he was powdered. "I have plowed my way to your barn, and stabled my horse there, but I was afraid you would leave me on the doorstep all night to freeze to death. This is bitter weather, and I have been delayed."

The woman laughed, as she flew across the room to place another chair before the cheerful fire, and into the pantry to fetch sugar and tea.

"There seems to be a gathering of the clans!" she said merrily. "You are the third man this evening who has accused me of leaving him to freeze, Master Sutherland. Yet the other two—Wells Goodwin and Peabody Ladd, who took not tea but rum for their toddy!—are both sleeping snug enough now in my best feather-bed. There may be nothing left for you but the trundle!"

"Is that not full too?"

"Aye," Elizabeth's eyes softened. " 'Tis ever full, thank God.—But we will find you a place somewhere."

"Despite the space which Jeamie and Davie and Charlie take up? Are the little laddies all well?"

"Aye, and the great lassies, too. Sue and her husband were with us all last week from McIndoes, and Agnes and Hugh and their bairns are in and out all the time. Jane says she will never marry—her heart is all in her teaching—and truly she mothers all the children of the neighborhood!"

"And the baby, Barzillai?"

Elizabeth's eyes softened. "The sweetest and sonsiest I have ever borne!"

The Priest laughed. "You have said that as each one has come along, these five and twenty years! But I saw for myself when I christened him that he was a very bonnie boy!—But it was a strange name you chose for him, Elizabeth!"

"It was adapted from the name of a long-lost friend," she said quickly, "to whom Jim and I both owe much." Then as if preferring to change the subject, she added, "You are very late to be traveling."

"No later than you to be working! A busier housewife there is not, I believe, between here and Hanover.—Is your husband away?"

"No, sleeping. When the last of the harvest was gathered in, he went off on a hunting party at Armington with the Folgers and the Brocks and two of his brothers.

242

Jeamie managed the farm like a man while his father was gone, and it was a grand outing for all. They made their headquarters at William Tarleton's fine tavern on the nearby lake, and brought back such a store of venison that my larder will be stocked for the winter. I shall be busy with curing and drying after we have had our fill of fresh meat. But, praise be, Jim was safely home again before this heavy storm set in! I rest more easily when he is beneath the shelter of our own roof, though I say this in no disparagement of Master Tarleton's good cheer!"

She handed the Priest his steaming drink, sucking the grains of sugar that had stuck to her own small hands as she did so. "Since I must be barmaid to all itinerant vendors," she murmured mischievously, "those of souls as well as those of soles, it keeps me stirring late—stirring drinks and stirring myself.—Will you have another cup? And will you not come into the parlor to drink it? I have a fine set of rosewood furniture upholstered in horsehair that I must show you—and a new square piano of ebony inlaid with mother-of-pearl."

The Priest settled back in his comfortable rocker. "Later, later," he murmured; "for the moment I am well content here. It seems more like the good old times to sit in the kitchen. But I will gladly have another cup of tea, and a slice of your thick fruit cake to go with it.— And while I drink take up your knitting again, and tell me how it has been with you and yours since I last saw you—a long time now. Since I have had the chaise I go seldom on horseback. And I am getting old——"

"In body, perhaps, but not in spirit!—All has been well!"

"You have no more to say than that?"

"There are no great changes here except of season!"

"Nay, but there are! Think what this Coos County was when first you came—a savage wilderness with only here and there a settlement! Now goodly buildings rise on every side—although 'tis said that Ryegate is a town of three-story barns, and one-story houses: the barns bespeak prosperity, and the houses comfort; and agencies of advancement and progress surround us on every side. Think of the splendid seminary in Newbury, and the center of

243

fashion that has sprung around the sulphur springs found there! Think how Samuel Morey's invention has borne fruit: ships and cars propelled by steam travel on many waters and in many parts of the land; and since this is so, that strange vapor to alleviate suffering of which Samuel White once dreamed may soon be found, too. Henry Keyes, who came to Newbury with his brother from Vershire well-nigh penniless, has prospered so greatly in his affairs, and is so progressive of outlook that he talks of building a railroad through this very valley! And he has bought the Dow farm, which is no longer an abode of gloom, but one of cheer and plenty—belike some day a man will live there yet who will be unafraid to take his place within the walls of the National Congress. Indeed, Henry Keyes himself has been elected to the state legislature, and that on the Democratic ticket!"

Elizabeth laughed. "And he a good Vermonter!" she said mockingly. "Well, there *are* wonders about us, even in this quiet valley!"

"David Johnson's son, Edward, has graduated from Dartmouth College and gone to New York City to practice law," Sutherland went on enthusiastically, as if unmindful of her gentle satire, "and there his fortunes are already so far favorable that he is betrothed to one of the most beauteous young ladies I have ever seen. Her name is Delia Maria Smith, and I waited upon her when I myself was last in the metropolis. Her father is Adon Smith, a mighty merchant and the owner of great bonded warehouses. It is said he is worth a million dollars! He received me with much show of friendliness and bade me stay for dinner and overnight, which I was pleased to do. You cannot think how lavish is the table he sets and how princely is his home. It is illumined by the flames of gas, and there is a room in it set apart for bathing, where at the turn of the hand water is released from pipes and gushes forth from faucets!"

"And are these faucets the wellsprings of love, and do the flames of gas kindle Edward's ardor?"

"You may jest if it pleases you, Elizabeth Burr! And while Delia Maria's beauty is not to be denied, neither do I deny that Edward has greatly bettered himself in worldly ways. Meanwhile his crippled sister, Nancy, whose nose is ever in a book, has penned verses and sketches herself with a skill so delicate that were it seemly a gentlewoman should become an authoress, I do not doubt that she would do so. In fact, her father's fears are great that she may, seemly or not, though she has promised him she will conceal her identity under some fancy pseudonym and thus spare the family pride of the Johnsons." [1]

Elizabeth smiled. "I know all this, and I am well content it should be so. But at the crossroads here the times seem much the same as they did before all these changes came to pass. The farm is fertile and we prosper, and friend and stranger still take refuge with us. The death of Indian Joe has grieved me greatly. But I shall never forget 'twas here that he crept in to die, when both his feet were frozen in the Great Storm of February last.—I still turn instinctively to the corner where Nannie used to sit and spin, but I have taken up her fallen distaff, as you see! The children thrive and grow. Jim is content."

"And you?"

She stroked the fur of the sleeping kitten, now cuddled in her lap. "I am busy," she said, "as you say. But I am not so shut in as once I was. Now and again I go junketing about the countryside to see my friends, taking my quiverful with me. And the work does not hurt me. I am very strong."

"You are always that."

"Nay—" She looked across at him, read the double meaning in his words, and flushed, shaking her head. "You have been good to me always," she said gratefully, "and in your charity have thought better of me than I deserve. In that you are like Jim."

"That Jim thinks well of you we all know," replied the clergyman with a pleasant laugh, "and has, ever since he first set his startled eyes upon you. Nothing like our little Scotch lady had ever crossed his vision before. I warrant

---

[1] Nancy Johnson, writing under the name of Minnie Myrtle, became one of the best known "lady-novelists" of the "timid fifties" and foreign correspondent for the *New York Times*. Her fame did not outlive her generation, but her career was a remarkable one and some day I shall tell her whole story.—F.P.K.

that if he could write like Solomon we would have a new chapter about the virtuous woman and her price! And I know that he subscribes to the sentiments of the great reformer, Luther, who declared that honorable marriage is an art, and a privilege. You have made it the one and James has found it the other! But that anything he said about you could be one whit exaggerated I do not grant.

"The children also," he went on, as she did not answer. "Verily, when they are like yours, they are, as the Bible says, an inheritance unto the Lord; blessed is the man who hath his quiver full of them. In the days to come, when this scantily settled country is become one of the great nations of the earth—aye, the greatest of them all, perhaps—who can say?—the descendants of the sons and daughters whom you have borne and reared will be among the elect of the earth. Something of your sweetness, something of your strength, shows in every one of them. It is a great work which you have done, Elizabeth Anderson—to make a fair garden out of the barren wilderness of a man's heart, and to plant there fragrant and fruitful trees which shall increase from one generation to another."

Again she did not answer. The Priest waited in silence for a few moments, then asked gently, "can you think of anything better for a woman to do—anything that would bring to her, as well as to those whom God has entrusted to her care, more of a sense of work well done, of fulfillment, of the peace which passeth all understanding?"

"Nay," she said at last, "there is nothing better——"

"And yet there is something on your mind, my daughter. Will you not speak freely to me?—It is now many years since first I felt——"

He left the sentence unfinished, and for a moment Elizabeth Anderson did not answer him. At last, lifting her eyes, she looked at him and met his level gaze.

"As you have guessed, there is a story which I have long wished to tell you," she said quietly. "Tonight, perhaps is the appointed time."

The tall clock had struck the midnight hour before either of them stirred again, before the Priest of Bath spoke. Meanwhile, as if in a mirror, he saw for the first time all the events which had led to this woman's marriage—the friendless girl riding up beside the wild Ammonoosuc for the wise counsel which she was not to find, waiting for the letters which did not come, struggling to free herself from the drunken beast on the stairway, giving herself finally to the man who had served her so patiently and so long; saw the grief-stricken and tortured young wife, torn in body and soul, the mother finding at last her first great joy in maternity; saw her losing this joy again in the desolate times of loneliness and sorrow and famine; saw her after years in exile, standing upon a high mountain looking down upon all the kingdoms of the earth—the promised land of love for which every woman longs and waits; and saw her finally turn away from that fair country and return to the wilderness, which, as he said, she had caused to blossom like a garden——

The glowing embers were turning to gray on the hearth. Elizabeth stooped and stirred them into fresh life.

"So the name of Barzillai," the Priest said as she turned to him again, "is in memory of——"

"Yes. It was Jim's wish as well as mine."

"It is strange," he mused, "that your husband should have chosen the time he did to go and talk with Master Barstow of a colt. The hand of the Lord must have been in it."

Elizabeth gave a little laugh. "Perhaps," she said smiling, "but be that as it may, the hand of Indian Joe was in it! He could not overcome his distrust of the other man who called himself an Indian; and no sooner had he seen me inside the tavern with Hazar Mir Khan than he struck out apace for Newbury to tell Jim what had happened. He found him seated at David Johnson's counter discussing meteorology. But that was one discussion of David's which was cut short!"

The Priest smiled in his turn, then gradually grew grave. "And have you ever heard from him again—this man whom you so loved?"

"Nay."

"Do you long to?"

"Nay," she said again.

The Priest forbore to question her. But she divined the question none the less.

"After that day what words could be needful between us? All that there was to say had been said in that one brief hour."

The Priest rose, and laid his hand on her shoulder. "You are right," he said, "and the man who went from you, alone and sorrowing, knew even then, and still knows, in his loneliness and his sorrow, that you are. This knowledge of your rectitude has given you peace and the strength to serve, and the happy heart which goes all day long, Elizabeth. To your husband it has given fullness of life such as few men have known, and faith in woman like unto his faith in God. You have robbed no one, my daughter, and you have bestowed much—even on Basil Keith, though it seemed that you sent him away empty-handed, to whom you longed to give most of all. But I cannot doubt, Elizabeth, that it is to you he owes the fulfillment of his destiny also. Ungoaded by the spur of despair, he might have succumbed to the idleness of a life of luxury, forgetting that loyalty to country comes next after loyalty to God and fellow man. But he has been driven to deserve the best that Britain can give him. He took up again the commission he had cast away, and rose, through reckless valor, to the rank of general. Now he hath become a mighty ruler in the Empire he helped to build."

She looked up at the Priest in swift surprise.

"How do you know?"

"The journals and the books which you see seldom here come to me often in Bath. The instant that you spoke his name I knew that it belonged to the man to whom supreme honors had been accorded. He is a great colonial governor—perhaps the greatest in the British Empire. Elizabeth—you could have been queen among women."

"I am a queen among women," she answered proudly.

Her voice rang out with a conviction that was compelling. She had risen too, and stood facing the Priest, her attitude one of authority. As he looked at her, he saw, with amazement, that she was indeed regal of aspect.

248

Her splendid hair, wound in a braid about the waves that framed her forehead, gave the effect of a crown; the distaff which she held in her hand might well have been a scepter; her full dress swept away from her like a royal robe. But the expression of her glowing face was even more arresting than these attributes of royalty. David Sutherland lowered his head before the glory of it.

"You are more than a queen," he said slowly and reverently. "Shall we give thanks that this is so?"

Side by side they knelt on the hearth, the woman's face uplifted as the Priest's.

"Our Father, who art in Heaven," prayed David Sutherland, "who hath been pleased to bring this woman Thy servant through the deep water of affliction unto the mountaintops of peace: Grant that the beacon-light of piety and purity which she hath kindled there may shine upon her descendants in this valley, and in all this land of America, from one generation to another; that the women following after her may be also of strong courage, of high loyalty, and of great faith. For the sake of Jesus Christ our Lord——"

"Amen," said Elizabeth Anderson.

———

The prayer seemed, then, all-complete and all-sufficient. But later, after Elizabeth had looked down, in the light of the tallow candle placed beside her bed, at the row of golden heads, laid close together in the trundle-bed, and the downy one that nestled in the cradle, she paused to gaze still longer at the dark one, sprinkled with gray, on the pillow beside her own, and knelt again.

Years had softened the somber splendor of her husband's face. Where once there had been bitterness and severity there was now serenity and strength. As if almost conscious that she was close beside him, he smiled in his sleep, and his look became transfigured. She took one of the powerful hands that lay outstretched upon the counterpane and held it to her lips.

"Dear Christ," she whispered, "I thank thee for all thy

goodness and mercy and loving-kindness to me. But most, with all my heart and soul, I thank thee, for the bridge which thou didst give me—the bridge which carried me safe over."

# AUTHOR'S NOTE

THE STORY OF ELIZABETH BURR and James Anderson which I have told in *The Safe Bridge* is true in every essential detail. Not only was each a real person, but so is every other character I have tried to portray. David Sutherland, "The Priest of Bath"; James Whitelaw, Commissioner of the Scotch American Company; Colonel Thomas Johnson and Colonel Asa Porter; General Jacob Bayley and General Moses Dow—all were men of distinction, whose fame spread far beyond the Upper Connecticut Valley; and even such minor figures in the plot as Wells Goodwin, the itinerant shoemaker, and Peabody Ladd, the itinerant musician, Joe, the Indian scout and Molly Squaw, Dr. Samuel White and Mary Dunn, the beautiful suicide, lived, breathed, moved and had their being during the early nineteenth century in the region I have described. This region was settled by my own forefathers; my mother still owns the house of David Johnson, which has now been in the family for six generations, and I myself live on the Dow Farm, which passed into the possession of Senator Keyes' family about one hundred years ago.

For reference material I am greatly indebted to *The History of Ryegate, Vermont*, by Edward Miller and Frederick P. Wells, *The History of Newbury, Vermont*, by Frederick P. Wells, and *The History of Haverhill, New Hampshire*, by W. F. Whitcher. But helpful as all these have been to me, the private papers placed at my disposal have been even more illuminating. Indeed, my sense of obligation to Mrs. Alexander Greer of Newbury, Vermont, who first told me the story of her grandmother—the heroine of my novel—and later placed in my hands invaluable family documents, is unbounded. Her daughter-in-law, Mrs. Charles H. Greer, who is herself the author of numerous historical sketches, has been equally coöperative. Without her assistance, I should not have known the exact details of Indian Joe's life, of the trial for heresy, the Psalms used on these occasions, etc. The indiscreet visit to the barracks, the mock funeral, the inscription etched with a diamond on the windowpane, the marriage on the rock, the "famine year," the portentous phenomenon in the heavens, the reappearance of the long-lost lover, and other episodes, are fully authenticated.

I am also deeply indebted to Mrs. Theodore Chamberlain of North Haverhill, New Hampshire, who now lives on the famous Asa Porter's place at Horse Meadow, for her information concerning this vivid figure, and for the loan of the unique diaries kept on sea and on land by her great-grandfather, David Sutherland, who for half a century was so dominating a figure in Northern New England.

The real name of my Elizabeth "Burr" was Elizabeth Todd and she was called "Eliza" instead of Lisa; the change has been made in the story for the sake of euphony. Her father's Christian name was David, but as it did not seem wise to have two Davids appearing prominently in the story, this was changed also; and the hero's surname was actually Henderson instead of Anderson. Elizabeth never divulged the name of her English lover, and no record of it was kept at the Franconia Tavern. It could, no doubt, be unearthed in the records of the British Army. But for practical purposes, that of Basil Keith seems to serve as well as any other, especially as it is known in the family that Elizabeth had some special reason for naming one of her sons Barzillai. The causes of Mary Dunn's suicide have not been disclosed, but since no record of the period would be complete without some reference to the hapless plight of the insane, I took occasion to speak of it briefly in connection with this tragedy, using the name of a family which is now extinct in Ryegate. I have done a little "adjusting" of dates. Peabody Ladd, for instance, actually came into Elizabeth's life later than Wells Goodwin; and there has been consolidation of incident, in order not to overcrowd the scene with superfluous characters. For instance, episodes affecting persons not appearing in the story have been credited to persons who do. But all these took place in the locality and are characteristic of it.

F. P. K.

**AVON** ◆ The Sign of Good Reading

**AVON**  The Sign of Good Reading